Praise for *The Undiscovered*

'A dark, disturbing and highly ori...
McG...
Mark Billi...

'Dark, twisted and compelling'
C.L. Taylor

'[A] gut-wrenching thriller. There are jaw-dropping revelations and
startling assertions in C.S. Robertson's gruesome tale'
The Times

'A brilliantly original thriller, dark and brooding, with a real emotional
punch'
Doug Johnstone

'Clever, dark, unusual and full of genuine surprises'
Louise Beech

'A truly startling novel'
The Sunday Times

'One of the highlights of my reading year. A deliciously dark masterpiece'
Helen Fitzgerald

'Twisted, twisting, original and sinister. *The Undiscovered Deaths of
Grace McGill* is unforgettable'
Chris Whitaker

'A sharp and vigorous novel with a massively original theme'
On Magazine

'So original'
Crime Monthly

'This is an ingenious, disturbing and chilling thriller in which Grace is
an unforgettable character, and not what she seems. Superb storytelling,
with an elegant twist'
Daily Mail

'Dark and quirky – there's just something readers are going to love
about meeting Grace McGill'
Scottish Sun

C.S. ROBERTSON

The Undiscovered Deaths of Grace McGill

HODDER

First published in Great Britain in 2022 by Hodder & Stoughton
An Hachette UK company

This paperback edition published in 2022

2

A CIP catalogue record for this title is available from the British Library

Paperback ISBN 978 1 529 36763 8

Typeset in Plantin by Manipal Technologies Limited
Printed and bound in Great Britain by Clays Ltd, Elcograf S.p.A

Hodder & Stoughton policy is to use papers that are natural, renewable
and recyclable products and made from wood grown in sustainable forests.
The logging and manufacturing processes are expected to conform to the
environmental regulations of the country of origin.

Hodder & Stoughton Ltd
Carmelite House
50 Victoria Embankment
London EC4Y 0DZ

www.hodder.co.uk

To Ian, Lorraine, Paul and Rosaleen

Loneliness will sit over our roofs with brooding wings.
Bram Stoker

Chapter 1

I see the stranger's reflection looming in the café's window, large and uninvited against the rain streaks. Cringing inside, I hear the chair scrape back and the start of an unwanted conversation. I pretend I don't hear her and continue looking through the window, concentrating on the jogger splashing along Dumbarton Road. It doesn't work.

'Horrible day, isn't it?' she repeats.

I'm forced to turn my head and look at her over the rim of my coffee cup, nodding with a half-smile. It probably seems a bit rude, but not as rude as sitting down at a table when there's already someone there. She's in her sixties I'd say, coat dripping onto the café's linoleum as she wedges herself into the seat, her skin rosy and tight, glasses steamed up. Cheery. Friendly. Chatty. All the annoying attributes.

'I've only been out for five minutes and I'm soaked. Suppose I could have stayed in, but I get fed up with my own company. Prefer a blether with a cup of tea rather than sitting in front of the telly. Never anything worth watching anyway. I hope you've not had to come far in this. I'm Annie, by the way.'

All I want is a coffee and five minutes to myself. I think I'm entitled to that. My head's full of what lies ahead and none of it is pleasant. I'm trying not to think about it. Can't stop thinking about it.

'Not too far,' I tell her.

Glasgow isn't a good city to live in if you're not the sociable type. People talk to people here. Whether the other people like it or not. They always want to know if you're all right, they always want to know how it's going.

I went to London once. You walk along the street and no one looks you in the eye, no one makes conversation with people they don't know. On the Tube, at a bus stop, no one ever looks at anyone else, far less talks to them. It's great.

It's not that I don't like people, it's just that I shy away from talking to the ones I don't know. Inside I'm fine. Inside I'm all witty answers and searching questions, inside I'm lovely and friendly and caring and cheerful and interested. It just doesn't come across that way.

'Is it your day off, love? What's your name, anyway? I'm Annie.' I know.

'It's Louise. And no, I'm just about to start work.' I'm trying to get by with saying as little as I can and hoping she'll take the hint. She isn't taking the hint.

'Oh right. What is it you do then?' She looks at me and at her watch as if trying to make sense of it all. These clothes, this time of day, her mind working overtime.

'I'm a hairdresser,' I tell her.

'Ah right,' she smiles, as if her detective work was spot on. 'Are you in the wee place on Dowanhill Street, Louise? I've heard they're really good in there.'

'No … I work for my myself. Not in a salon. I do home visits.'

'Oh, that would be handy.' She nods appreciatively at the idea, although at the same time I can see her looking at my hair and wondering why it's such a mess. It's confusing her, but she pushes past it. 'Getting someone to come to mine to do my hair would be lovely.'

I make a face. It's supposed to be apologetic but could look like anything.

'I'm booked up. Sorry. For ages. And I do elderly people who can't get out to a salon.' She looks so disappointed. 'You're too young,' I tell her and do my best to smile.

She takes that. 'Who are you going to see? I probably know them.'

'Are you local?' I'm hoping that she isn't.

'Oh aye, all my days. Just live two streets away.'

I shouldn't. I know I shouldn't. But I'm curious. 'I'm going to see Mr Agnew. Thomas Agnew. On Modder Street.'

She shrugs with her mouth, tasting the name but not recognising it. 'Don't think I know him. Nice that he's still taking care of himself though.'

'Anyway, I better get going. Don't want to keep Mr Agnew waiting.'

I'm already on my feet, pulling my coat on and making for the door.

Almost none of what I told her is true. My name's not Louise and I'm not a hairdresser. I'd no idea what I was going to say when I started to answer her, but I was never going to tell her what I really do.

I don't like talking about me. So, sometimes, when I feel trapped, I think the only thing for it is to lie. It's wrong, I know, but it's easier that way. Safer too.

The only bit that is true is that I'm on my way to Mr Agnew's, but I'm not in quite the rush that I made out. Mr Agnew isn't going to give two fucks if I'm late. He's already dead.

Chapter 2

I park in an empty bay, a few doors away from the address I've been given. The street is like a hundred other Glasgow streets, a faceless stretch of red sandstone on either side, four storeys high, straight as a die for two hundred yards, every building identical, not an inch to spare between them.

These tenements are in Partick, a few hundred yards back from Dumbarton Road, but they could be in so many parts of the city. They make me think of camouflage. Of claustrophobia. The kind of place where, these days, everyone knows everyone else and no one knows anyone at all. A good place to hide and a lonely place to die.

I grew up in a street much like this one, just a few miles north and thirty-odd years ago. Two bedrooms, a bathroom and a living room, a communal back green. All the rooms with sky-high ceilings but still pokey enough that three people who didn't get on couldn't easily avoid each other.

I've done my homework on Modder Street, same as I always do. I like to know who I'm dealing with, how it came to be that someone could go unmissed for so long. Most of the flats are rented, either from housing associations or private landlords; just a handful are owner-occupied. One hundred and twenty-one people – sixty men, sixty-one women. Just a handful of kids, just a handful over seventy-five. Seventy-four single people, five widowers. All but eighteen of the people are white, all but twenty-five of them were born in Scotland. Students outnumber workers, who outnumber the retired.

Those figures are out of date now. They include one old, white, widowed Scotsman who'd owned his home but is no longer with us.

Thomas Agnew had lived in 22/8, so top floor, right-hand side, and I strain my neck to look up. White roller blinds lowered to half height, bright sun stinging the glass, the man's flat is as anonymous as any of its neighbours.

I've got keys for number 8, but they haven't given me one to get past the communal front door. It's locked and I'm going to need to buzz the door entry system and ask someone to let me in. I dread it. It's almost as bad as speaking to someone on the phone. I need three attempts before I get a reply. The man's voice is gruff, local, straight to the point.

'Who is it?'

'Hi, my name's Grace McGill. Can you let me in, please? I'm going into Mr Agnew's flat.'

'Who?'

'Mr Agnew, 22/8. The man that died.'

'Oh.' A pause. 'Right.'

I think I hear a bit of embarrassment in the two words. Maybe some guilt. Or maybe I'm just hearing what I want to hear. Either way, the guy doesn't want to ask any questions, doesn't need to know who I am. There's a short buzzing sound then a click. I pick up my two cases and put my shoulder to the door.

As I climb the stairwell, my nose is tickled by the perfume of a traditional Glasgow close. It's not terrible, just the familiar aroma of stale air simmering in a lack of natural light, of something *fousty*. As I cross the second-floor landing, I hear a door squeak open behind me. 22/3.

I turn and see a tousled grey head sticking through the gap between door and frame. The man is in his fifties, in jeans and T-shirt, with a week's growth peppering the chin that he lifts to me by way of greeting. His voice is the voice from the door entry. And he's looking me up and down.

I don't like people looking at me.

Does anyone like people looking at them?

I'm a bit too tall and a bit too thin. My hair's too long and my face always looks slightly less happy than I feel. My smile is sort of … wonky. It's probably because I don't use it much, not enough practice to get it right. The more I try, the worse it is, overstretched or up at one side and down at the other, or just plain weird. I'm better off not smiling at all.

I should really get my hair cut, but that would mean going to a hairdresser, a real one, and that would mean unnecessary conversation. I'm not going anywhere on holiday; I'm not doing anything nice at the weekend; and I've absolutely no views on reality TV, so it would just be an eternity of pain spent fobbing off attempts to make me talk. Anyway, I got out of the habit last year during lockdown and am done with it. So instead, I tie my hair back, I pile it up, or else I just don't care and let it lie where it falls. It's dark and wavy and there's lots of it, a mane with a life of its own – which is more than can be said for me. I do like brushing it though. A couple of times a week I make sure I take a long bath then spend an age easing a brush slowly through it the way my mother used to. It feels good, easily the best hour or so I have.

I've always dressed the way I wanted to, which is to say without much thought as to what's fashionable or flattering. I wear flat shoes, never heels. I'm five feet ten and that's already tall enough to make men feel uncomfortable without making it any worse. I wear shirts and jeans, or hoodies and jeans. I own two dresses and haven't worn either of them in three years.

I've been told I'm pretty, but that was mostly by my mother, or men who probably didn't mean it. All I can see is my wonky smile and too much hair. And green eyes that are a little too big for my face.

So that's me. Too much of this and not enough of that. Pretty to some, pretty average to others, and never happier than when wearing a mask.

I don't know what the man from 22/3 thinks of what he sees but I know he wants to talk to me. And that's something I could do without.

'Mr Agnew,' he starts. 'That was the old boy on the top floor?'

'Yes.'

He's weighing that up. And taking his time about doing so. I'm forced to say something just to break the silence. 'Did you know him?'

'Not really. Saw him coming and going but not for a while. What happened to him?'

'He died.'

I know I'm just winding the guy up by stating the obvious, but something tells me he deserves it.

'*Aye*.' He's not pleased at my lip. 'So I heard. But what was it?'

'Natural causes. Old age.'

He sounds disappointed. 'Right. I heard he'd lain there for a long time before he was found.'

I think, *For someone so nosy you could have checked on him now and again.*

I say, 'Five months. Maybe six.'

His mouth drops. 'Jesus. I'm sure I saw him just last …' He thinks better of it. 'That's a sin, so it is. How could he be dead all that time and no one know? You'd think someone would have checked on him.'

I nod in agreement. 'You'd think someone would have.'

He twists his mouth in sympathy then straightens it again as he takes my meaning. 'I didn't know the man. I'd say hello if I passed him, but didn't know him to talk to. Didn't even know his name.'

I think, *Well, you should have*.

I say, 'We've all got busy lives.'

'Right.' It sounds defensive and so it should. 'I'm working most of the time. You know how it is.'

I do.

'Anyway …' The man's finally had enough of apologising for being himself and he's sounding his retreat, 'I hope he's … Are you his daughter or something?'

'No.'

'Okay, well … okay.' His grey head withdraws, and the door closes. *Prick.*

I climb to the top floor and take the flat's key from my pocket, slip it in the lock, then put on my protective gear. I pause, like I always do, never quite knowing why. My version of taking a deep breath while I can. I quietly say one of my prayers, one of the Buddhist ones.

'*With infinite oceans of praise for you, and oceans of sound from the aspects of my voice, I sing the breath-taking excellence of buddhas, and celebrate all of you gone to bliss.*'

A metallic creaking breaks the silence and my train of thought. I look back to see the letter box of the flat opposite open a couple of inches. I can't see eyes in the darkness, but they must be there, looking directly at me.

Whoever is there says nothing. They just prop open the letter box and stare out at me. I must be quite a sight. An alien in a white spacesuit, my hood and mask covering my face, standing outside a dead man's door. There's nothing else for me to do but stare back into the void of the flat opposite. It seems I'm braver behind a mask. Ruder too. I just look and look.

The silence fills the space between us. We stare at each other for a full minute, but it seems longer. I'm just about to give up and enter Mr Agnew's flat when the neighbour beats me to it. The metal flap falls closed with a clunk. As it shuts, a single muffled word escapes. I can't quite make it out but think it's *weirdo.*

I turn the key and push the door open, slowly.

The hallway is a sea of mail and fast food flyers. A narrow pathway has been cut through the middle of it by the feet and legs of police and paramedics, leaving knee-high mounds to either side. This is what you get when time stands still, when no one knows or cares that there's no longer anyone at home. I've seen it too many times, letters continuing to be sent because direct debits continue to be paid, pizza offers and takeaway discounts that can't tell the difference between life and death, and guilt-etched Christmas cards from people who can't find the time to call or visit.

It was a water leak that brought people to the door. A student in number six noticed a small sag forming in his ceiling and called his landlord. Three visits to Mr Agnew's flat brought no response so they'd little choice but to call the police, who put the door in and found the old man lying dead in bed.

That was two days ago. The cops have gone, what was left of Thomas Agnew has gone too, and only the smell remains. I'm suited up and wearing a respirator mask but there's still no missing the odour. I got used to it ages ago, I've had to, but that doesn't mean I'm unaware of it.

I know the science. The very second that life ends, decomposition begins. The gases and chemical compounds that get released from the body all have their own smell. Cadaverine and putrescine smell like rotting flesh. Skatole smells like shit. Indole is mustier, like mothballs. Hydrogen sulfide is rotten eggs, methanethiol is rotting cabbage, dimethyl disulfide and trisulfide are like the worst garlic you can imagine. They all smell bad, but together they smell like nothing other than death.

This one is bad. The boys in blue would have got it full blast when they put the door in. Some of them can't handle it and you hear the odd tale of tough-guy cops throwing up, eyes streaming, stomachs heaving. If they're lucky it might be so bad that the underwater unit gets called in with breathing apparatus to get the body into the shell.

I start, as always, with an appraisal of the property, doing an initial walk through and hazard assessment of the scene. Moving quietly through the flat, I head for the bedroom. Mr Agnew's final resting place. His deathbed.

It's where the dangers are; potential biological hazards like bloodborne pathogens, human body fluids and tissue. They could be hiding in grout, cement, wood flooring, sub flooring, you name it. The entire room has the potential to emanate death odours, so my first task is to use cross-contamination protocol to control it by securing and separating it from the rest of the flat. I seal it off, then set about making it safe.

It's my job. I'm a lonely death cleaner.

To give it its Sunday name, I carry out bioremediation. I do the deep clean that's needed after a body has lain decomposing for so long. It's smelly, it's sad, it's messy, and it's dangerous.

People almost always want the clean-up done quickly. It's another thing out the way, something else they don't have to worry about, and it helps their grieving process and their sense of guilt if they don't have to think about their loved one lying alone in their own dirt.

From the door, I can see a chest of drawers topped with a ragged line of framed photographs, a large pine wardrobe with its doors half open. There are more unopened letters, discarded socks, and a small stack of yellowing newspapers.

I pick my way carefully across the room until I'm standing by his bed. I can't help but stare. When someone has lain in the same place for five months, you can still see where they've been, still see their shape, long after they've gone.

I don't know how many people have taken the time to remember him, but the bed has. The bed holds his memory, his length, his width, his final outline. It holds hairs on the pillow and his depth in its contours. It also holds a dark soup of bodily fluids. Mopping them up is my next job.

The police are waiting on post-mortem results, but they've told me there are no suspicious circumstances, sure that Mr Agnew just passed away in his sleep. I kneel by the bed, the only sound the rustling of my protective suit. As I look closer, my breath catches in my throat and I'm aware of my skin tingling and my heart rate rising, but nothing else. The room, the house, the outside world, all shrink into black silence and the only thing I can see or think of is the tiny object on the corner of Mr Agnew's pillow.

My hands are gloved in blue as I pick it up. A dried daisy. I hold it up to the light, turning it between two fingers. The petals used to be white but now they're a murky grey. The yellow centre is dull and burned out. I stare at it for what could be seconds or minutes until the spell breaks and I bring it near to my mouth and kiss it through my face mask before dropping it gently into a clear plastic bag. Mementoes must be kept or else there's nothing to trust but memories.

I've only been told three things about the man. His name, that he'd lived alone, and that he lay undiscovered for an estimated twenty weeks. The police are appealing for family members to get in touch as there are no known relatives.

I use a fogger to get rid of the insects, flies mainly, that have infested the room. I don't mind them particularly, it's maggots that I can't stand. I can't even allow myself to think about their feasting.

To do this job you have to be two things that seem at odds with each other; professional and compassionate. Sometimes I'm too much of the second one, and that's my curse. I do what I do because I care.

That's why I say a prayer for the dead, why I'll sort through the man's things and find mementoes as a permanent reminder of his life, something to pass on to those that come after him. It's why I'll light candles in the house and place flowers by the bed, why I'll say another prayer before I leave. If I do it right, I'll make order from the chaos, make right some of the wrongs that loneliness brought. I'll make it the way I think he'd have wanted.

The bigger companies don't have time for this and, often, neither do the owners of the properties that need to be cleaned. It costs me some jobs but gains me others. Those who care enough, or feel guilty enough, will pay a little extra or allow a little longer to have me do it my way.

I move the bed and begin ripping up carpeting, knowing it's saturated with contaminants that no amount of cleaning will make safe. It has to go.

As I do so, I study the photographs on the dresser, six of them in all, three in black and white and three in colour. Snapshots of a long life that ended in solitude.

The first photograph is a young Mr Agnew, I'm sure. He has his arm around a girl, raven-haired and dark-eyed. They're on a wide sweep of beach, not anywhere warm by the clothes they're wearing.

The couple are married in the next frame. Him in a suit and dark tie, her in a white dress and veil, his arm tightly around her waist, their eyes glued to each other's. They age slowly in the next three photographs, morphing into colour as they get fuller and, eventually, greyer. Dancing cheek to cheek in one, eating dinner in another, at their ruby wedding anniversary party in the third. A man and his wife growing old together as their images edge along the dresser's top. The final photograph is Mrs Agnew on her own, slimmer, frailer, smiling at the camera.

No photographs of children, none of grandchildren. No friends on show. Just him and her. Then, just him. Old and alone.

Old people all look the same when you're under forty. They tend to wear the same uniform; colourless clothes in too many layers, fashions of all decades and none, with the same grey faces. It's too easy to think that's how they've always been, that they were born old, that they lived frail and died frail. And, of course, it's not true. Every single one of them has a back story.

They've all loved and lost, chased dreams, made mistakes, done good things and terrible things. They fought in wars, had affairs, stole and cheated, stood up to bullies, started businesses, saved lives, took lives, learned stuff, forgot stuff, and had plenty of sex. If they hadn't, none of us would be here to underestimate them, patronise them, and ignore them.

They might look the same to people my age, but they're not. They might look like they've never done anything interesting, but that's bullshit. If they look so tired, it's because they've done so much.

They've all got stories to tell, but most of us are too busy fucking up our own lives to listen.

I kneel and take a closer look at the pile of newspapers. There are six of them, neatly stacked, all corners matching, all copies of the same newspaper, the *Scottish Standard*.

Leafing through them, I find each copy is from the same day in different years. July 23, 2004 and then every July 23 from 2016 to 2020. His birthday or his wife's? The anniversary of the day they met, or their wedding? Maybe. I don't know, but I know it meant something to Mr Agnew. I'll make sure these are kept, just as he'd kept them.

Once I'm certain that I've removed every stain, every drop of fluid, every ounce of the soup that was once Thomas Agnew, it's time to clean, disinfect, and de-odorise all the affected surfaces. That requires an ex-pensive assortment of special disinfectants, degreasers, brushes and squeegees. People don't realise how much some of this shit costs. I have a special vacuum cleaner that set me back over a grand just because it has a filter that stops bacteria being pushed out into the air. A reg-ular vacuum cleaner throws out some of the particles and when you're dealing with corpse dust, that's not a particularly good idea.

This part of the process is time-consuming, expen-sive, monotonous, and life saving. It tips over from one day into the next, defying all haste, and sees me grafting at the clean again the next morning, the rooms secured in my absence.

With it done at last, I move around the room with an eye for anywhere else that might harbour danger or bugs or something personal that should be retained. Most houses have all three, a dead person's home has them in spades.

It feels intrusive, poking around among his things, even though he's long gone, but I know I'm doing it for the right reasons. I work my way through the chest of drawers, but it's full of socks and underpants, vests, and a lot of woollens, V-necks, crew necks and tank tops. The second drawer from the bottom has a surprise though. There's something wrapped in what looks like old newspaper, black type on off-white paper, a part of an advert for a car showroom facing up at me. It's rectangular, like a book but thinner, wrapped like a last-minute birthday present.

I peel back a layer of newsprint and reach inside, immediately regretting it as something stabs me through my glove, pain flashing into my thumb like a needle. I instinctively drop the wrapped object and it falls back into the drawer, nestling on a striped V-neck jumper. I'm bleeding.

I pull the glove off and suck on my thumb, drawing out the excess blood until the skin is translucent with the ruby red glowing beneath. It stings, but I'll be fine. I reach for the wrapped item again, more carefully this time, and turn back the newspaper. Inside is a photograph in a frame, its glass smashed, broken slivers screaming out in violent, jagged lines from the centre.

It's a plain wooden frame, a black-and-white photo inside. A group picture of five young men, late teens or early twenties, arms over each other's shoulders as they stand in a cheery, sunburned line, the sea behind them. I recognise the place, I'm sure it's the pier at Rothesay on the Isle of Bute. Going by the other photos, Thomas Agnew is the one in the middle, tall and skinny with sticky-out ears and a huge grin on his face.

The newspaper is the *Scottish Standard*, the same as those stacked in a neat pile on the floor. This one is dated

Friday, August 28, 1964. The advert is for Callanders in Kelvinside, a sketch of a car for sale, something called an Auto Union 1000. There's a story about Glasgow City Council announcing that all men with Beatles haircuts would have to wear bathing caps in swimming pools after a committee said their hair was clogging up filters. That, and a report saying the new M8 motorway linking Glasgow and Edinburgh would open that November, and little else of note. I rewrap the photo frame and place it on top of the chest of drawers.

The wardrobe is a tall, dark wood affair, a serious piece of furniture. I open the doors and immediately take a step back in surprise. Inside are newspapers. Hundreds of them. Three tall, fading stacks of them.

I've long since stopped being shocked by people and what they do, particularly in the privacy of their own homes. One thing I know is that they collect stuff. With some, it's teapots or watches, others it's carrier bags or stamps, beer mats or postcards. I cleaned a house once where the old lady who'd died had an enormous collection of used train tickets. There were bags and bags of them strewn around the house. It seemed she'd kept every ticket she'd ever bought. Automatic barriers had probably been the death of her.

Poor Mr Agnew clearly collected newspapers. The stacks are just too big to simply have been something not thrown out yet. He was either a collector or a hoarder. Some people are one and tell themselves they're the other.

I look through stacks of papers, flipping up front pages and seeing the dates. There's not just the *Standard*, but the *Daily Record*, the *Express*, the *Sunday Mail*, and the *Herald*. They're not in any order, but almost all the copies are from different dates in July, with some from days in early August. As I delve into the piles, I find copies from 2014, 2018, 2012, 2019 and more; a jumbled selection of summer days from every year since 2011.

Whereas the six copies in the room were piled with precision, these have been thrown in haphazardly, copy onto copy, edges all off kilter. They've not been cared for or considered important, but he kept them. These newspapers are screaming at me, hundreds of different screeching voices drowning each other out, all unintelligible. I close the wardrobe doors and the noise stops immediately. I can't deal with whatever it is they're about. I'm going to leave them locked away to be disposed of.

Instead, I'll take the copies that meant something to him, whatever it was. Fetching clear plastic bags from my case, I carefully, respectfully, slide the six newspapers inside in the order they're stacked. I'll take these and the cross on the wall, the daisy that was by the pillow, the photographs from the dresser and the smashed framed photo from the drawer, the neat, blue-and-red striped tie that was hanging in the wardrobe, plus another couple of items, and fill a box with them. They were his things and, as best as I can tell, they represent his living if not his life.

I'm nearly done. I've installed air purifiers, I've disinfected, I've double bagged and removed contaminated items for disposal. Finally, I've tested for ATP. Adenosine triphosphate is an enzyme that's present in all organic matter, so blood, saliva, bacteria. The luminometer tells me it's clear and I'm good to go. So do my body and mind. A clean, done properly, is exhausting physically, mentally and emotionally.

I put down my cleaning cases and the box of mementoes, and take a moment, much the same as I did before I came in. I turn and face into the room, close my eyes and pay my respects.

'God bless.'

The thing is, I don't believe. Not any more. I stopped that nonsense a long time ago. Too many lies and broken promises, Gods and Jesuses who hadn't come for me when I'd prayed for them to. It was okay, that was done and dusted. I don't hold grudges, I just don't believe.

So, praying is a bit odd, I know, but it's just me and the shape where the old man had been, no one to judge me other than the god I don't believe in, so nothing lost. Mr Agnew had believed, so it's the least I can do. Do good or do nothing, that's how I see it.

I close the front door behind me and turn to see a woman standing in the doorway of the flat opposite, arms crossed over her chest, appraising me over a cigarette. The letter-box peeper, no doubt. The woman is looking at me as if trying to work out what I am.

She's in her thirties, roughly my age I'd say. Dirty blonde hair pulled back on her head, and laughter lines that don't look like they've been caused by laughter.

'You the one that's cleaning Mr Agnew's place?'

'That's right.'

I get a judgemental shake of the head in return as the woman makes a disgusted face. 'Don't know how you can do that.'

I think, *And I don't know how you can live next door to someone for five months without knowing they're dead. Takes all sorts, doesn't it?*

The neighbour's mouth opens and closes, opens again, then closes for the final time. Her front door slams shut with a bang. Wait, did I say that out loud?

Oh well. Never mind.

I gaze back at Mr Agnew's flat, my head turning to follow my train of thought, and I have to wonder just how disgusted the neighbour would be if she'd seen what I'd seen.

Chapter 3

Three weeks later

I'm still slowly simmering when I get back to my flat on Brunswick Street after an aborted attempt to deliver the box of mementoes to Thomas Agnew's sole living relative.

Three weeks were time enough for the post-mortem to come back as an open verdict with no suspicious circumstance and for the police to trace a man named Kevin Durham, Mr Agnew's sister's daughter's son. The man's grandmother is long dead, his own parents emigrated to Australia. It's him and only him within five hundred miles with a known family connection to the dead man.

Okay, so maybe I understand that he can't get too emotional about someone he didn't know, but he was still a *person*. Even if you didn't know them, love them, like them, surely it would bother you that anyone can be left to rot, unmissed and uncared for? Turns out it didn't bother Kevin Durham and I've returned home with the box of memories still in my arms.

I need to calm down and not take this inside. It's our unwritten law, George and me, that I do my best to leave my work and my worries on the doorstep. I pause outside the front door, breathe in some calm air, and breathe out a lungful of frustration.

George can usually tell how my day's been by the way I close the door, and I'm determined not to go there. I shut it as slowly and calmly as I can, but the flat is so quiet that the noise echoes through the stillness anyway. I don't want a fanfare and a marching band, but welcome-home silence is always a downer.

'George? I'm home. And I could really do with a hug. *George?*'

There's no answer and I make my way to the kitchen with a sigh, dumping the bag and the box on the table. I fill the kettle and leave it to boil, searching the fridge for a snack. I edge aside some cold meats that might make a sandwich, disregard the cold chicken as well, and settle on some Greek yoghurt and a tub of diced fruit.

'George?' I call louder this time.

As I close the fridge door, he's there. Standing a few feet away and looking as if he's wondering where the fire is. I can't help but smile. He's as handsome as ever and just what I need after a day like I've had. We hug and I immediately feel better, some of the day's dirt washing away.

'I had to deal with this selfish prick tonight. Wasn't interested in taking the stuff I'd collected from his great-uncle's house. You think people might care, but this guy didn't give a damn.'

George scolds me with his withering stare. I know I'm not supposed to bring this home with me but …

'The old boy, the great-uncle, had lain there for five months. I told you about him. Five months and no one missed him. That's not right, is it? At least I've got you. You'd miss me even if no one else did, right?'

Instead of answering, he slips from my grasp and winds his way around my leg before heading to his dish and looking up pleadingly. I've no doubt this cat loves me, but he never loves me more than when he wants to be fed. I have food therefore I am loved.

'Is that a no? I need to know you'd miss me. Can you imagine having no one? What a crappy life that would be. George?'

He's not going to engage in this conversation, or any other conversation, until he's been fed. I do my duty and he duly loves me for it. I then sit at the kitchen table and close my eyes.

There's not a sound in the place, not the pad of paws, not the swish of a tail. If George is still there, he's abandoned me to my thoughts. My mind blackens as it fills with images of Thomas Agnew and Kevin Durham, of loss and selfishness, of empty homes and unseeing neighbours. I slump to the tabletop, my head on my folded arms.

I let the darkness take me, swimming in it, drowning in it. Why do I do what I do?

The ping of my mobile drags me rudely out and I reluctantly lift my head. When I see his name on the screen my heart sinks. I read the text but push the phone away. I don't need this right now.

I get up and walk away, leaving my mobile in case it goes again, and wander through to the living room.

Looking around, I remember how bare this room is and promise, yet again, to do something about it soon. When it's done deliberately, as a style statement, they call it minimalism and it's meant to be a good thing. When it's done by inaction, by not bothering, by not having a reason to make an effort, it's called empty.

There's my chair and there's George's chair, the television, and a small table with a lamp. On one wall is a framed photograph of my mother and on one of the others is a single shelf with ornaments and keepsakes. That's it.

It's supposed to be the main room of a house, yet I spend so little time in it and no one else ever sees it, so I've never felt the need to add unnecessary flourishes. I know there's supposed to be more, that most people would have more, but I'm not most people. I'm very much aware of that.

I go over to her photograph. It deserves a wall to itself. It was taken in a restaurant in town, a rarity, and she's pictured sitting behind a large plate of spaghetti and a glass of red. She's smiling. Happy. And it makes me happy to look at it. That's why it's there.

The shelf with the knick-knacks on it isn't quite the same. It doesn't exactly make me happy, but then not all memories are going to do that. I look at them and sigh, eyeing one after another, and close my eyes for a moment. They're still there when I look again; the carriage clock and the little statue, the paperweight and the glass candle holder. The last one's the one that means the most and I pick it up, running a finger softly over

26

the pale blue glass, holding it up to the light and seeing the colour change. When I can't look any longer, I place it carefully back on the shelf.

From the kitchen, I hear my phone ping again. I know it's him and I'm not going to answer it.

The box of stuff from Mr Agnew's flat is lying on my kitchen table and that wasn't the plan, not how it should be. The stuff is for *them*, for the family, not for me. Now I have it and some unwanted responsibility. I can't throw it out, that would be disrespectful, but I can't keep it either. Not like this. Like this it's just a box of questions without answers, gnawing away at me. I need to do something to get it out of my system. I need to work on my model.

The model of Thomas Agnew's bedroom.

It's something I began doing a few years ago. My own way of remembering things, a sort of tribute and a form of therapy. Truth is, I don't know why I make them, but I know I feel better for doing so.

I've always taken photographs to document the scene. Often, relatives don't have the stomach to visit the place where the person died, but then want to see what it all looked like once their conscience gets the better of them. But I came to realise that the photos only show so much. They show what's there, not what you *feel*. Photographs can't capture sadness; they can't properly convey the pointless bleakness of it all. So, I started making the dioramas.

Not that I knew that's what they were. I thought they were just models, if I thought they were anything at all. I'd never heard the word until I started googling for help on how to make them – and to try to make sense of why I was doing it.

I'm still not sure there's much sense to it, but there it is. Thomas Agnew's bedroom is taking shape on my kitchen table.

There's a bed in place, headboard against the middle of the back wall, door in the front left corner. That's the bare bones of it, a skeleton that I can fill and furnish until it has the look and the feel of the room on Modder Street.

My miniature version of it – my diorama – is 30 centimetres by 30 centimetres. Mr Agnew's bedroom was 4.8 metres squared, so a scale of 1:16. Everything I put inside it must be as near to that as possible. Wardrobe, chest of drawers, photographs, clothes, the stack of newspapers, the discarded clothes, the wallpaper, the carpet. All the things that are imprinted on my brain.

I can't stop thinking about it. About him. About how long he was left alone. About the neighbours and family, no matter how distant, who let him lie undiscovered. About the long life left untold, the people who had filled it but slipped away one by one until the solitary end. Until he lay dead in that flat for five months. And I can't stop thinking about all I saw there.

I already had a scaled-down wardrobe among my collection of stuff that is a near fit for his. The size, shape and style are right, but the colour is off by a few shades so I'm darkening it with wood stain to make sure it replicates the original. I've already washed it down using a rag and trisodium phosphate, and now I'm drying it with a paper towel. If I want the feel of Mr Agnew's room – and I really do – then it's important to get it right.

The little plastic wardrobe is dry to the touch now and clean enough to allow me to stain it. I'm using a tinted polyurethane, laying it on in parallel lines with a fifty per cent overlap using a foam paintbrush, keeping the brush moving, keeping the coverage even.

Five months he lay in his deathbed with no one no-ticing. Twenty weeks. Every time the thought crashes through my mind I get angrier, and I squeeze the brush a little harder.

The polyurethane gives a topcoat to the plastic wood, letting the fake grain show through underneath. Not the truth, just something that looks like the truth. It's darkening before my eyes, morphing shade upon shade into the mahogany shadows of Mr Agnew's wardrobe.

I'm going to make a little pile of newsprint to sit out-side it, tiny rectangular cuttings from one of the faded *Scottish Standard*s that I rescued from the flat. That pile of papers has been bugging me since I first saw them, one day in time that meant something significant to the old man, but I couldn't guess at what. I'll cut out a lot more miniature copies from the same old paper and fill the inside of the wardrobe with them, stuff them in hap-hazardly the way he had.

I've found a fabric online that's a good match for his red plaid bed cover, sourced a paint colour that's as close as I can get to the vintage off-white shade of the walls, and ordered a little chest of drawers that will be the image of the one in his room.

I remember that Mrs McCrorie had a very similar cabinet in her bedroom. Mrs Helen McCrorie, a widow who lived and died in a flat in Allison Street in Govanhill. It was six months before she was found, dead in her bath. She suffered a pauper's funeral, and no one came except me and the priest and a red-faced man who'd obviously been promised a tenner if he went along to boost the numbers. I've been thinking about Mrs McCrorie a lot since I cleaned the Modder Street flat.

I'm going to make a daisy for the pillow while the wood stain is drying on the wardrobe. I've decided it will be the last thing I place in the room when it's finished, but I want to start making it now because it's playing on my mind.

I don't want to place it on the doll's house pillow on the doll's house bed until I'm satisfied that everything else is right. So far, I've taken care of the furniture and fittings, and that's been the easy bit, giving me the look of the place. For the feel of it, I'll add the mess around the bed and print off some tiny replica photographs to sit on the chest of drawers to give more of a sense of the sadness and abandoned despair that filled that room. But I feel the need to make the daisy.

I've got to make one because the smallest replicas I've been able to find on the crafting websites are silk flower heads, cute little things, just 3.9 centimetres by

3.9 centimetres, perfect feathery petals with golden sun centres, the daintiest of daisies, but still too big.

I need one a sixteenth of the size of the one from Mr Agnew's pillow, so I'm going to make it from a polymer modelling clay called FIMO Professional that's great for holding detail and gives me the flexibility to make pretty much anything I want.

George is brushing against my legs, talking impatiently, doing his best to break my concentration as I pockmark the round flower head with the point of a needle. He's making demands for attention or more food as I carve out delicate petals and lay them on the flower disc in two alternating layers. I'm going to ignore him best I can until I've placed the clay daisy on aluminium foil in the oven to harden. Eighteen minutes at 110C, a little paper tent over the model to prevent scorching.

I feed George a little more and think about Mr Agnew. I make myself a sandwich, pour a glass of milk, and think about Mrs McCrorie. The sense of despair that hung in the air in both houses, the impression of something not being right.

Eighteen minutes and there it is: a miniature daisy, freshly baked and ready for painting. My mum called them gowans, said it was what her mother, my Granny Davidson, always called them. An old Scots word for daisies that I still use sometimes because it makes me happy.

I need to get the colour right so I'm mixing some brown paint in with the yellow to take the heat out of the glowing centre, stripping the life from it. Then the same with the petals, making them grubby and listless. But even as I painstakingly apply the paint, I know. The gowan's still too big.

Allison Street runs west to east through Govanhill, from Pollokshaws Road to Polmadie, hundreds of identical sandstone flats hiding in plain sight above the busy road. Mrs McCrorie lay dead in one of them for half a year before anyone bothered to look.

It takes half an hour for the paint to be dry to the touch. I pace the floor, driving George to distraction. I can see him watching, wondering what's wrong with me. I blow gently on the clay petals, hastening the process by seconds, then walk around some more.

My phone has pinged twice more with texts and twice more I've ignored them. My head's full of Mr Agnew and Mrs McCrorie and there's no room for him as well right now.

I'm not going to wait until the rest of the diorama is finished. I can't. The itch that's been clawing at my skin demands an answer and I've given in to the urge to see the daisy where it should be.

I slide my hand into the model room and immediately it seems weirdly otherworldly, like a fairy-tale giant invading a home. My fingers are quite long, piano-playing hands my mum said, and the tiny painted gowan is held firmly, gently, between forefinger and thumb, ghosting past the wardrobe and reaching for the pillow.

The daisy is still too big. I place it on the miniature pillow on the miniature bed in the miniature room and it's still too bloody big. It's sticking out like a sore thumb, like Gulliver in Lilliput, like a grown man on a kid's tricycle. It's half the size of the pillow and screaming out to be seen. Unmissable.

Unmissable. How could the cops or the SOCOs not see it and think, hang on that's a bit strange, something's not right here, it's not what it seems? Instead, all they saw was an anonymous old man dead in his own mess and they couldn't care less. How could they miss it?

Mrs McCrorie had a neat little flat. It reminded me of my gran's. Same kind of carpet, much the same ornaments, similar curtains. All bought from the same granny shop, I guess. I've been thinking about Mrs McCrorie a lot since I cleaned the Agnew flat. It's been hard not to.

Reaching carefully back into the model room, I pluck the daisy from the pillow, feeling it stick a little, tacky to the touch because I'd rushed it. I slide it back out and hold it up to the light for a few moments before stepping on the bin pedal and dropping it inside.

All the little mementoes I save from the houses of the undiscovereds mean something. Whether they find a home with the family of the deceased or are stored away by me, it's important that they're kept, looked at and thought of. It's said that we all die twice: once when we breathe our last, and then again when the last person we know says our name. My undiscovereds were forgotten in life, I don't want them to be forgotten in death too.

I've been doing my best not to think about Mrs Mc-Crorie, trying not to see things that aren't there. I've been trying so hard that I can't think of anything else. My head's a mess of guilt and accusations, memories and associations. I'm trying to keep them all alive by saying their names.

I have a drawer of little things. Rescued items. They're not labelled because they don't have to be. I remember, and that's the whole point of them.

I know, without looking, that the bag I want is at the back right of the drawer. It's behind a holiday postcard sent from Ullapool to the home of Mr John Taylor in Steel Street off the Saltmarket. It's next to a lucky sixpence that belonged to Ms Margarita Dunlop who was found in the living room of her upmarket tenement flat in Walmer Crescent in Cessnock.

I reach for the bag, eyes closed, feeling for it with my hands. I ease it out and hold it up to the light. Inside is the object that I lifted from the edge of Mrs McCrorie's bath.

A dried daisy. The petals once white but now a murky grey. The yellow centre dull and burned out.

Chapter 4

Six months Mrs McCrorie lay undiscovered. Five months before Mr Agnew was found. *Daisy, Daisy.*

I turn it between two fingers, studying the faded petals and the dried-out disc flowers. I remember every house I clean and have a memory of every person whose remains I bagged and prayed over. Even though this daisy is dead, the florets still form a perfect pattern, hundreds of them flowing from the centre. Some clients stay with you more than others. Mrs McCrorie is one of those.

I realise I'm crying, tears trickling down my cheek. I'm scared.

Daisy, Daisy. Give me your answer do.

Wiping at my eyes, I make the start of a decision. I get paid to clean. I get paid to remove and disinfect, to soak, decontaminate and dispose. I don't get paid to think and I don't have the courage to wonder.

Some things are better left alone. Some questions are better left unanswered. Right?

I slide the plastic bag back into its hiding place in the back right corner of the drawer, the daisy inside. Out of sight, almost out of my mind.

My hand is still on the drawer handle though and I'm wrestling with my conscience when my phone beeps once more, dragging me back into the room.

I reluctantly pick it up and look at the messages, seeing it's the sixth text from him in the last hour. It's angrier than the one before, and much angrier than the one before that. I wonder how much he's drunk between text one and text six.

I make the same decision that I make every time this happens. The only one I can make. I push the drawer firmly closed. The cat sits and watches and I know he's judging me.

'Don't look at me like that, George. It's not like I have much choice. He's my dad.'

George just looks back at me. He knows the old bastard has given me hell for years. And he knows what he did to my mother. And I guess he knows that I'm going to go anyway.

I fetch my coat and my car keys and head for the door.

His flat is just a few hundred yards away from where we lived when I grew up. I'm sure he'd rather have been back there on Avenuepark Street if he could, but those bridges were burned a long time ago. Instead, he's above the shops on Maryhill Road, the traffic plaguing him all day long and giving him something else to complain about.

I drive around the back and park on Hathaway Lane, the bit people don't see as they charge past on the main road. From there the walls are red and rough, there are green squares of grass, tight cobbled spaces you can squeeze your car into, and dark openings into the tenements. I sit in my car until I can't put it off any longer, swear at myself under my breath, and go inside.

His door needs painting, and the name plaque belongs to the people that lived there before him. I knock and wait.

I hear his voice, raspy, loud and demanding. 'Who is it?'

He knows it's me. He commanded my presence, he recognises my knock, and no one else ever visits him. He knows it's me. I've got a key but he makes me knock.

'It's Grace.'

'About time.'

The last line, spat out like phlegm, makes me think about turning on my heels and going home again, but I won't. I never do. He opens the door and turns away without waiting to see my face. I follow him inside and make my way through the hall, entering the living room just in time to see him fall back into the worn armchair that will forever hold his shape.

'I could have been dead by the time you got here. Could have been lying on the floor for hours. Not that you'd have cared.'

I think, *You texted me half an hour ago. You couldn't have been lying there for hours. And if you could text me you could call an ambulance. If it was needed.*

I say, 'I'm sorry.'

He's not the intimidating sight he used to be. Not the bad-tempered bastard who used to sit at the kitchen table in a vest, with scars and tattoos visible, muscles ominous. Not the man who sent plates and cups flying with the back of his hand, breaking crockery, glass, and hearts. He's scrawnier now, more bone than brawn, and there's a greyness to his skin. The temper is still there, burning darkly in a wasted shell, now too big for the body that holds it.

The eyes are the same too. Cruel and green, still capable of delivering a glare that can shrivel your soul. He's still got most of his hair, greyer and longer than it should be for someone in his late sixties, but clinging to his head like a man overboard.

He was never a good-looking man my dad, but he had a presence that made up for that, something about him that made women look and wonder. Trouble was, it wasn't the something that they thought it was.

I see the glass on the table by his chair, half full or half empty, and he catches me looking.

'Something to say? Can't a man have a drink in his own house without getting a lecture? If you're going to come round here with that attitude you can fuck off again. I don't need to be told how much I can fucking drink.'

I think, *Yes, you do. You need to be told it every night. You're an alcoholic. A pain in the arse when you're sober and worse when you're drunk. I should just leave you to drown in it.*

I say, 'You know what the doctor said. You need to cut back. For your own good.'

'I'll decide what's for my own good.' He tugs the glass to his mouth, the whisky swilling, and downs it. 'Here,' he thrusts his arm towards me, 'you can fill this up again. Do something useful for a change.'

He hasn't shaved for a few days and the grizzled grey spikes his jutting chin. Of course I'd love to slap it, and of course I won't. Instead, I take the glass to the kitchen and quietly ease as much water in alongside the whisky that I think I can get away with. He looks at it suspiciously on my return but takes it anyway.

'Have you taken your pills?'

'Aye.'

'All of them?'

'I said so. Not that they do me any good. I've been sitting here in agony. Worse than dying, so it is. If that doctor had any idea what the pain was like he'd give me twice the dose. Doesn't give a fuck that guy. Just wants me out his waiting room as quick as possible and then not see me for another six months.'

I've heard this tune before. It gets played every time I visit. I'm going to stop dancing to it one of these days.

'D'you hear me?'

'I hear you, Dad. I'm sure the doctor's doing his best.'

'Oh aye, sure he is. What took you so long anyway? Six times I had to text you. No point in me having that phone if you don't answer. What were you up to? It's not like you were on a date, is it?'

I think, *Fuck you*.

I say, 'I was working late. I had to go see a relative of a man whose house I'd cleaned, and by the time I got back and had some food I was knackered. I think I must have nodded off.'

His eyes light up. 'You're a fucking liar. My phone shows me when you read the messages. You read them. You weren't sleeping. You're a fucking liar.'

Shit. 'I was tired.'

'*Tired*. Get yourself a proper fucking job then. No wonder you're tired, wading around in dead people's shit all the time. That's no job for a woman.'

I think, *No but you're happy for me to clean up your shit. Happy for me to be tired tidying up after you, cooking for you.*

I say, 'I like my job. I'm good at it and I like it. I'm doing something good.'

He gives me the look. Sneering. Scornful. Unbelieving that I even have the gall to say that. 'Something good? You're a cleaner. And for fucking *dead* people. You know what that is? That's embarrassing.'

'It's a job. My job. And I make sure people get to go out of this world with a bit of dignity.'

'What? Like your mother did?'

There's silence. A horrible noisy silence like the world has suddenly stopped and you can hear its brakes screeching. For a moment I think even he regrets saying it, then I see the smirk creeping onto the corner of his mouth, and I know he's the bastard he always was.

I have to leave the room, get out of his sight and him out of mine. I'm going to clean. It's what I do for a living and it's what I do when I'm angry. The greater the anger, the greater need to punish myself, so I'm going to clean his bathroom.

He's not careful about much in his life and that's undoubtedly true about his aim and his hygiene. I get bleach, rubber gloves, toilet brush, spray and cloths and set to work. It will be spotless when I'm done, every surface disinfected, scrubbed and refreshed.

The problem is that I'm out of his sight but not out of earshot. He's in his chair, criticising, insulting, harping on and on about my failings. The badgering is constant. I'm trying to shut most of it out, but words and phrases still sneak through my defences and the bathroom door. *Selfish. Ungrateful. Bitch. An embarrassment. Bitch. Liar. Waste of space. Uncaring. Bitch.*

It continues relentlessly for half an hour. Every word makes me scrub harder, wiping every stain of him from the surface. I finally finish, the bathroom will be immaculate until ten minutes after I've gone. Maybe it's because I've stopped that I hear his latest barb, and it pushes me over the edge.

'You're a fucking waste of space, just like your mother. I don't know why I put up with her as long as I did and I'll not be putting up with you as long, that's for sure.'

I tear off the rubber gloves, throw them to the floor, and storm into the living room. I don't say anything but lift the whisky glass from the table before he can stop me. It's not much of a protest but it's all I can think of in the moment. He's surprised so doesn't move, and slow once he does. I'm in the kitchen and the booze is down the sink before he gets near the kitchen door.

'What the fuck are you doing you stupid bitch?'

I think, *What does it look like?*

I say, 'What does it look like?'

'That's my fucking whisky you're wasting.'

His voice is lower, rougher. His eyes are half closed. Like a wolf. He's edging towards me. That's when I realise my big mistake. He's between me and the kitchen door. Between me and my only way out.

He lurches forward and I know he's going to swing his arm. He's old but he's still strong when he wants to be. He's old but he's also drunk and he's slower than me. I take two steps to the side out of his reach and race for the door. He lashes out as I pass him, just catching me on my shoulder.

He's shouting, raging so much that it's just a noise, the anger scrambling words I can't make out and don't want to. But as the front door closes behind me, I can clearly hear his last yell before it's swallowed up by the darkness of the close.

'You're your mother's daughter all right, you fucking bitch.'

Chapter 5

It was lashing down as I ran from my van to the Fiscal's office on Ballater Street at Gorbals Cross. The sky had rumbled, black as night, tipping down a month's worth of rain in a heartbeat. By the time I burst through the front door, my hair was soaked, and my clothes streaked wet.

Now I'm waiting for one of the admin officers, idly watching the water pooling at my feet as it drips from me to the floor. If the rain that's stolen its way into my coat had fallen a couple of hundred yards to the north it would have hit the Clyde and would now be heading out to sea to start again. Instead, it's dying a slow death on a mind-numbingly dull office carpet.

The sound of my name being called snaps me back into the room. I look up to see Harry Blair standing a few feet away with a folder in his hand. This makes me happy. Harry's one of the good guys and can be relied upon not to give me a hard time just for the sake of it.

'Hey Grace. Is it raining?'

Okay, maybe he won't give me a hard time, but he's Glaswegian so he's still duty bound to take the piss where he can. Harry is in his late forties but lean and fit, a marathon runner, and married with a couple of kids. I'm a regular visitor so he looks after me like I'm a customer. Today, I've got to return the key to a property so that they can sign off on it and release it back to the landlord. I also want a favour.

I hold up the key so Harry can see it, then lay it on the countertop.

'Rahul Agarwal. The IT guy who died in the flat in Jordanhill. Job's all done.'

Harry gives a brief shake of the head and purses his lips. 'Poor guy was young wasn't he?'

I say, 'Yes, just thirty-three. Heart attack. He worked from home so it took two weeks before anyone noticed or worried enough to check on him.'

Harry blows out hard. 'Living with this virus and working from home the last year or two was bad enough,' he says. 'I can't imagine doing it full-time. I need people around me.'

I think, *Lockdown wasn't that bad. Staying at home is the easy bit.*

I say, 'Yeah. Me too.'

I felt about lockdown the way alcoholics must feel about Hogmanay. Suddenly everyone else thinks they're in the same boat and makes this whole song and dance about it. But getting wrecked on New Year's Eve gives you zero insight into life as an alkie, and living on your own for a few months of lockdown doesn't give you the first clue of what's it like to live a lifetime of loneliness.

For the likes of me, lockdown was a sideshow, something that was happening to other people apart from the dreadful increased workload it brought. Too many lonely people dying undiscovered as everyone was locked away on their own. The human cost was awful, although I'll admit to seeing an upside if it means the end of people wanting to hug each other. I've never been a hugger.

'Harry, do you remember Thomas Agnew? The five-month undiscovered in Partick.'

'Modder Street?' he asks, and I nod. 'I remember. Cops said it was a bad one. I don't know how you do it, Grace.'

I think, *Yes, it was a bad one. Maybe worse than you know.*

I say, 'Someone's got to. Might as well be me. Can you check on the funeral details for me, Harry?'

'Sure. Why do you want them?'

'I'm thinking of going.'

Harry laughs softly. More with me than at me. 'Of course you are. Never change, Grace.'

I'm not sure why it's funny, but I know that it seems to be. Someone needs to go to the man's funeral. I'm still angry that no one cared enough to notice he'd died. And I'm still on edge at the memory of the daisy and all that it might mean. I can't tell Harry that though.

He starts to look for Mr Agnew's file in the database but stops himself.

'Have you fixed a date with Doug Christie yet?'

'*What?*' I know I sound flustered and I'm mad with myself for it.

'For the interview he wants to do. Come on, Grace. He's really keen and you know he won't mess you about. You can trust him.'

'No way, Harry. I *don't* know I can trust him. And you know I don't like talking about myself.'

He looks sympathetic. 'You wouldn't be talking about yourself. You'd be talking about your models. You don't have to open up about anything you don't want to.'

My models. The dioramas. I wish I'd never mentioned them to Harry, never mind shown him the photographs on my phone. But he was interested and persuaded me, so I did.

They're not art. Not to me anyway. What would I know about art or how to make it? But that's what Harry says they are. When he saw them, he said he thought they were amazing. I was surprised, flattered, and a bit embarrassed. Then he said he'd told Doug Christie about them and I nearly died.

Christie is a journalist. I saw him a bunch of times over the years on either side of police tape, and we've chatted. Well, he's had to do most of the chatting, but he's easy to talk to and kind of easy on the eye. Now he's more of a feature writer, but still has an eye for the darker stuff.

He seems a nice guy, but the idea of opening a door that I've always kept locked is terrifying. I'm a private person, and the dioramas are almost the most personal and private part of my private life. So, I'm reluctant to say the least, but Harry keeps pushing it and … it's Doug Christie.

The biggest problem with Doug is that I like him. He's a journalist and funny, and has broken all kinds of stories. And journalists are sort of glamorous. Well, interesting at least. And he talks to me like I'm a real person. And, well, you know, he's a good-looking guy. And. And. And. And he's married. That's a plus though. Married makes him unavailable and means he's not interested in me, which is fine. If he wasn't married, he wouldn't be interested in me for an entirely different reason and that would hurt. My track record with men is unsurprisingly awful.

I've had the grand total of four boyfriends in my life. Danny Moran, Greg Fotheringham, Lewis 'one week' Wilson, and Matt Aitken. There was also what I guess you'd call a one-night stand with a guy called Paul Cairney, which I sort of regret and sort of don't.

So, I'm more than okay that Doug Christie is married. I fancy him, he doesn't and couldn't fancy me, and that's how it is. Despite all that, Harry is still intent on shoving us together, platonically, to show the world my dioramas.

'Come on, Grace,' Harry says. 'Your models are incredible, and more people should see them. These things should be in an art gallery, not stuck in your flat. And you know Doug.'

'No. I've met him,' I say defensively. 'I don't *know* him.'

'Grace, he's a good guy. You do know that. And he works for the *Standard* now, not one of the red tops, he's not going to sensationalise your stuff.' The *Standard*. The same newspaper that Thomas Agnew kept copies of. Newspapers keep archives, don't they? Someone who worked there would probably have access to all the editions of July 23 that there ever were. But it's still a no.

Harry huffs. 'Why don't you at least think about it while I'm digging out the funeral arrangements for your Mr Agnew. Co-op job, I'd assume?'

'No chance. I'm not doing an interview. But yes, bound to be the Co-op. He's got no family.'

Co-op job is insider parlance for a public health funeral. Basically a local authority provides funeral arrangements as there is no one else to do it. They're what are sometimes called pauper's funerals. It's an ugly phrase. In Glasgow, the council has a contract with Co-operative Funeral Services, and they do all of them, around sixty or seventy a year. They're usually done first thing in the morning, minimum of fuss, and burials are in a common, unmarked lair. I've been to a few. They're grim, sad affairs. Usually no people there except those who are there to work. A minute's silence that there's no one to hear, then the coffin is lowered, or the curtain closed. Job done. Duty performed. Life over.

Harry looks up from his computer screen, a bemused look on his face.

'Looks like we were both wrong. It's not a public health funeral at all. It's been paid for.'

'*What?*'

'There's a service for Mr Thomas Agnew at St Simon's on Partick Bridge Street on the 15th. Followed by a cremation at Daldowie. Privately paid.'

'Who's paid it? Is it a guy named Kevin Durham? Agnew's great-nephew?'

'Not that I know of. It's listed as anonymous. Name withheld.'

My mouth drops open and I clamp it shut again as soon as I collect myself.

I'd been thinking of attending Mr Agnew's funeral. Thinking of newspapers and daisies, of photographs and uncaring relatives, of things known and unknown.

I'd been thinking about it.

Now, there's no doubt in my mind. I'm going.

Chapter 6

St Simon's is a little church on the slope of Partick Bridge Street. It was built in the 1850s by a priest named Daniel Gallagher who taught Latin to David Livingstone and set him on his way to Africa. It's the third oldest Catholic church in Glasgow, but is now surrounded mainly by new builds, a blond sandstone oasis in a desert of gentrification. Many people know it as the Polish church because of its links to exiled soldiers in World War Two, and there's still a mass said here in Polish every week.

It really is small, only just bigger than the rectory next door. There's no one going in or out, and for a moment I wonder if I've got the right time and place. I hesitate before the tall, dark wooden doors, then slip inside, immediately sensing the still solemnity of a funeral. I have to fight the instinctive urge to cross myself, scolding my hands for beginning to move.

The church is musty and echo-quiet, my footsteps ringing off the floorboards. There are just two other people inside – no, I correct myself, there's a third. Mr Agnew's coffin sits before the small altar; red, blue and yellow rays streaming across it from the stained-glass windows above. The coffin makes him look small. Smaller than the man in the photographs, smaller than the indentation left in his deathbed.

Being at a stranger's funeral feels like gatecrashing a wedding. A guilty voice inside me wants to tell them I'm not here for free sausage rolls or communal comfort. It begs the question why I *am* here, but I've learned sometimes it's better not to ask. I take a seat about halfway towards the front, better to see, less chance of being seen. The two other mourners are sitting well apart, one front row centre and the other on the right of the third row. They're hunched and both wearing black overcoats, both old from what I can see, most likely contemporaries of Mr Agnew's and, I hope, friends of his if not each other. There's no great-nephew, no Kevin Durham, and I curse him under my breath.

I'm here because I'm angry and I'm here because of the daisy. I'm here because my undiscovereds stay with me. I'm here because no one else is, because they couldn't be arsed to care enough in life or in death.

The words of a Beatles song drift through my head and I realise I'm humming it, hopefully not aloud, although I can't be sure. Eleanor Rigby. Buried along with her name. Nobody came.

The priest walks in from stage left, head down and businesslike. He's young but balding, wiry and solemn. I christen him Father McKenzie in my head. He stands in front of us and introduces himself as Father O'Dowd but I prefer McKenzie. He's not the usual priest, he's just filling in, he says. I'm not sure any of us care. I'm not sure that he does either.

He begins the words of a sermon that he probably thought no one would hear. He's going through the motions and I can't help but think he could be reading his shopping list for all the emotion he's putting into it. He obviously didn't know Mr Agnew at all nor has he taken the time to find out anything about him.

He says Mr Agnew was a good man, says he lived a long and fulfilling life, that it was a life of joys and sorrows, and that he is now safe in the arms of God. I can only assume McKenzie has a pro-forma sermon tucked away in his computer so that he only needs to cut and paste the name of the deceased.

McKenzie asks us to stand and pray. The man in the front row gets slowly to his feet, his weight on a walking stick, and as he rises, I see he's probably in his seventies, stern-faced and ruddy with a thick, white moustache. The other man is taller and slimmer, seemingly fitter. Both are as grey-haired as doves. I watch them as they bow their heads to pray, and can't help but wonder what they know.

As McKenzie makes his final remarks, a burly bald-headed man in a dark suit wheels a metal gurney in from the wings and positions it next to the coffin. With a nod from the priest, the two old men rise from their seats again and make their way forward, one shuffling, the other striding. They reach the coffin simultaneously and take a place at either end, neither making eye contact with the other. The stocky assistant and the metal gurney do most of the work, but the old men and the priest help manoeuvre the coffin onto the trolley, then the two of them accompany it down the aisle, one at either side.

I can't take my eyes off them as they walk towards, then by me. The shorter man has one hand pushing the trolley and the other gripping his cane. His eyes are fixed on the next step in front of him, his face looking more angry than sad. The taller man has a thousand-yard stare, head up, wet eyes gazing somewhere unseen.

Once they're past me, I stand and walk to the aisle to follow them and the coffin out of the church. It's only then that I see there's one more mourner, a younger man, perhaps in his fifties, sitting towards the rear of the church. He's pale, with cropped dark hair, smartly dressed, black suit and tie, and is staring forward. It's only as the coffin passes his row that he swivels his head and fixes his gaze on the cortège. As soon as they pass, he turns his attention back to the altar, or something beyond it. I try to catch his eye as I leave but he won't have it, continuing to look straight ahead, expressionless.

I'm outside on the pavement of Partick Bridge Street, rain beginning to fall, and see the coffin being slid slowly into the back of a hearse. I look left and right and across the street, but see no sign of the younger man with the intense stare, and it bothers me.

The two old men are standing well apart, not looking at each other, and I wonder if I have the nerve to talk to them, ask them where they were for the past five months. Even if I can somehow muster that, I know I won't say what I want to. That I'm glad they came to his funeral but where the fuck were they when he needed them?

I start towards the taller man, thinking he looks more approachable, but I get no more than two steps before the rain becomes heavier and he turns up his collar and turns away. I can only watch as he hurries to a car and gets inside. I spin, but the other guy has also gone, and I'm left alone in the teeming rain.

Fuckety fuck. I really hadn't wanted to go to the crematorium, it's not my favourite place, far from it, but now I know I'm going to. I want to know what their story is.

Daldowie Crematorium in Uddingston is a familiar end place for thousands of Glaswegians, a beautiful, traditional stone building with a decorated copper dome, set in sweeping lawns and well-maintained flowerbeds. It is a lovely place in many ways, but it chills my bones. It's maybe because it's exposed enough that the wind can rattle through the grounds like memories, or the thought of bodies being something one moment and nothing the next. Maybe it's the overwhelming fucking sadness of the place.

Most likely of course is that it's where we said goodbye to my mum. I will never forget sitting transfixed as that curtain closed, my mind filling in the blanks, seeing the flames engulf the coffin and her body within. For at least fifteen years, I could close my eyes and see, all too vividly, that which I'd never seen.

As I pull into the car park, there's a host of cars already there and I briefly let myself think there's been some sudden discovery of friends and family of

Mr Agnew. It takes one breath to realise that they're much more likely to be there for the cremation before or after his. There's only Daldowie and the Linn serving Glasgow, so it's inevitably a conveyor belt, a heartfelt, dignified conveyor belt of one service after another.

The scene inside is heartbreaking. Row after row of empty seats, stretching from deep at the back of the room all the way to where Mr Agnew's coffin sits at the front. It's just as it was in the little chapel except bigger and brighter, making the coffin and the two mourners seem smaller and sadder. They're still sitting far apart, one in the second row and one in the fourth. The dark-haired man is nowhere to be seen.

Father McKenzie has made the trip over from St Simon's, the final bit of the job, the last right and the last wrong. He's wiped the dirt from his hands, and no one is saved. Maybe I'm too hard on him, maybe it's just his face. And his voice. And his tone.

It's not going to take long. One reading, one prayer, and McKenzie will be done, we'll all be done. I realise I've not heard what he's been saying for the last few minutes. I'm just waiting. Dreading the closing of the curtain. I close my eyes but all I can see is another fire for another coffin. And a daisy. I can't help but see the daisy.

I can't take it any more and get to my feet. I retreat, quickly, quietly, down the aisle, to the door. I know what I'm going to do. Much as I'm not going to like it, I'm going to talk to them.

Two minutes later and the tall man is first out. He's not as tall as he should be, a bend in his back seeing to that. His face is creased with age and bags are holding up his eyes. I take a half-step across so that he can't go any further without knocking me over.

'It was a nice service,' I lie. It's no time to be telling the truth. 'I hope he'd have liked it.'

There's a glimmer of recognition in his rheumy eyes and I realise he must have seen me at St Simon's. 'Yes, I guess it was nice. Not sure Tommy would have liked it, he was never one for funerals. Not after Liz went. Are you …?'

He's letting the question slide in the hope I'll fill it in for him. I do, sort of.

'Yes. I'm Cathleen. A great-niece. On Liz's side.'

I hold out my hand and he's little choice but to shake it. 'Oh right. I'm Bob Meechan.'

His forehead creases and I know he has more questions, but luckily the other old man appears at the doorway before he can ask them. He's out of breath from the effort of shuffling up the length of the chapel, and ready to head off without speaking to anyone.

I put my left hand on his arm, consolingly, and reach for his hand with my right. It's so much easier pretending to be sociable when you're already pretending to be someone else.

'I was just saying to Bob. Nice service. I hope Tommy would have liked it, but then, I suppose he was never one for funerals.'

'Aye,' the man looks unsure at what's going on and distinctly uncomfortable at being trapped with Bob Meechan. 'It was … nice, right enough.'

'Jackie,' Meechan says in a brusque greeting, as if forgetting they'd carried their friend's coffin together just an hour earlier. There's an odd edge to what's passing between them and I can't understand it. But I know I want to.

The florid-faced Jackie has no option but to respond. 'All right, Bob?'

'Yeah. Fine, fine. You?'

'Okay. Thanks.'

That's it. They fall back into awkward silence and I know they're both about to leave. I'm anxious, fretting at the prospect of them walking away in different directions, taking with them any chance I have of learning anything about Tommy. I need to do something, say something.

'There's a wake,' I announce, the words out of my mouth before I have the chance to think them through. 'Food and drink for Tommy's friends and relatives.'

They both look doubtful. 'And I don't think there'll be any other relatives. So, it would be good if you could make it. A last chance to pay respects. Someone should really be there. As many as possible.'

I'm out of emotional blackmail, but I can see it's working. Both men look uncomfortable and unable to come up with an excuse in time. Their mouths are twitching, chewing words and thoughts, then they nod half-heartedly.

'Where is it?' the taller man asks.

Good question. 'The Lismore,' I tell him, giving him the name of a pub I know of near Tommy's flat. 'Okay,' Meechan nods, 'I'll be there. What time?'

I look at my watch. 'Two o'clock.'

He and I look at Jackie, who shrugs. 'Two o'clock. Okay.'

I'm wondering what the hell I've said and how the hell I'm going to do it. The why is easier; I want to know more.

I see the two men properly look each other in the eye for the first time and know that whatever it takes, I'll do it. Something in the look they give each other bothers me and intrigues me. They both look scared.

Chapter 7

I'm still Cathleen, the lying great-niece, when I phone the Lismore from my car. The woman who answers the phone is a bit surprised to be asked to arrange a wake at five minutes' notice and more surprised it's for just three people. But she says sure, they can do sausage rolls and sandwiches for three. And we'll have a few rounds of drinks, I add. Tongue looseners, I hope.

I'm not sure the two men will turn up. The easiest thing was for them to say yes to get rid of me then bugger off home. But as I go inside the pub, the first person I see is Bob Meechan, tall but slightly stooped, standing at the bar with a pint in his hand. He's looking around warily, seeing who else might be there. I'm about to go across to him when the other man, Jackie, comes through the door behind me. He doesn't look like he wants to be here, but at least he's made the effort.

'Hi Jackie, thanks for coming. I'm sure it would mean a lot to Tommy to know you're here.'

Jackie doesn't look so sure about that. He doesn't look so sure about me either. He nods with his mouth twisted. I watch as he sees Meechan at the bar and the expression hardens.

'Why don't you take a seat and I'll fetch you a drink? They've reserved a table for us. What can I get you?'

'Whisky,' Jackie relents. 'I'll have the one. Ardbeg if they have it. For Tommy. Just a drop of water in it.'

'Great,' I smile. 'I know he'd appreciate that. I didn't catch your surname, Jackie.'

He hesitates but tells me. 'Stevenson. Jackie Stevenson.'

Jeez, Cathleen is a lot bolder than I am. It feels weird. Empowering in one sense but tiring and alien. I'm not sure how long I can keep it up. I go to the bar where Bob Meechan is still standing. He's seen the other man arrive and seems glued to his spot.

'Let me get you another one of those, Bob. You get a seat. They've got us a table. Jackie's there.'

He smiles like a hostage making the best of it. 'I'm driving.'

'You only go to your friend's funeral once.' Cathleen is a fucking terrible influence and I mentally apologise for her.

He gives in. 'I guess I can leave the car. Get it tomorrow.'

'Good thinking. Not far to go then?'

His eyes narrow. 'Not far. I'll have a pint of Guinness. Thanks.'

He leaves me, maybe to get away from me. But he's going to sit, and I'll take that. I order up the beer and the whisky, plus a Diet Coke for myself. I briefly worry about all the aspartame in it but figure my head is already messed enough that it won't make much difference.

I tell the woman behind the bar that I'm the one paying for the sandwiches and sausage rolls and she takes my card and fetches me a receipt. I apologise for it being so last-minute, me taking over from Cathleen again and becoming tongue-tied and contrite.

I turn, job done, a tray of drinks in my hands, and stop in my tracks. Meechan and Stevenson are deep in conversation, heads close together, not for anyone else to hear. That's a change, that's not the pair that couldn't even look at each other before. I can't work out if it's good or bad, but I know it's different. Jackie Stevenson's index finger is jabbing at Meechan's chest, forcibly making a point. Meechan is shaking his head and the tips of his ears have turned crimson as his blood has risen.

Stevenson's eyes are wide, his face getting more furiously red as he leaves Meechan in no doubt what he's thinking. There's a lot of anger, a lot of rage and spluttering. I can't see Meechan's face but am guessing it's a mirror of Stevenson's. I don't know what to do. If I go over, they might stop, and I don't think I want them to do that. They're being the way they are because they don't know I'm watching. Then, just as suddenly, they do. Stevenson sees me and stops, says something quickly to Meechan and sits back in his chair with a half-hearted attempt at a smile on his face.

I walk over and ease the tray between them, taking my own seat at the table. The silence is so off-the-scale awkward that you could scratch it. It's going to have to be me that says something. Fuckety fuck. I raise my glass of Diet Coke, the ice chinking.

'Here's to Tommy.'

Both men nod soberly. 'To Tommy.'

They raise their glasses and nod them, one toward the other, then Meechan scoops back a lungful of his Guinness while Stevenson sips tightly at his Ardbeg. They sit their glasses back down and stare into them.

'How did you hear about the funeral?' I ask. Initiating conversations is killing me, they really better start talking soon.

'There was an ad in the local paper,' Meechan says. 'Not sure I'd have known otherwise.'

'Same,' Stevenson adds. 'Was it you that placed it?' he asks me.

It wasn't and I don't want them to ask much more. 'Tell me about Tommy,' I say. 'I'd like to know more about him.'

A look passes between them again. That's natural enough, I guess.

'He was a good guy,' Meechan says. 'You always knew where you were with Tommy. He was never the sort to say one thing to your face and another behind your back.'

Stevenson bobs his head in agreement. 'Yeah. Straightforward, that was Tommy. Salt of the earth. Maybe that's an old-fashioned phrase but true all the same.'

I think, *Okay that's a start. But you could be talking about anyone. I want details and I want to know why you bailed on him.*

I say. 'That's lovely. Did you two know him a long time?'

Another shared look. 'It's how well you know someone,' Meechan says. 'Not how long.'

I think, *Fucksake.*

I say. 'Yes, you're right. Tell me something about his life, his jobs, the things he liked.'

The hesitation is long enough for me to be sure they're thinking carefully about it. 'He loved his football,' Stevenson says.

'Yes,' Meechan seizes on it gladly. 'Loved his football, Tommy did. He was a big Partick Thistle fan. I mean, a proper one, not like when you don't want to admit you support Celtic or Rangers. He'd watch them on Saturdays, and Mansfield Park on Sundays. He used to give a lot of time to that wee team.'

This is more like it. It makes Mr Agnew real. *Tommy*. I want more.

'And what did he do with his days?' I ask. 'I guess he wasn't out much after Auntie Liz died.'

I turn and see Meechan studying me over the rim of his Guinness glass. I don't like the look on his face.

'I don't remember Liz ever saying she had a niece,' he says.

'Great-niece,' I correct him, thinking it's a trap.

'Aye, right enough. Great-niece. I don't remember her ever having one of those either.'

Stevenson has the same expression now. Like he's looking at me properly for the first time and wondering what I am.

'Is that on her sister's side?' he asks thickly.

Oh fuck. I'm sure *this* is a trap. Or is it? Why did I lie in the first place? The two men are staring at me, demanding an answer. The right answer. I can feel my skin reddening and my heart is skipping.

'Her brother's side,' I tell him.

'Right …'

'Joe Pearson,' I say. 'My grandad.'

They look at each other, making some unspoken calculation amid their silent conversation. They signal agreement with heads and shoulders. I pass the test.

'I didn't know Joe,' Meechan says. 'I remember Liz talking about him though. That was a long time ago now, of course. Sorry about your loss, hen.'

I make a sad, grateful face. And inside I'm glad of my homework on Tommy and Liz, the online trip through ScotlandsPeople that showed she was born Elizabeth Pearson and had one brother, Joseph. I took a bit of a guess thinking he was known as Joe, but it seemed a good bet.

'I hadn't seen Tommy in six years,' Meechan admitted. 'But I heard he didn't go out much any more. Shops and back, and that was it. He hadn't been involved with his football team for a while. Problem with his hip, was what I heard.'

'Heard he was waiting for an operation,' Stevenson confirms. 'Don't know if that's true but it's what I heard. I don't get out much myself these days but a guy I know says he saw Tommy hirpling along Dumbarton Road. That was probably two years ago, mind.'

'Sounds right,' Meechan agrees. 'He had to pack in the bowling club too. Couldn't bend properly. He was a good player in his day, by all accounts.'

I think, *So why didn't you go to see him if you knew all this? Why didn't you do something to stop him being alone?*

I say, 'Did he change a lot after Liz died?'

They both breathe out hard, as if synchronised. I can feel the emotion coming from them.

'Broke his heart,' Stevenson says. 'He was never the same after it. Didn't really want to know anyone. Not like before.'

Meechan nods. 'It was like half of him had been ripped out. He was in bits and never got over it.'

'They were that close?' I ask.

'Like limpets,' Stevenson says. 'Never away from each other more than they could avoid.'

'I guess they had such a long life together,' I say. 'They got married quite young, didn't they?'

'That was the way it was done then,' Meechan agreed. 'People didn't hang about like they do now. Get married and stay married. Way it should be.'

I think, *Yeah right.*

I say, 'You're right.'

Meechan is enjoying his Guinness. I'm already eyeing his glass and ready to buy him another. Stevenson is going at his whisky more slowly, but I think he's getting a taste for it. Maybe he could be persuaded to have one more while I look for the courage to shame them about abandoning their friend and try to drag some information out of them. I want to be inside their heads.

'Did you know Tommy and Liz when they were young?' I ask them.

The shrugs are non-committal but they're warming up. 'Fairly young,' Meechan admits. 'But then we're old, so everyone seems young.'

'I remember seeing a photograph of them,' I white lie. 'They were on a beach somewhere. A black-and-white photograph but not anywhere warm by the look of it. I think it might have been Bute. Would that be right?'

Meechan stiffens and he leans in a bit towards me. 'Bute? No, I don't think so. Don't remember them ever going to Bute. Do you, Jackie?'

Stevenson frowns firmly and shakes his head. He answers with a snarl, his moustache twitching. 'No. Never.'

I don't like Jackie Stevenson much. Too angry, too touchy and grouchy. They say don't judge people by their looks, but I think by the time you get to his age, you've grown into your face and the outside shows the inside.

'He liked horse racing too,' says Meechan. 'He wasn't what you'd call a gambler, but he liked a bet. Just a couple of pounds a day. It gave him an interest. Tommy could tell you the name of just about any favourite running any day of the week.'

'Liz wasn't so keen, mind you.' Stevenson says it like it's meant to be a joke, but I can't hear much humour in his voice. 'He'd tell her he was taking the dog for a walk, but he'd never get further than the Ladbrokes on Dumbarton Road.'

'And he loved that wee dog he used to have,' Meechan says. 'What was his name again?'

'It was a Westie, wasn't it? The wee white one. Hamish, was that it?'

'Aye! Hamish, that's it. Fat wee thing.'

'No wonder. It never got walked far enough!'

I know a change of subject when I hear one. And I'm itching at the way they dismissed my mention of Bute so quickly. I think they're lying and I want to know why.

'I remember seeing another photograph of Tommy when he was younger,' I say. 'Maybe in his early twenties. He was on Rothesay pier with some friends. All young guys together.'

Stevenson is mid-sip, the glass rim kissing his moustache. He stops, just ever so briefly, but I catch it. Even when he moves again and drains the malt, his eyes have changed and they're like a thunderstorm.

The thought genuinely hadn't occurred to me till those words came out of my mouth, but I suddenly find myself trying to picture the two old men beside me as they might have been when they were so much younger. I'm desperately remembering the broken photograph and matching the shadowy black-and-white faces of youth with the older, fleshier faces in front of me. Maybe. Maybe not.

Neither man has answered me, so I wait. Then I realise I haven't asked a question. So, I change that. 'Did either of you know him back then?'

'Back when?' Meechan isn't looking at me, but at the table. And although he's asked a question it's more like a challenge.

'I'm not sure. Before colour photographs.' *God that sounds stupid.* 'I mean, Tommy was in his twenties, so mid-sixties I guess. Were you all pals back then?'

'That was a long time ago,' Stevenson snaps. 'What do you want to know about all our yesterdays for?'

I hadn't asked a question and now he hasn't answered it. 'I'm just interested in knowing more about Tommy. Because he's gone.'

'Fair enough.' Meechan chips in. 'But why about back then?'

I think, *Because you're lying to me and I want to know why.*

I say, 'I don't know. I just remember that photograph. From Rothesay.'

I see a tic. A flicker in the corner of Meechan's eye when I say Rothesay. So, I say it again. 'It was Tommy and four other men. Boys really. On the pier at Rothesay with that sign behind them. Haste Ye Back. You know the one?'

There it is again. Right on cue. *Rothesay.*

'No, I don't know it.'

'This photograph that you're talking about,' I turn my head and see Stevenson staring at me hard. 'Is it yours? Have you got it?'

I lie. Of course. 'No, I just saw it at Tommy and Liz's flat. When I was wee.'

Meechan's brow furrows in thought. 'And you remember a photograph after all this time?'

I think, *Good point.*

I say, 'I remember it because I used to go to Bute on holiday with my mum and dad. The first time I saw the photo, I got all excited because I recognised the pier. So, it stuck with me, I guess.'

'Right.' Meechan isn't completely convinced. 'Well, you'll know more about the photo than us. Can't tell you anything about it.'

I catch sight of a look from Stevenson to Meechan. It's clearly a warning shot. *Shut it.* He bangs his empty glass on the table and pushes his chair back, taking a misstep as he gets to his feet. 'Time to go.'

Meechan downs the last of his Guinness and he stands up too. They're both ready to leave. I'm exhausted doing so much talking and don't have much more of it left in me. But I'm still channelling my inner Cathleen and she has one more thing to say.

'Hang on. Please,' we say to them. They look reluctant, Stevenson still breathing hard and angry. They glance at each other and shrug. They'll hear me out.

'Which of you paid for Tommy's funeral?'

I see both men frown in confusion, foreheads wrinkling.

'What are you talking about? I didn't pay for the funeral,' Meechan tells me. 'I couldn't afford it even if I wanted to. Jackie'll be the same.'

Stevenson nods furiously, redder than ever. 'Nothing to do with me. He must have had insurance or something. Funerals are expensive. An insurance policy, that's what it'll be.'

I think, *They're not lying but it's not life insurance. Harry Blair said someone paid for the funeral privately. Harry wouldn't get something like that wrong.*

I say, 'Yes, you're probably right. It must be an insurance policy. Obvious, really. But one more thing … there was someone else at the funeral, a man about fifty or so, dark-haired and tall. Do you know who he was?'

They look at each other again and I can see that they don't know who or what I'm talking about.

Stevenson shakes his head, his mouth twisted. 'I've no idea. I'm going.'

With that, he turns and storms out as fast as his limp will let him. Bob Meechan is still standing by the table, seemingly stuck between staying and going, looking apologetic.

'Jackie's got a temper,' he says. 'Always has had. Try not to blame him for being a bit short with you.'

He wants to say something else to me. I can feel it. 'What about you, Bob? Are you going too?'

He pauses as if he's not sure. 'Yeah. I'm going, but no rush. No one to go home to.' His voice cracks slightly and I can hear the plea for help in it.

'Where do you live, Bob?'

He's itching to leave but nowhere to go. 'Shawlands. Brought up in Partick but got posh and moved to the southside thirty years ago. I kind of regret it now.'

'You miss where you grew up?'

He makes a face. 'It's more that the reasons that took me there aren't there any more.'

'You could move back.'

He shakes his head. 'I'm too old for moving. And far too old for running. No point in going back because the people that were there, they've gone too. Get to my age and all your friends are dead or dying. You know how it is.'

I do.

Chapter 8

Five young men in black and white, framed in broken glass.

Worse than that, in grainy, faded black and white that was probably never quite in focus in the first place. Five young men frozen in time. Back before mobile phone cameras, before taking twenty photographs in two minutes, when they had to make every shot count and take it to a chemist before they could see what they had. My mum used to tell me off for taking too many photos, as if they'd run out.

There's an easy companionship between them, hanging onto each other's shoulders like brothers. Three of them with shirts off, comfortably skin to skin, arms over arms. No casual acquaintances these. Of course, they might just have been drinking, the one thing other than funerals capable of turning west of Scotland men into Californian hippies.

No, these are a band of brothers. They didn't meet that day; they went there together. One for all and all for one.

Tommy Agnew in the middle. Is that just where he was standing, or was he leader of the gang? Men make a big deal of hierarchy, alpha this and alpha that. He's taller than the other four, and they're all obsessed with size at that age. But he's skinnier than them, green twigs for arms and legs. But it's definitely Tommy.

So long ago and far away. I look at the man-boy on Tommy's right. Stockier, grinning, carefree, shirtless. Can it really be Jackie Stevenson? I try to see the corpulent Toby jug man that was at the funeral and the Lismore, try to see him in the years before life soured his mood and his face. It could be. Someone that age could grow up to be anything.

I look for Bob Meechan. Tall, slender, stooping Bob. None of these guys are tall enough, but boys grow weird and late and fast. The one on the end, quieter than the rest, shirt unbuttoned, less shouty. Maybe, the face is sort of similar. Surely not though. I pick the photograph up and bring it close. Maybe.

The one to Tommy's left has what I'm guessing is red hair and freckles, pale skin, and a wide, almost manic grin. He shouldn't be out in the sun. And he looks like trouble. I didn't think that before, but now I know other things.

The last one is also shirtless. A chubby, cheery, dark-haired boy, shamelessly flaunting his puppy fat. He's got a nice face. Life all before him, like the others.

I put the photograph in a drawer. Then take it out again. I stare at it some more.

Chapter 9

Death gets in places you wouldn't think. Blood and fat have a life of their own.

It doesn't bother me any more, if it ever really did. The trick is to close your mind to where the stuff came from, where and what it used to be, and just scrub. To me, it's no different from cleaning an oven. It's messy, it's yucky and sticky, but with the right cleaning solution and plenty of elbow grease you get the job done.

And like in an oven, the messiest, the yuckiest, the stickiest, is fat. When the human body decomposes, it basically dissolves. It becomes fat, oozing and seeping where it pleases.

You know the saying that water finds its own level? Human fat is the same. I've had to remove it from cracks in floorboards, from electrical sockets, from ceilings, light fittings and grouting, from the legs of beds and the arms of chairs. It gets everywhere. And every single drop of it is a potentially lethal cocktail of pathogens and microorganisms that can make people sick months and even years later if it's not removed completely.

It's been three weeks since Tommy Agnew's funeral. Three weeks of wondering and trying not to wonder. Dreams of daisies and old photographs.

I'm in a flat in Baillieston. On my hands and knees in the bedroom, where the body of a woman in her early thirties was found dead on the floor. She overdosed on a street benzo called etizolam and wasn't found for a month. Her place is chaotic and bare, like a one-bedroom Mad Max movie.

Wallpaper is peeling from the living-room walls, a glass ashtray is overflowing with stubbed-out butts and ash, the worn and yellowing couch has cigarette burns, and the TV is propped up on three legs and a cardboard box. The floor is covered in a carpet so bare in parts that the pattern is unrecognisable as belonging to the rest of the room.

The tiny kitchen is dirty, and the window crawls with flies. There's food-turned-mould that's continuing to grow on the cracked Formica tabletop. In the fridge, there's a litre bottle of Coca-Cola, half empty, with another full one beside it. There are two ready meals for the microwave, both out of date by over six weeks, four cans of beer and a tub of creamed rice. And that's it. In the lone wall cupboard, there's four cans of soup, six packets of digestive biscuits, and a multipack of crisps.

The bathroom is a biohazard all of its own. Stains and spills, streaks and splashes. It's as bleak as a prison cell.

There's no bed in the bedroom. Amanda McHugh was found in a torn red sleeping bag. A bag of bones. The sleeping bag is in the lab and I'm removing her leaked remains from the nylon fibres of a lurid pink carpet that must have been put down for a young girl that's not slept here in many years.

I can switch off from the blood and the fat. That I can deal with, it's my job. What I struggle to do is switch my head off from the person. Right now, I'm wondering which is the greater tragedy, the woman who died young after choosing a lifestyle that she knew could kill her, or the old man who chose a straighter path and lived a long life, but died with no one to care for him? It's not a competition and maybe it doesn't matter at all, but it doesn't stop me thinking.

Tommy Agnew was old enough to have been this woman's grandfather. He lived in a very similar, very different, flat just eight miles away. He lived a very different life, yet the end was just the same. Alone. Undiscovered.

I've not been able to get Tommy out of my head. I clean many properties, clean up after many people, and I simply don't have the room to let them all live in my head, and mostly they don't. They are with me when I do the clean, then I close the door on them when I leave. Tommy Agnew has hitched a ride.

He's whispering to me now, asking if I'm still wondering about the photograph on his dresser. Asking if I can make sense of Bob Meechan and Jackie Stevenson's reaction when I mentioned Rothesay. He's asking me if I've read those newspapers yet. Asking me if I've looked again at the photograph by the pier and if anyone looks familiar.

This flat smells. Not just the usual stink of death, although that's here for sure, but something bad that preceded decomposition. Damp, decay, despair. They all have their own odours, and I can recognise each of them.

Drug users make up a high percentage of my clean-up jobs. Addicts, pensioners and suicides, they're the three groups most likely to go undiscovered. For me, the users are potentially the most dangerous. By the nature of their lifestyle, they represent a much greater biohazard than the general population.

My personal 'record' for an undiscovered death was also an addict. A young man who overdosed in a bed-sit in Kelvinbridge. He'd lain there for fourteen months until a debit card expired and his rent stopped being paid. Police tracked down his parents in Bearsden who'd disowned him because of his habit, and I delivered them a box of items that had them in tears on their doorstep. Top of the box was a framed photograph of them.

I also once spent an entire day removing the blood of a suicide victim who bled out from her wrists, painstakingly mopping it up from a carpet that the landlord refused to throw out. A week later, tox reports showed the woman had high levels of morphine and diazepam in her system. They also showed that she had hep B and hep C. That was the point when the carpet was finally removed and replaced, and when I got scared as to what I might have missed.

There's blood in Amanda McHugh's flat too. A rusty spatter near the door, unconnected to her death and, given the disordered lives of users, it could have been there ignored and uncleaned for who knows how long. It will be cleaned now though, and properly.

Seeing a blood stain may seem like bad news but it's not as bad as not seeing it. People think if they can't see the stain that means the blood is removed, but it's so not true. Blood is capable of seeping deep into surfaces and can prove nearly impossible to get out. So many areas of your home are porous and welcome blood with open arms, things like carpet, wood, fabric, and concrete. They'll hide blood till the end of time.

And blood, like red, means danger. Spills carry the risk of bloodborne pathogens, so as well as hep B and C, there's the risk of HIV, MRSA, brucellosis or syphilis. So, I have my own checklist for blood clean-up, a ten-step programme that never varies, no matter how big or small the spill. *Equip. Remove. Soak. Disinfect. Soak again. Dispose. Decontaminate. Check. Wash hands. Report.*

Equip means industrial-grade disposable gloves, suit and mask with respirator. Anything else is just asking for it. *Remove* any sharp objects. Imagine that you're wearing a condom and use forceps to get rid of any broken glass or shards that could puncture your protection. Cover the spill in cloth towels to *soak* up as much blood as possible. You need to do this before you *disinfect* because what is called a 'broad-spectrum kill claim' won't be effective if the surface is still wet. *Disinfect*, ditch the towels in a biohazard bag, then *soak again* and allow the area to dry. *Dispose* of all protective equipment in a biohazard bag. *Decontaminate* by using registered disinfectant to clean any equipment like dustpans, forceps or buckets that you will use again. Do a final *check* of your body for any contamination. Blood might have splashed onto your shirt or the back of your elbow. *Wash hands* with warm water and disinfectant soap. Be prepared to have red skin and to always smell overly clean. Finally, fill out an incident *report*. All done.

I do all of that now, even though it's not easy having someone with me, whispering in my ear, taking my mind off the task at hand. What about that daisy, he says. You know that was wrong. What about Bute, he says. You know they're lying, don't you?

I do know they're lying, Tommy. I sensed it at the time, the way they were so offhand about it and yet so sure you'd never been to Rothesay, never stood on that pier. How they were adamant you and Liz hadn't been on a beach on Bute.

After the wake, I went home and googled like crazy. I had the photograph of the two of you to hand, ready to compare, and as soon as I put Ettrick Bay into image search, I knew I was right. A long sweep of golden sand, the water glistening, the mountain ridges of Arran visible across the Kyles of Bute. The same place as in the photo. No doubt about it.

Have you read those newspapers, he repeats? Yes. And I've found nothing. Nothing but a series of random, surely unconnected news stories; local, national and global. July 23, 2004. Then 2016 to 2020. Murders, robberies, politics, scandals. A drowning, a missing toddler, a hit and run.

I wonder if Amanda had friends other than the ones who sold her the tablets that killed her. If there wasn't even one BFF that could have phoned or called in and found her before it was too late. I do this not unaware of the irony that there would be no best friend, for ever or otherwise, who'd drop in on me.

My timeline of female friends is similarly tragic to my history with boyfriends. One or two close friends when I was younger plus a handful more to say hello to, friends dropping in and out depending on arguments, job changes, house changes, whatever.

I think I always felt a bit different to most of them. At first, that was simply because I didn't realise that most other people suffered the same anxieties and insecurities that I did. Once I'd figured that out, it was a bit too late. I was already on the outside of so many cliques, had painted myself into a corner of awkwardness. The biggest problem with being shy is that you accept that's who you are because it's still easier than talking to people, no matter how much you want to.

I got better as I got older, but my mother's death sent me into hiding; from the world, from myself. I climbed out of that hole just enough to keep up with a few friends from work and old school pals, but only online. I can chat to the likes of Cath McDonald and Susan Shaw for an hour on Facebook, but if I see them by chance in Tesco then I'm likely to hide in case I've nothing to say after 'hello'.

So, that's how it is. In real life, just me and George. Online, a few people I can talk to. And at work, in real death, just me and the lonely lost.

Amanda McHugh's flat makes me sad. I'm going to do my best to put some things together, scrape a memento box from the few bits I can find in the hope that the cops will trace someone to take them. She was only thirty-two, three years younger than me, forty-three years younger than Tommy Agnew.

Amanda's story, at least the end of it, is written on the peeling walls and the threadbare carpet. It screams out from the chaos and despair and the absence of friends.

Tommy's story is wrapped in old newspaper, hidden from sight for decades. Maybe I've spent so long with dead people that I'm seeing ghosts where there are none, but I'm sure Tommy Agnew had a story to tell.

He just won't stop whispering to me, and it's driving me crazy.

Chapter 10

Death smells different when you know the person who's died.

It's two weeks later and I'm fretting outside a tenement in Grantley Gardens in Shawlands, struggling to remember how to breathe naturally and rehearsing how to make my feet work. I'm stuck to the spot as if my batteries have run out.

When you smell something, it's science that's happening. Odorant molecules – bits of the thing you're smelling – travel inside your nose and bind onto receptor cells. They then generate electrical signals and send a message to your brain.

The moment I saw the death notice in the paper, I got on the phone to Harry Blair and requested the job. Harry was surprised I asked for the clean because I rarely pitch for work, but I told him I knew the deceased, wanted to do the right thing by him. Harry said, sure.

So here I am. Glued to the pavement, heart pounding, and steeling myself for the prospect of my nostrils being infiltrated by tiny decomposing fragments of someone that I knew.

The front door to the tenement opens and a young woman exits onto the street, stopping abruptly at the sight of me dressed top to toe in my white protective suit. I can see it's taken all of two seconds for her to join the dots and know why I'm there.

Her neigbour. The dead man. The shame of the un-discovered.

She's in her late twenties, fresh-faced and friendly, blonde hair pulled back in a ponytail, and dressed to go running. She sees me and I know she's thinking of death as I watch remorse spread across her face.

'Are you here for … I mean, of course you are. Oh God, I'm so sorry. It's such a terrible thing. Poor man.'

People don't know how to handle second-hand grief or second-hand guilt. This woman's got no idea who I am but feels the need to apologise. And maybe she should.

'Are you cleaning out his flat?' she asks.

I think, *I am if I can. If I can remember what to do and how to think straight.*

I say, 'Yes.'

She blinks nervously, needing more from me than a monosyllabic grunt, but it's all I've got.

'He was a nice man,' she tells me. 'Not that I knew him well, but he always said hello and asked how I was doing. A really nice man. Always well dressed. Took care of himself.'

The last line hangs there. A well-meant platitude that suddenly sounds stupid. He couldn't have taken that much care of himself. He's dead, and lay there for two weeks undiscovered. I can see she's thought better of it and been bitten by fresh guilt.

'Sorry, I'm babbling,' she says. 'Ignore me. I've not … this is the first time anything like this has happened where I've lived. It's your job so I suppose you must be used to it.'

I think, *I'm not used to it. Not today. Not this time.*

I say, 'Yes. I guess so.'

'If there's anything I can do to help …' She thinks better of that too, the thought of being in the man's flat overwhelming her. 'I mean if I can …'

Whatever it is, she can't, and she knows it.

She has one last shot at making amends. 'I'm so sorry this happened. Mr Meechan really was a nice man.'

The sound of his name shocks me. Like it's news, like it's a confirmation of worst fears and more. I've been trying to shut my mind to so many things in the last two months, trying not to see death and daisies every time I close my eyes, but just the mention of his name shatters all my pretences.

Mr Meechan.

Bob Meechan.

Dead and undiscovered.

The set of keys is hot in my hand and my palms are moist. Going into a dead person's home is a well-trodden path for me, but my heart's racing as I climb the stairs. This is different and I don't like it.

The front door is well tended, the nameplate polished and the mat neatly in place. I get stuck again as I see MEECHAN engraved in the brass plate, my feet grinding to a halt in protest, the name jarring, poking at me. I breathe out hard and push on past it.

As soon as I turn the handle, the smell attacks me, foul and familiar. Molecules of Meechan. Bits of Bob. It invades my face and my senses, screaming at me that something's wrong. Everything's wrong.

There isn't too much mail inside the door. He's only been dead for two weeks. *Only.* Long enough to decompose, long enough to stink, long enough to need the place deep deep cleaned. It was the smell that did it this time. A neighbour called the landlord, maybe the woman I'd met on the street, maybe concern or complaint, but at least she called. The cops found him slumped on the floor of his living room, flies buzzing.

Even the insects are dormant now though, and Meechan's home is still, and as quiet as the grave.

I'm three steps inside, ready to start a walk-through, when I realise I didn't say a prayer before I came in. I never go in without saying a prayer, but I'm not thinking straight.

I turn, open the front door and go back out. I'm not sure what fate I'd be tempting, but I'm not risking it, not today.

Bob Meechan was a Protestant and that makes prayers for the dead trickier, given that purgatory is off the table. My go-to are words from Martin Luther and they're a cop-out but they suffice.

'*Dear God, if this soul is in a condition accessible to mercy, be thou gracious to it.*'

I reopen the door and go back inside, heading as straight as my legs will allow to the room where it happened. As I look around, it strikes me that apart from the smell, which is significant, most people would look at this and have no inkling of what happened here.

There's no body of course, and no blood spill. It looks like an older person's front room minus the older person. The venetian blinds are half open, the carpet is in good condition but looks like it would be at home in a Wetherspoons, the television isn't what you'd call smart, and there are ornaments and seat coverings that my granny would have approved of. It's like Bob's just walked out of the room. But I know he hasn't.

I know too that there are potentially lethal pathogens on the carpet, microorganisms hiding in the threads. There will be larvae and eggs in there too, a greenhouse of infestation.

A massive heart attack, that's what the police and coroner have said. A conclusion yet to be tested in the lab, but that's their thinking. My thinking is different. They say he was watching television when death grabbed his heart and squeezed it, forcing him to his knees, leaving him on the floor. I say they're wrong.

I'm standing in his house, standing over the spot where he died. And there's about as much air to breathe as there was when his name leapt off the page and grabbed me by the throat.

I have the police photographs in my case and the images imprinted on my mind.

Bob lay here with his head by the armchair, one leg tucked under the other, his right arm across his chest and his left by his side. Navy blue flannel trousers. Blue slippers. A white shirt and dark cardigan, a T-shirt underneath. His mouth open, his eyes staring into eternity.

There are two framed prints on the mantlepiece of him with his late wife and I can't help but stare at her. Smiling shyly under a fringe of short silver hair, high cheekbones, rimless spectacles, eyebrows plucked. He's got his arms wrapped around her and she around him. Inseparable but separated by death. Now reunited beyond.

People think men usually die first because of their lifestyle; drinking more, smoking more, worrying more, more physical labour. But that's not it at all. Nature makes sure men are likely to die before their wives because they're useless at living without them. Can't cook, can't clean, can't sew, can't cope with being alone. It's changing, slowly, but for men of Bob's generation, it's the truth.

He had lung cancer and it would have taken him soon enough, just that he'd have endured the pain for longer. Small mercies.

It feels weird and wrong, being in his house without him here. Like I'm intruding. I got used a long time ago to being in other people's homes, but sometimes, like now, I feel like I'm a thief.

I steal photographs first, taking shots of the living room; of the carpet and his chair, of his television, his sideboard and ornaments. The room is a museum to his loneliness and has probably never changed since he was widowed.

I've worked the flat and put the moment off until I can't escape it any longer. My heart is throwing itself at my ribcage and my breathing is heavier inside my suit, loud enough that I can hear it above the blood rushing in my ears.

I drop to my knees, the unseen soup of pathogens in the carpet fibres being displaced, the remnants of Bob Meechan's death shifting beneath my weight.

This is where he lay, where he breathed his last. The man whose old friend died undiscovered just two months before. The man with a history, with a secret, stories wrapped up in stories. The things that could be explained as coincidences had been wearing thin, but they were shredded the moment Bob's death appeared in the newspaper. I can't close my eyes to it any longer.

I'm crouching on the floor. I look. And I see it.

My breath catches in my throat and a noise escapes from my mouth and into my suit.

There. Half hidden and completely ignored, by the chair leg, by where his head was. Half expected maybe but no less startling.

A dried daisy.

Greying white petals, fading yellow heart. I pick it up, shakily, and bring it close to examine it.

Daisy, Daisy. Give me your answer do.

I'm crying. Stupid, stinging tears inside a mask and I can't even wipe them away with the back of my gloves. I'm scared. Trembling and nervy. At what happened and what might happen.

I somehow manage to manoeuvre the flower into a plastic bag and seal it. I need to work, need to get my head back in the game, not to think, thinking will get me nowhere. I need to do everything I would do if this were a clean-up the same as any other. I'll equip, I'll remove, I'll soak, I'll disinfect, I'll soak again, and I'll dispose and decontaminate. I'll wash my hands, and I'll wash them, then wash them again. And again and again and again.

I'm singing tunelessly, mindlessly, under my breath. *I'm half crazy. All for the love of you.*

Suddenly, I'm agitated that I'm kneeling where he lay dead and I push myself to my feet in a rush, anxious not to be sitting on his remains, needing to be on my feet and off him. It's like I'm being shouted at from all sides, thoughts and memories all around me, screaming to be heard.

I stand still and close my eyes, trying to close out some of the noise and gather myself. It's a mistake. Instead, I sway and wonder, my mind flooded with the image of the man splayed across the carpet, seeing his mouth hanging open and his eyes wide.

I think I'm losing it. I can't work out if I'm remembering the police photograph of him on the floor or seeing the real thing lying there. A chain of thoughts jumbled up in my head. Tommy Agnew. Bute and bodies. Daisies and dioramas. Dread and dead.

Poor old Bob Meechan lying dead where I stand. A faded daisy by his head.

Chapter 11

I finally leave Meechan's flat with my cleaning cases, a small box of belongings, and my head still spinning. It's going to need two trips to get it all in the car, so I leave the mementoes outside the flat and take the cases first.

My car is parked on the other side of the street, just four strides across the narrow road. I put the cases down and fish my keys out of my pocket. As I'm pressing the fob to open the door, I notice a car about thirty yards behind mine, with someone sitting at the wheel. I can't see the person properly as the sun is shining on the windscreen and the visor is down. It bothers me and feels like I'm being watched.

As I put the cases in the boot and close the lid, I don't look around but take a glance in my kerb-side mirror. The person in the red Octavia is looking straight ahead, not moving, not getting out or driving off, just sitting there, looking.

I ignore it, sure that I'm just rattled by Meechan's death and being in his flat, and triggered by seeing the daisy on the floor. My head is all over the place. I can't think straight but need to.

Up the stairs again, down the stairs again, the memento box in my hands. I head straight for my own car, open the boot again and deposit the box. It's only when I'm in the driver's seat that I look in my rear-view mirror. The Octavia has gone.

I sit with my eyes closed for a minute, trying to compose myself, trying to slow my heartbeat and my breathing. I squeeze my eyes tighter, forcing everything behind my eyelids to black and then to shiny, sparkling fireworks. I'm squeezing tighter and tighter, wondering what it would take to burst them, when my phone beeps and ruins it.

I take it out and look at the screen. My father.

Got no milk and no dinner. I need you to bring me some. Please.

Please? Well seeing as it's the middle of the afternoon, peak politeness point for the old … I stop myself, thoughts of Bob Meechan checking my scepticism. I know he's used please sarcastically and as an afterthought, but at least he's used it. And I'm feeling guilty enough without making it worse. I'll do it.

I start the engine and check in my rear-view before I move off. Just in time to see the red Skoda pull into the space thirty yards behind me again. The visor is down, and I can't see anything above the neck of the driver, who sits there, not moving.

Handbrake off, car into gear, go. My eyes are on the car behind me for the couple of hundred yards to the first corner. It hasn't moved. I turn right onto Hector Road, breathe, and head for Maryhill.

★ ★ ★

We have to go through the same stupid game every time. He knows it's me.

'Who is it?'

'It's Grace.'

'Right. Hang on.'

I hear the chain being released and the snib turning. He pulls the door back like a magician revealing a trick. Shit, he's in a good mood. That can only mean one thing – between texting me and now, he's had his first drink of the day.

'It's my wee Grace. Come to save me from starvation.'

Even when he's being one-drink nice he's also being a sarcastic prick. I ignore it and take the two bags of shopping to the kitchen. I put milk and orange juice into the fridge door and four ready meals onto the shelf alongside some veg that he probably won't eat. I put away the carrier bags and begin to empty his bin.

From behind me, I hear the fridge door open and close, swiftly followed by the sound of a ring pull. My shoulders tense and it must be obvious.

'I'm just having a beer, darling. Got nothing else to do with my afternoon except this and the shite on the television.'

Just a beer. I know how the progression usually goes. One-drink nice, two-drinks overly-nice, three-drinks not-so-nice, four-drinks arsehole, five-drinks violent arsehole.

'I'll do a washing for you while I'm here,' I say. 'What have you got that needs done?'

He waves an arm airily towards his bedroom with a half-smile. 'Knock yourself out.'

It's not exactly what I want to be doing but I'm still high on contrition and need to burn some of it off. The moment I step into his room, I'm regretting it.

It's a tip. There are clothes on the floor, clothes on the chair by the bed, clothes piled in the corner. There are five empty glasses, all smeared with booze, sitting on the bedside table, alongside an overflowing ashtray. The bedclothes need washing too but I'm not touching those.

He's a sixty-six-year-old man with a teenager's bedroom. I don't want to think what's under the bed.

What's not here or in the living room or anywhere else in the house is a photograph of my mother. Of his wife. It's an almost ever-present in the older undiscovereds. A photo of the one who went first, a photo of them together. Not here. It would have been understandable if she didn't have one of him, but he's got no excuse.

The absence of any physical reminder of her always angers me. This time it works away at my lingering guilt, channelling it into blame. Much healthier.

I collect the clothes from where they lie and put them on the bed while I vacuum the room, then I deposit them into his washing machine, closing the door with a click that coincides with the sound of another beer can being opened. Drink three.

'Aye, you're a saint right enough. I don't know what I'd do without you.'

I ignore him but with teeth clenched.

'So good of you to give up your time for your old dad. You could be out with your friends or on a date but instead you're here looking after me. What did I do to deserve such a wonderful daughter?'

It's a familiar tactic. It's not enough that I shop, clean and cook for him. On top of that, I have to be castigated as a martyr. It's not enough that I'm at his beck and call, he has to resent me for it too. It's not enough that I have nowhere else to be, he has to relish reminding me of the fact. And he knows I *have* to be here.

I turn and see there's already a glaze to his eyes and a change to the way his mouth's working. Part slur, part sneer. It's an ugly addition to his face, but it keeps talking. I turn away again.

'Your mother would be proud of you. Working so hard, taking care of me. Don't you think?'

I think, *Don't bring her into this. Just shut your vile mouth.*

I say, 'I don't know. Maybe she would.'

There's glee greasing his voice as he replies. 'Oh, don't be so modest. Of course she would. She'd be so proud to see you on your knees.'

I think, *Fuck you.*

I say nothing.

'Do you ever wonder how things would be if your mother was still with us? If she was still alive? Do you think she'd be on her knees doing that and you'd be fucked off somewhere else just doing whatever you pleased?'

I think, *Don't even talk about her. Shut your mouth before I shut it for you.*

I say, 'Just leave me alone. I'll get this done then I'll go.'

'What?' He's feigning innocence, of course. 'It was just a question. Fine state of affairs if you don't even want to talk about your own mother. Maybe you're not such a saint after all.'

I let that remark simmer before I slowly stand, turn, and face him.

'I cleaned a house today. A nice old man. Maybe he didn't live a perfect life, but he seemed to be decent. He died alone, wasn't found for two weeks. He had no one to look after him. Is that what you want?'

'Is that a threat?'

'Take it any way you want.'

He bristles at me answering him back. He isn't used to it, doesn't like it. As with most bullies, he only wants to play by his own rules. I can see him debating the consequences now and he doesn't like those either. He makes one last, defiant jab.

'Well, you've done your duty like a good girl. Maybe you should just fuck off now. I know you can't wait to get out of here. Go home and talk to your cat.'

I think, *One of these days, you'll push me too far. And I can't wait for that day.*

I say, 'Yes. I'll do that.'

'Don't let the door hit your arse on the way out. I'll see you tomorrow.'

'Maybe.'

'Oh, you'll be here. We both know you need to be.'

Chapter 12

It's only a fifteen-minute drive from his flat on Maryhill Road to mine in the Merchant City but it feels longer right now. My head is everywhere other than the road in front and I'm probably a danger to anyone around me.

Maryhill Road is long and largely straight, so it doesn't require much thinking other than the many traffic lights along the way. Not thinking isn't good though, it encourages the mind to wander and mine doesn't need much encouragement right now.

I'm thinking about dead people and daisies.

Images are flashing through my mind as I make my way across the junction with Bilsland Drive. I'm not paying attention at the lights and get stuck on the yellow box junction, causing cars to blare their horns at me. I wave apologetically.

I can see the daisy on Agnew's pillow as clear as day. In my mind's eye it's flashing neon yellow, like a cartoon, screaming with klaxon sound effects. *Shit*, the lights have changed again and now I'm getting beeped at from behind.

Drivers in the next lane are trying to catch my eye, shouting and gesticulating at me. Oh just please fuck off. I pass the fire station, then the shops and Jaconelli's.

I can see the daisy by Bob Meechan's chair. See it, smell it, hear it rustling in the wind. I take the left fork and head along Garscube Road, traffic tight on my tail. I know I'm dawdling.

I'm approaching what they used to call Rockvilla, the old stretch of buildings standing oddly alone at the junction where Garscube Road, Possil Road and St George's Road intersect. My mind's busy picturing police officers swarming over Meechan's flat picking at all the evidence but not seeing it.

There are three lanes and I realise I've wandered lazily into the right-hand one, which is right turn only, except I'm going straight on. I don't look, I just swing back into the middle lane and cause chaos. I only just stop short of hitting the car in front. There's a loud screeching as the black car immediately behind has to slam on his brakes to avoid going into the back of me. I hold up a hand in more apology but get no response.

My nerves are shot. I need to calm down and I need to concentrate.

I'm passing through Cowcaddens without incident and into the city centre, quickly getting snarled up in traffic on Renfield Street. *Daisies.* I'm inching around George Square. *Meechan.* Montrose Street. *Agnew.* Candleriggs. *Daisies.*

I know I'm rattled. Can't deny it. I park the car and fetch the box of Meechan's mementoes from the boot. Looking into the box doesn't settle my nerves any.

It's just a couple of minutes to my flat and I walk, wondering what to do, what to think. I'm probably not paying as much attention as I should. I suddenly realise I'm about to walk into someone and hurriedly sidestep to the right in case he barges me over. I apologise but now see the man has his head down and maybe he was the one not looking where he was going.

I'm a few steps further on before it clicks. *That guy. I know his face.* I turn and look back but he's just disappearing around the corner.

When I get inside the flat, I put the box on the kitchen table and contemplate going through the stuff. My head's messy enough as it is though, and I'm not sure I need any more stimulation. Anyway, George wants me. He's meowing noisily, demanding attention and food, talking human as best he can. I talk back to him. I always do.

'How's your day been, George? I know, I'd rather have been here with you, believe me. But I'm back now and I'm in for the day. Just you and me.'

George was a rescue cat and sometimes I wonder how much effect that's had on him. He's loveable and loving and needs to know he's loved. Maybe that's not so different from any of us, but I know he regularly needs the reassurance of a cuddle or a conversation. He feels the need to wake me in the middle of the night just to tell me that he loves me, and that I should love him back. Which I do, unconditionally.

I found him, or he found me, one Sunday afternoon in the city as I wandered past Ramshorn Cemetery. I stopped to say hello and he let me scratch his ear and admire his handsomeness. He was timid and bold at the same time, in the way that only cats and certain humans

97

can be. I tried to walk on, but he followed me for ages, until I ran into more human traffic than he was comfortable with and he turned back. I met him again a few days later and the same thing happened, and so it was that I got to look out for him any time I was in that area. I started calling him George because he was handsome, like Clooney.

It was a month or three later that I saw he was hurt. He was limping badly and carrying his front right paw. I stopped and he came towards me slowly but when I reached for the injured foot, he jumped like he'd been electrocuted and hissed viciously at me. I took no offence; I was used to that from those I tried to help.

It took three attempts before I managed to wrap him in my jacket. He drew blood twice at my wrist and once with a slash to my left cheek, but that was okay. He calmed down a bit when he was tight to my chest and the pain was worth it for the chance to do some good.

When we got to the vet, it turned out George didn't have a fracture as I'd thought, he had an infection. The vet asked if he was mine and I said no, but I was paying, being as sure as I could be that he didn't have an owner, or at least not one that cared enough to look after him. The vet shrugged and said fine. He drained the infection and told me George would need to be off the street for a while. So, I took him home.

I did try to set him free again once his isolation period was over, I really did, but he was having none of it. Either he liked me, or he didn't like it out there; either way he stayed and has been shacked up with me ever since. Sure, we're both on our own, but now we're on our own together.

Sometimes I wonder if I rescued him or if he rescued me. Maybe it doesn't matter.

Once he's fed, I scoop him up in my arms and we walk to the window to gaze down on Glasgow. I like living where I do. We're right in the heart of the city centre, George and me, yet so high above it that we can see it all without having to interact with anyone.

Down below is the Merchant City, bustling and businesslike during the week, bustling and boozy at weekends, although being Glasgow it's the weekend at least four days a week. On the Wilson Street side, I can see the old sheriff court that's now the Citation bar, a beautiful blond sandstone structure with six huge pillars at the front. I can see new buildings growing out of old ones, phoenixes and gentrified ghosts, elegant avenues built on old tobacco money and slavery.

Wait. There, by the corner of Citation. Looking up. The same guy who nearly bumped into me when I came from the car. The guy who was keeping his head down. The guy whose face was familiar, but I couldn't place.

It's him. The same guy. I'm sure of it. And …

And he's gone. I don't know if he saw me looking, but he's turned on his heel and walked around the corner. Cropped dark hair, fifty-something, about six feet tall. Very familiar.

And now I know where I've seen him before.

I don't remember walking across the floor from the window, but George and I are in the chair and I'm hugging him close, my knees pulled up towards my chest.

'I'm scared, Georgie.'

He looks up at me inquisitively, sensing my unhappiness, his nose twitching towards mine. I bend forward and rub noses with him. It helps, but not enough.

'I know where I saw him before, George. But I've no idea who he is or what he wants from me. And I'm terrified.'

I lean further forward so that George's head is under my chin and he's wrapped up in me completely.

'Whatever this is, I can't deal with this on my own,' I tell him. 'I'm going for help.'

Chapter 13

The nearest police station to me is at Stewart Street in Cowcaddens, up by the Passport Office. I can't face dragging the car around the traffic lights of George Square before I even start to get anywhere, so decide to walk. Across the Square, up Buchanan Street and West Nile Street, the city centre is just far enough away that you can start to breathe as the bodies thin out.

Past the Station Bar. Turn left at the fire station, right at the St Andrew's Ambulance place and there it is, a big building in squares of pale blue and navy, looking like it's made from Lego. 'A Division' Police Headquarters the sign says. Except the A is faded and the U has gone altogether. It doesn't fill me with confidence.

I know a few cops, nature of my work, and I'm both hoping that there will be a friendly face I recognise and hoping that there won't. The sergeant on the front desk, a heavy-set man in his late forties, is looking down at some paperwork but I can see enough to know I haven't seen him before.

Deep breath. Just do this. Just get the words out then leave it to them.

I stand in front of the desk and wait for him to look up. He knows I'm there but he's doing that authority thing of making me wait because he can. He wants me to know he's in charge from the start. Most days, almost all days, I'd stand there and say nothing until he's proved his point. Today's not most days.

'Excuse me.' He doesn't flinch so I repeat myself. Louder. 'Excuse me.'

'Can I help you?' He doesn't sound full of eagerness to help.

'I'd like to speak to someone, please.'

'I'm Sergeant Cochrane. You're speaking to me.'

I think, *Maybe I should just go. I'd be better doing that than talking to this one. But I can't. I need to see it through.*

I say, 'I need to speak to a detective. It's important.'

He stifles a sigh. 'If you'd like to tell me the nature of your enquiry, then I will see if there is anyone from CID who is available to speak to you.'

Here goes.

'I want to report a suspicious death. Two of them.'

'*Two?*' Now he's interested. Still sceptical, still world-weary, but interested.

'Yes. Two deaths which I believe are related.'

I can see his interest shrink immediately at the word *believe*. I think, I suspect, I imagine, codewords for the paranoid and the crazies. But he has a duty and now has a pen in his hands.

'And what is your information regarding these two deaths?'

I think, *Daises. Three of them. But I'm keeping any thoughts of Mrs McCrorie to myself for now.*

I say, 'I'd like to speak to a detective.'

He sighs, doesn't try to hide it this time. 'I will need more information before I can ask a member of CID to speak to you. What makes you believe the two deaths you're talking about are related?'

'I cleaned both houses after the deaths.'

His face contracts into a confused frown and freezes there until he's able to recompose himself.

'What's your name?'

'Grace McGill.'

'Sit over there please, Ms McGill, and I'll get someone to speak to you.'

Ten minutes later, I'm deeper inside the building and sitting opposite two men in smart suits. One is Detective Constable Phelan and he's being very nice. He probably thinks I'm a nutter. The other is Detective Sergeant Carsewell and he's looking at me as if I'm wasting his valuable time. He's certain I'm a nutter.

Phelan is young, mid-twenties maybe, fair-haired, fresh-faced and not yet worn down by the job, still thinking he's in an episode of *Taggart*. The sergeant is about ten years older, his dark hair receding from his forehead, and he's seen every episode and every repeat. Phelan is doing all the talking. Carsewell can't be arsed.

'You told the desk sergeant that you have come to report two suspicious deaths.' His voice is nasal and irritating.

'That's right.'

'Okay. Well that's obviously something extremely serious and we're very interested to hear what you

know. You understand that we'd need something sub-
stantial from you in order to initiate an inquiry of this
nature?'

I think, *I'm not sure what I understand any more.*

I say, 'Yes.'

'Okay. Let's start by taking some details. What's your
full name?'

'Grace Margaret McGill.'

'And your date of birth?'

'March 13, 1987.'

'What's your address Ms McGill?'

'Seventy-four Brunswick Street. G1 1TB.'

I'm aware of Carsewell leaning forward, studying me
more closely, but I try to ignore it.

'And your occupation?'

I think, *This is where you become sure that I'm crazy.*

I say, 'Well that's what I was explaining to the sergeant on the desk. That's how I'm sure the deaths
are connected. I'm a cleaner. A crime scene cleaner.
I …'

'I knew I knew you from somewhere.' Carsewell
speaks for the first time. 'You're a cleaner. You specialise
in houses after people have lain there for months.'

The last sentence comes laced with some contempt.
I'm used to it.

'Yes. That's right.'

Phelan looks to the DS then back to me. He's a bit
confused but he continues. 'So, Ms McGill, you're em-
ployed to clean houses after people are found dead in
them. Is that right?'

I think, *No, not really. I deep clean the ones that need it. And why do you say that as if it's weird? Have you already been talking about me behind my back?*

I say, 'Basically, yes.'

'And you believe that two of these deaths are somehow connected?

'Yes, I think they are.'

'Okay. Talk us through it, please. In as much detail as you can give me.'

He doesn't think I have any detail. He doesn't think I know the difference between Friday and fantasy. He's wrong.

'The first is a man named Thomas Agnew. He was found dead in his flat in Partick. Modder Street. He was seventy-five and had died five months earlier but hadn't been found.'

I see DS Carsewell's lip twitch. He doesn't like the thought of someone lying dead that long. He doesn't like the thought of having to clean up the mess. He wouldn't want that on his nice suit.

'I was called in to clean Mr Agnew's flat. I deep cleaned it, removed anything hazardous, made it safe for habitation, documented the scene with photographs, and collected some items for the deceased's family.'

Phelan nods. I think he's getting bored.

'Among the items I removed from Mr Agnew's house was a dried daisy which I found on his pillow.'

The two cops share a look. 'Right …' Phelan says. 'And there would have been a post-mortem into Mr Agnew's death as he was found at home. Is that right?'

'Yes.'

'Do you know the results of that? We can check.'

'Natural causes. No suspicious circumstances. But …'

'Right.' He makes a show of taking notes. 'And the other death?'

'Robert Meechan. He lived in Grantley Gardens in Shawlands. He was … I think he was seventy-four. He'd been dead for two weeks before he was found. I got the job to clean his flat too.'

'When was this?'

'Yesterday.'

'Okay,' Phelan makes another note. 'Carry on, please.'

'Well, I know it might not sound much but there was a daisy there too. Not just a daisy, but the same …' *Oh fuck*, '… the same kind of dried daisy. Where he died.'

Carsewell has slipped his hand over his mouth and I know he's hiding a smirk. Two daisies. I must sound like a complete zoomer.

Phelan is still trying to be professional. They must get all sorts in here. They probably have a competition for nutter of the month. They'll be going back upstairs to see their mates, telling them they have a contender.

'Do you have this daisy?' Phelan asks. 'Either of them?'

'Yes. I brought them with me.'

I place the two clear plastic bags on the table between us. I stare at them a moment longer than I should, suddenly back in the two houses, smelling death and loneliness.

The detectives gaze down on them. Two faded, ordinary, unexceptional daises bleached by time and lack of life.

'How do you know which is which?' Carsewell asks. The prick is being sarcastic but thinking he's being oh so clever by keeping his voice oh so sincere.

'I've labelled them. Name and date.' I hold one up to show the white-stickered evidence.

'And one of these was on the pillow of the men who passed?' The lack of belief is stretching Phelan's voice.

'Yes! There was one on Thomas Agnew's pillow, and one on Bob Meechan's floor. Don't you think that's a bit of a coincidence?'

'Oh I do,' Carsewell agreed. 'Quite a coincidence. Murray, get the incident reports, will you?'

The DC pushes his chair back and leaves the room. Carsewell leans forward again, his head on his chin.

'How long have you been cleaning houses, Ms McGill?'

'Eight years. The last four with my own business.'

'Do you not find it ...' he's struggling to find a word that won't be too offensive, '... a slightly odd way to make a living?'

'Someone's got to do it. Might as well be me.'

'It can't be easy. Spending all that time surrounded by death.'

'There's worse things.'

'Like what?'

I think, *Like life. Like living alone.*

I say, 'Like doing a job you don't enjoy. I like mine. I get satisfaction from it, from helping people through a bad situation. Would you like to go clean up a house after one of your parents had died in it?'

I see the answer in his eyes before he says it. 'No. No I wouldn't.'

'And would you prefer that I did it for you?'

He just makes a face but it's as good as a yes. 'But I'm wondering,' he says, 'if you're in that kind of environment all the time, if you maybe sometimes lose sight of how other people view things. People that wouldn't be able to face doing what you do.'

'What do you mean?'

'It must be very stressful. And you work alone?'

I'm bristling. 'Yes.'

'And you live alone?'

'Yes, I do but …'

'It would be understandable if you felt the need to reach out to people. To feel more involved with … living people.'

He thinks I'm crazy. Maybe I am crazy.

'The daisies were there. I didn't imagine them.'

He doesn't say anything. He just looks at me until the door opens and Phelan walks back in. The DC looks across to Carsewell and gives a quick shake of the head before taking his seat.

'Ms McGill,' Phelan says, 'there's no mention in the incident report into either death of a daisy, or any other flower, being at the scene. No mention at all.'

'They *were* there. They're in these bags.'

Both men just look at me.

'A little flower's not the kind of thing police are going to notice at a scene like that when there's no reason to think anything untoward happened,' I tell them. 'It's natural they'd think the old man had just died. And the place would have been stinking, they'd have wanted out as quick as they could.'

'Is there anything else at all, Ms McGill?' Phelan asks me. 'Other than the daisies.'

My heart sinks and my mouth bobs open. They're not going to do anything.

'Look, you don't understand. There's something going on here. These men knew each other. Tommy Agnew and Bob Meechan were friends.'

Carsewell looks exasperated. He probably has a cup of coffee to get back to. 'They knew each other? If this is true, why didn't you mention it before?'

To be fair, that's a good question.

I think, *Because I don't want you to know everything.*

I say, 'I didn't think it mattered. Not as much as the daisies. But they did know each other. From years before. I think there was something they were involved in.'

'Involved in?'

Oh shit. I want *them* to do this. Not me. I don't want to have to explain what I think it is. It's their job to go digging, to do what I can't.

'Yes. I found a photograph. Of Agnew and Meechan together with friends. I think they were on holiday in Rothesay.'

'Rothesay.'

'Years ago. The sixties.'

'Ms McGill …' Carswell is rubbing at his eyes. 'People are often nervous when they come to the police. Maybe not thinking straight. Sometimes they can't remember everything they want to tell us. So, I'm asking you now, what is it that makes you think there was something suspicious about the deaths of these two men?'

I think, *I just know.*

I say, 'I spoke to Meechan at Tommy Agnew's funeral. He and another man, Jackie Stevenson, they weren't being honest about whatever happened back then, I know they weren't. And now Bob Meechan has died just two months after his friend. And that's too much of a coincidence and I know there's something that happened in Rothesay and …'

'You cleaned the man's house and then went to his funeral?' Carswell is looking at me like I'm wearing my shoes on my ears.

'It's what I do. Sometimes. And I think someone's been following me. I've seen this man twice and …'

Carswell holds a hand up as if he's on traffic duty. He's staring at me long enough that I'm uncomfortable before he finally turns to look at Phelan. 'Murray, what time are we due to go to HQ to talk to DCI French about the Hopeman case?'

Phelan looks at his watch. 'Oh right. Actually, we should have left five minutes ago.'

That's code. I know that it's code. Code for let's get the fuck out of here. Carswell makes a poor attempt at an apologetic face. 'I'm sorry but we're going to have to go. We've got your details and I think we've got enough to take it from here.'

I could try to tell him about Meechan and Stevenson lying. About any or all of it. But I know I'd be wasting my breath and their time. They've made their mind up. My statement is going to be filed under N.

The two cops are on their feet and I've little option but to do the same. Carsewell has the door open. At least Phelan looks slightly embarrassed at bailing on me. 'I assure you that we'll look into it, Ms McGill.'

They won't.

I'm back on the street, outside the station and feeling stupid. Stupid and angry. I fetch my phone from my bag and call.

'Harry? It's Grace. Okay, I've changed my mind. Tell Doug Christie I'll speak to him.'

'You're going to do the interview?'

'Yes. God knows I don't want to, but I will. But tell him I want something from him in return.'

Chapter 14

When I hear the knock at the door, I take a deep breath, nervously blow out hard, then answer.

It's been a while since I've seen Doug Christie but he's looking good. Not that I should think that and I'm not thinking that.

'Hi Grace. Thanks for agreeing to talk to me.'

I think, *I'm not sure I ever really agreed. You agreed and Harry Blair agreed, I sort of got forced into it. And I'm still not happy.*

I say, 'Sure. Come in.'

I stand back to let him past then close the door behind him. He lets me lead on into the living room and I notice his eyes go immediately to the table where my five finished dioramas sit. To his credit, he doesn't rush over to gawk at them.

'Harry said you were nervous about this,' he says. 'So, thanks. I know being interviewed is a bit of a nightmare for most people. But your models sound amazing. I'm sure people will find them fascinating.'

I think, *They'll think I'm weird is what they'll think.*

I say nothing.

'How long is it since we first met, Grace? Must be years now.'

I think, *You don't remember? 2015. A ninety-year-old woman whose body had lain undiscovered for five years. You photographed outside, I cleaned up inside.*

I say, 'Not sure. Must be five years at least.'

'Yeah, must be. Grace, are you okay talking about this?'

I think, *Well, to be honest, no I'm not. I'd rather you didn't, but I don't really see how I can back out now. And I do want your help.*

I say, 'I guess so. Just a bit nervous. And you remember the deal?'

'I get you into the archives at the *Standard*. Okay, but I still don't get why you want to.'

'I'm doing my family history,' I lie. 'And there's things I'd like to look up. From the sixties.'

'Well, yeah. We can do that. I've got to warn you that they're in a bit of a mess. We used to have a proper archivist who curated them, but she retired, then costs got cut, and now they're piled up in a cupboard.'

'Oh right. I'd still like to look through them.' *Even though I'm not sure what I'm looking for.*

'No problem. And listen, I won't write anything you don't want me to. I don't do that kind of journalism. And, in case you're worried about it, I'm not going to write anything taking the piss either. So, should we maybe take a look at your dioramas and you can tell me a bit about why you started making them?'

I think, *Oh shit.*

I say, 'Okay.'

I don't say anything else as I walk to the table and he follows me. I let the models speak for themselves for now. Five rooms. Five resting places. Five little spaces of disarray and despair. Five emotional train wrecks in miniature.

I watch him. He stalks around the table, staring at them intently. Soon it's like he's forgotten that I'm here. He's crouching down, getting closer, looking from different angles, his face creased with fascination.

I'm nervous. It's all of it; opening myself up, letting people in, showing them me and showing them my stuff. But there's something else. I'm nervous about whether he *likes* them or not.

He pauses and looks up at me. 'These are incredible. Harry was right, they're definitely art and they're amazing. They're … *real*. There's a sense of sadness from them that's overwhelming. Tell me the story of this one.'

He's squatting in front of a modelled bathroom. Mrs McCrorie's bathroom. The tiny daisy on the edge of the bath.

I think, *I'm not telling him about her. I'm not telling him about it.*

I say, 'They each have a different story. But the people who lived and died in these rooms deserve their privacy. The people who hired me to clean them put their trust in me. I'm not going to breach either of those things.'

He looks me straight in the eye and nods, making sure I know he means what he's going to say. 'And I'm not going to ask you to. No names, no details. I don't want to know where any of those rooms were, except maybe in very vague terms, like in Glasgow. Maybe the part of the city. You don't have to tell me whether the people who died were men or women. But if you can tell me something about each one without giving much away then it would …'

He loses the sentence because he was going to say something that would have sounded inappropriate. *Bring them to life? Put flesh on the bones?* Metaphors are fuckers when you're talking about dead things. Anyway, I get his point and I give in. I'll be careful.

'Okay. The person in this one died in their bath. In Glasgow. The person wasn't discovered for a very long time. The um … mechanics … of decomposition caused the mess you see to come over the side of the bath and onto the floor.'

He can see that much. The little ceramic doll's bath I've placed in the corner of the room is swilled in a blood-brown mix that I manufactured from red Play-Doh and coffee. It spills over the side and onto the green tiled floor. What he can't see and doesn't need to know is that the bath was fitted with a reheating mechanism that caused decomposition to accelerate and poor Mrs McCrorie to turn to sludge.

'These details,' he gestures with his pinkie, 'these are as they were in the room?'

They are. The wilted vase of daffodils, the shelf with bottles of shampoo and conditioner, the photo frame, the neat little stack of white towels. The daisy.

'Yes. Everything that you see.'

I want him to ask me about the daisy. I don't want him to ask me about it. I don't know what to think.

'How do you make …' he pauses. 'Maybe what I really mean is *why* do you make them. But I'd like to know both. In any order you like.'

Here we go. So difficult. Sigh.

'There's a book by a lady named Frances Glessner Lee. It's called *The Nutshell Studies of Unexplained Death*. I came across it when I was on the internet, looking for information on home deaths.' I look to see if he thinks that last bit is strange but if he does, it doesn't show.

'She was quite a wealthy lady, from Chicago, and was in her fifties when she started a career in legal medicine. She inherited the family fortune and set about developing an interest in how detectives solved cases. They say she was the most influential person in developing forensic science in America. And was the first female police captain in the US.

'In the forties and fifties, she held seminars in homicide investigation. Everyone would go. Detectives, prosecutors, private eyes, they all wanted to know the latest methods, as she was reinventing the whole game. That's where she introduced the Nutshells.'

'The dioramas.'

'Right.' I'm warming to it now, my enthusiasm for the project overcoming my fears. 'She presented the investigators with these incredibly detailed miniature models. Hers really were amazing things. They were based on real autopsies and real crime scenes that she'd visited herself. There were twenty of them, and the idea was they'd test the students' ability to collect all the relevant evidence. They were like doll's houses and she did everything by hand, everything *exactly* as it was in the scene. Tiny bullet holes entering at the same angle as in the case, window latches placed just as they were, blood spatters replicated, everything precise and perfect.'

He is nodding, drinking in every word. 'But you're not using these to solve cases, right?'

My mouth falls open and I stammer a reply like an eejit. 'No. Nothing like that. I'm ...'

'I'm sorry,' he smiles. 'I was just joking. I shouldn't have. So, when you learned about Glessner Lee's models you decided to make your own?'

'Yes. I mean, mine aren't anything like hers. Nowhere near as good. But they're not meant for anyone else to see, they're not meant to be so accurate you can solve crimes. They're just ... for me.'

He looks from me to the dioramas and back, nodding, thinking. 'These are incredible. They have ...' He waves a hand at my dioramas. 'They have soul.'

'*Soul?*' I'm flattered and scared and excited and curious.

'Yes. You know I've been to hundreds of crime scenes, accidental deaths too. So, I know what they're like. They're more than blood and broken bones, more than police tape and blood spatter. They're ...' he gets lost for a moment and I know he's gone there. 'They're bleak. Stark. Chaotic. Heartbreaking. All of those things twisted around each other. And you get that. You get the *feel* of them.'

I think, *Shit. That scares me. I don't like that you get it. But I like that you get it.*

I say, 'Thanks.'

'How do you go about making them?'

I breathe and tell him about being a regular at the art supply shop on Queen Street, about making things from stuff I have lying around, crafting websites and everything miniature. When I finish, he looks at me for an age, as if trying to look inside me, then slowly nods, accepting. 'Okay. You've told me how and it's fascinating. But you haven't told me *why*.'

'Do I have to know why?'

'No, you don't have to. But do you?'

I sigh. 'How can we be sure why we do anything? Best I can do is guess.'

'Do you want to guess?'

'No. Okay, maybe. A little. But I don't *know*.' He nods to accept that for what it is. 'Harry Blair has a theory. Maybe he's already told you it. He told me that what I'm doing is art therapy.'

'Art therapy?'

'Yes. Obviously, I told him he was wrong, that my models weren't meant to help the departed or the families, they couldn't do that, especially as I never intended anyone to know about them. I said they were for me, not for other people. Harry said, yes exactly, they are therapy for me.'

'What do you think of that?'

'Well, I'd never thought of it till he said it, but … yeah maybe. I guess it makes sense. I don't *know* if that's why I do it, but it makes sense. Right?'

'Yes. So, the whole idea of Frances Glessner Lee's models was to learn how to solve crimes, and the idea of yours is to learn about yourself?'

I think, *That's a step too far. Way too personal, buddy.*

I say, 'I don't want you to put that in your story. That's a guess, remember. I don't think journalists should be guessing.'

He nods. 'Neither do I. It won't go in. So, your models … is there one you're working on currently?'

I find words stuck in my throat. Only one struggles out. One that I regret immediately. 'Yes.'

He leans forward, very interested now. 'Is it a recent job you've worked on?'

'I … it's not finished.'

'That doesn't matter. I'd love to see it. In fact, it would be great to see one in progress to see what your process is and how it changes from the finished model.'

'I don't know, it's …'

I can't stop myself from looking. Over to the corner worktop where Tommy Agnew's flat is in construction. His eyes follow mine and he sees it. He's on his feet and moving before I can say anything.

'This is it? Wow. It's so … sad. This is astonishing.'

'Is it?'

'Jesus, yes.'

I've added a hallway to the model and Doug's staring at that now, seeing the replica of the sea of mail that I walked through. I've fashioned tiny flyers from the pages of magazines, modelled little envelopes from bigger ones. In the bedroom, the doll's house dresser is in place and I've put miniature reproductions of the photographs along its length. I've even pressed Mr Agnew's shape into the bed, imitating as best I can the indentation of the man himself.

And there's a daisy, of course. A new, smaller gowan resting on the pillow.

I'm nervous just looking at it. Watching his eyes. Waiting for him to spot it, for a memory to click in his brain, see his eyes widen in surprise.

I'm waiting for him to say, *'Wait. That daisy on the pillow … wasn't there a daisy by the bath in the other model? There was! That can't be a coincidence. I need to look into this. There's something very wrong here.'*

It doesn't happen.

He doesn't see the daisy because he's not looking for it.

'I really want to photograph this,' he's saying. I don't hear him at first because I'm still watching, waiting for a reaction that isn't coming. 'Is that okay, with you, Grace? You don't have to tell me where this happened, or who or when. Just let me show it. The model speaks for itself.'

I think, *No. I'm scared.*

I say, 'Okay …'

Crime reporters must be like detectives, surely? Same instincts. Seeing clues and connections. He's looked at Mrs McCrorie's diorama, now he's staring at Tommy

Agnew's. Surely he can see what's there. I could tell him, of course I could, but that's his job. *His* job, not mine. And I'm scared of what might be.

'It's a crime. Don't you think?'

I blurt the words out before my brain catches up with my tongue.

He looks confused and starts to smile before stopping, eyes narrowing, unsure of my meaning. Which makes two of us.

'It's a crime,' I say again. 'That old people, anyone really, can die and not be discovered for weeks, months. Don't you think?'

He stares at me for a moment. 'Well, yes, it doesn't say much about society, I guess. We're not as good at looking out for each other as we should be.'

I think, *That's not enough.*

I say, 'Yes, but it's not just old people dying, it's more than that. The police should be involved. Can't you see?'

He smiles. Condescendingly. Not only doesn't he see, it's the wrong thing that he's not seeing.

'Yes, we should be doing more,' he says. 'But at least you're highlighting the issue by building these models. The feature will get people talking. We need to have a conversation about this, as a society.'

Oh fuck. He's full of shit. I give in. None so blind as those who will not see, my mum used to say.

Maybe he senses my unhappiness. He starts gushing, rolling out the flattery.

'This really is amazing, Grace. I've been to homes where people have died, terrible accidents, murder scenes, and there's a feeling that you can't miss. They might not make front-page news or television headlines but they're tragic, even if only in their own small way. There's tragedy in this model. You've put it there.'

I stare back at him. Unsure. Bothered.

He's full of shit but I'm still falling for his fawning. I maybe wouldn't be but for the fact this will be my best one yet, once it's done. Maybe that's because Tommy Agnew touched a nerve and I can't get him or his story out of my head, day or night.

'It's not finished.' I can hear how half-hearted that sounds.

'It's amazing. I just hope my pics can do it justice. Okay?'

I nod.

He works his way around Tommy's diorama, photo-graphing the mini rooms from every angle, producing a foldable, white reflector that he uses to get the light right. I watch and see the diorama come to life under the flash, and part of me smiles inside.

Another part of me says, *What the hell are you doing? What are you letting him do?*

But it's too late now.

Maybe Christie can't see what's in front of him, but his camera can. And surely his readers will. I just don't know if that's a good thing or not.

Chapter 15

The copy of the *Standard* is in my hands. And my hands are shaking.

The front-page story is about a legal challenge over Scottish independence. There's a photograph of a mass rally, thousands of saltires and marchers. I can barely see any of it.

I realise I've no idea where a story like mine – whatever that is – would be. It's not news, surely, so it will be further back I'd think. I open it near the middle and go page by page. When I don't find it, I go again from the middle until, suddenly, shockingly, there it is. Two pages of it.

Pages 28 and 29. All me. *Shit.*

Grace McGill creates miniature replicas of lonely deaths

Macabre models give insight into final despairing moments

Oh my God.

My name. My photograph. But it's even worse than that.

Most of the right-hand page is taken up with a photograph of my new diorama. The unfinished one. Tommy Agnew's one. It's huge and horrifying and detailed. I can only stare at it, my breathing stalled. This was a big mistake.

I'd hoped somehow that maybe his photograph wouldn't have shown too much detail.

Yet there it is in inglorious technicolour. The hallway littered with mail. Tommy's bedroom. Tommy's bed. You can make out the fading daisy on his pillow and the indentation where he'd lain. This is too much, too invasive, too personal, too private, too risky.

Fuck. You can see the photographs on Tommy's dresser. You can see the photo of him and the four others on Rothesay pier. I'm being paranoid. I *hope* I'm being paranoid. Can you make out what it is? I can, but that's because I know. Maybe I'm not the only one who knows.

The caption labels it as *a deadly diorama: the final resting place of an unknown Glasgow pensioner*. My stomach flips.

Tommy's death was in the same newspaper. And all the others. My diorama is unfinished and so it's obviously recent. It's not going to take a genius to put these together. And anyone who knew him at all will recognise the flat.

I told Meechan and Stevenson that I didn't have that photograph. I told them that I was Cathleen. His great-niece. I don't like my lies being found out. I don't like being made public.

The photograph is so bloody big.

I realise I haven't even looked at the words and I'm not sure I can bear to.

Grace McGill from Glasgow runs her own company that cleans up after people who have suffered a lonely death and have lain undiscovered in their own homes.

It's difficult and often dangerous work and most certainly not the job for everyone. To cope with the psychological stress of such a traumatic occupation, Grace spends a large portion of her free time recreating detailed miniature replicas of the rooms she has cleaned. A word of caution: although recreated without the corpses, some of the replicas can be disturbing.

The finished results are both art therapy and social commentary. Despite having no art training or background, the thirty-five-year-old has created stunning models that capture the sadness and quintessential loneliness of a death undiscovered.

Grace has been cleaning death scenes for eight years, three of them with her company, LastWish Cleaning. She cleans around 100 rooms a year. As part of the process, she photographs the rooms in the deceased's home in case relatives want to see them but soon realised that those didn't reflect the true sadness of the incident. That's when she decided to make the dioramas, the macabre miniatures that so skilfully and emotionally capture the tragedy of lives that end alone.

She is self-taught, buys supplies from her local craft shop, and creates replicas with them. She sometimes uses copies of the photographs she's taken, which she then sculpts into miniature objects.

Grace says that she spends about one month on each replica. She explains that she does what she does – both her work and her modelling – in an attempt to offer some respect and dignity to those that have passed.

'People end up lonely for many reasons. Some choose it, some are chosen, some deserve it, but most fall into it without even noticing. This is Glasgow, some drink their way to being lonely, with others it's illness, the death of a loved one, or just that they've made bad choices somewhere along the line, or that they've run out of options. Whatever the reason, if they've died with no one to notice or care, then the least I can do in their death is to show them the respect and dignity they may not have enjoyed in their final days.

'The real tragedy is not that they have lain undiscovered for so long, that's someone else's problem. That's an issue for property owners, for police and medical professionals, it might be a health risk for neighbours, and it's an unpleasant task for someone like me. None of that matters to the person who died alone. Their problem was in their lives not their deaths. The real tragedy was in the last of their living when they had no one to visit, no one to talk to, no one to care. Sometimes, a lonely death is a release from a lonely life.'

I can't believe I said all of that. He's made me much more articulate than I am. If I said all of that … Oh God, I said all of that.

Saint Grace of the Lonely Hearts. Fucking martyr on a fucking soapbox.

And that photograph, *shit*. That photograph.

Chapter 16

I still have the newspaper open on the kitchen table, lying next to my diorama of Tommy Agnew's flat. I've been pottering around trying to find things to do to take my mind off it, but I keep coming back, keep looking at it in the hope it will disappear in front of me.

Instead, it taunts me. Worries me. I feel my agitation crawling over my skin.

I'm staring at the story when my phone rings. A mobile call from someone not listed among my contacts.

Unknown numbers on my phone are the bane of my life.

It's bad enough when I have to talk to people I don't know, but when they're trying to sell me a new boiler or funeral care or scamming me with PPI or computer problems then it's even worse. I'm useless at getting them off the phone, and listen to far too much of their patter before finally, apologetically, finding a way to end the call.

The problem is that my phone is my living. Some of my jobs come via the PF's office, but lots of others through private bookings. I need to answer the unknowns.

'Hello? LastWish Cleaning.'

There's silence on the other end of the line. Another spam call? I'm trying to decide whether to speak again or hang up. Then there's a voice, thick and hoarse.

'Is that Grace McGill?'

I'm immediately wary. Partly because I don't get many work calls asking for me by name, and partly at his tone.

'Yes.'

'That was you in the story in the newspaper? The one who cleans dead people's houses?'

I think, *What? Who the hell are you and why are you calling me?*

I say, 'Yes. Who's calling?'

'You don't need to know who I am. I know who you are, that's all that matters.'

I think, *The voice sounds muffled, and I think he's making it lower than it is.*

I say, 'Is this … is this a work call? Do you need a place cleaned?'

'No.'

'Then why …'

'Do you think it's right to put people's houses in the newspaper like that? Even models of them. Do you think it's okay?'

I'm freaked. It's been three hours since I saw the article in the *Standard*. Probably another five since it landed in the shops and newsstands. Already there's backlash and I don't like it.

'I said, do you think it's okay?' He sounds angrier, more aggressive.

'No. I mean, there was no way for anyone to know whose houses they were. It could have been anyone's.'

'You sure about that?'

My breath catches in my throat. It's the way he said it. My mouth hangs open. I don't want to reply, to ask what he means. I want to hang up. Am I sure?

I think, *No*.

I say, 'Yes.' And I hear how weak it sounds. 'It's just a room and a hallway. Could be anywhere.'

'It's not anywhere though, is it? It's Modder Street in Partick. Flat 22/8.'

I can't speak. My mind is flooding with images of Tommy Agnew's deathbed, of a sparsely attended funeral and the man who I think's been following me. The caller lets the silence hang between us, knowing it's slowly strangling me. I can barely breathe or think, but eventually find some words to puncture the hush.

'How do you know that?'

'I just know. I can see things I recognise.'

'Who … who is this?'

The voice gets lower and jaggier. 'You need to be careful. Very careful. You don't want to end up like Agnew.'

'What do you …'

I can't finish the sentence, but it doesn't matter. The call has been ended. He's gone.

Chapter 17

The *Standard*'s office is on Waterloo Street in the city centre, the grand frontage of Central Station standing guard at the end of the road. I loiter across the way for an age, partly worrying that an imposing newspaper office like this is no place for the likes of me, and partly just worrying.

I've spent most of the way here glancing over my shoulder and looking into darkened corners, looking for something and nothing, someone and no one.

The office is in an old red sandstone building known as Distillers' House; a survivor, a slightly battered but still grand exterior amidst the modern glass fronts of its central business district neighbours. All ornate arches and pillars, it curves around the corner to the right where a tower rises above the third floor. There are two statues on lookout duty above the front door, and another, which someone once told me was the Lady of the Lake, above the first-floor corner. The building is old and daunting and so is the prospect of going inside.

I'm not sure I can do it. Or should do it. As I think it, the tall, dark wooden doors push open and Doug Christie strides out onto the street and is crossing the road towards me. I want to run but I can't.

'Hi Grace. Glad you made it. Come on in and I'll show you around. Like I said, the archives aren't what they were, but you're welcome to have a look.'

I think, *I've got to go. Can't stay. Sorry.*

I say, 'Okay, thanks.'

Inside, the building feels even older than it looks from the street, and distinctly less grand. All fur coat and no knickers. You can see what it once was though. Marble stairs worn, mahogany bannisters chipped and needing varnish, stained-glass windows that have seen better days and seen them more clearly.

'Were you wondering about the statues above the door?' he asks me. 'I saw you looking at them. The building was originally built for a whisky company, Wright and Greig, who made Rhoderick Dhu named after the chieftain of the Clan Alpine. He's one of the two. The other is supposed to be James Fitz-James, the Knight of Snowdoun. Both of them appear in Walter Scott's *Lady of the Lake* and she's …'

'The statue on the corner.'

'Yes. That's right. Okay, I see you know your Glasgow. Well, the *Standard* used to be a much bigger building than this, long before my time, and had ten times as many staff. And that was just the journalists. Now an office upstairs is big enough for us to rattle around in. Changed days.'

His voice echoes on the stairwell, our footsteps too, ensuring no one is likely to miss the fact that I'm here.

'The archives used to be quite something by all accounts,' he tells me as we climb the stairs. 'The public would come in regularly to look through the back issues to find out anything they needed to know. I guess we were all they had in a world before Google. Now of course, they can get anything they need from their phones. It's the death of knowledge through the rise of the machines.'

He's talking, but I'm looking around. We're approaching an office, editorial according to the sign, and I manage to glance in, seeing maybe eight people, all hunched over desks, staring at screens. The machines have taken over here too, Doug.

'Has anyone told you what they thought of the feature?' he asks.

I think, *Just the one death threat.*

I say, 'No. Sorry.'

He laughs. 'Don't be sorry. Sometimes you're better off not hearing from some of the nutters out there. The people who like it don't usually say much but they'll be the majority. It's the odd few who are noisy.'

'Right.'

I think, *Right. Fine. Just a crazy person. Who knows things.*

I say nothing and he carries on.

'So, the cuttings library … to give you a bit of history, they used to be organised by a lady named Eleanor. She was the librarian and a bit of a legend around these parts. She was laid off about ten years ago but everyone still refers to them as Eleanor's Cuttings. My boss always bangs on about them, saying they'd been put together by professionals, done with journalists in mind, whereas search engines just produce what they want you to find. *Google isn't for real journalists*, that's his line. As well as Eleanor's Cuttings, there are bound editions of the back issues of the paper. They're kind of old and musty mainly but they're still in one piece.'

He's leading me along a narrow corridor that doesn't seem to get much traffic, taking us to the back of the building. There's a set of stairs and we go down again.

'Seems a long way for a short cut, I know, but it's the only way to get there. In the good old days, in the old offices, Eleanor's Cuttings had its own library and they hung in rows of purpose-built shelving, all arranged by topic and alphabet, cross-referenced on master files with military precision. Now … well, see for yourself.'

He pulls back a door and I stop in my tracks. We're staring into the dark recesses of a walk-in cupboard. And a mess.

There are piles of boxes dumped all over the place. It's like one of those cupboards most homes have where you just squeeze in yet one more thing, close the door and forget it. There are boxes stacked against the wall, boxes on top of each other, boxes tipped over, and files spilled on the floor.

'It's worse than it looks,' Doug says. 'Even within the boxes, the files are sometimes in the wrong order. I think they all fell out at some point in the move from the old place and whoever put them back was working off a different alphabet from the one we use. Sorry.'

'Okay. I'll … see what I can find.'

'The back issues of the paper are at the back of the cupboard, so you'll need to work your way towards them. Do you know what year you're looking for?'

I think, *Not really. Sort of.*

I say, 'Yes. Thanks.'

He's a journalist. He has a nose for this sort of thing. A story. Lying. He suspects there's more to this than I'm telling him. He stands for a moment, waiting for me to tell him something else about my search. I'm not going to.

'Okay, well I'll leave you to it Grace. I'll be in editorial, back where we passed at the top of the stairs, so if you need anything come give me a shout.'

Still nothing from me other than, 'Thanks.' So, he goes. I close the door behind me, a single bulb lighting the gloom of the cupboard. Jeez, what a mess. I don't even know if there's a needle in this haystack, far less how to find it. But I know I want something to make sense of things, something to connect Tommy and Bob and Bute to some July of yesteryear.

I reach into boxes as I pass them, finding folders neatly labelled but not necessarily bearing much relation to the ones next to them. Devolution next to Missing People#3 next to Aberdeen#2 next to Murders#2 next to Floodings. It's a guddle.

I leave the boxes and the folders for now and go right to the back to find the dusty bound copies of the past papers. Of course, they're in no obvious order, just lying where they were abandoned in disorderly stacks. I look for 2004 and read about the body of a young man found dumped in a bin.

He isn't named in the original story, probably waiting until he was formally identified by his next of kin. But I read on through the next few days until I find the update. Martin Crossan, eighteen years old, of Easterhouse. Stabbed fourteen times. By this time, it's been labelled by police as probably gang related. There are quotes from his mother, pleading to anyone shielding Martin's killer to give them up. *Someone knows who killed my son. If you're a mother like me, do the right thing, imagine it was your boy. Give him up. Don't protect a murderer.*

I look at the thick volume of copies between July and the end of 2004 and sigh. So, I make a silent apology to the blessed Eleanor of the Cuttings and reach for my phone. Google has only a brief BBC news report of the killing, less than in the file story.

I go to other years, other July 23rds. I read and I read, and I read. An hour later, then another, and I'm still reading, knees burning and legs cramping. I don't really know what I thought this may go like, but the reality is a lot duller than I'd hoped. It's an endless, fruitless trawl and I think I'm getting word blindness. If there is something here, I'm worried I might just skip right past it without seeing.

The 2009 copy leads with fears over swine flu and a story about Osama Bin Laden's son being killed in a US airstrike. Inside there are photographs illustrating the previous day's downpour as a month of rain fell in one day, a political row over immigration and an anniversary plea from a mother to find her son's murderer.

She's Patricia Crossan, mum of the stabbing victim, Martin.

Anniversary. A mother's plea. Memories are nudged and dots join. The outlier among Agnew's smaller pile of newspaper copies is surely the 2004 edition. The run of yearly copies from 2014 makes some sort of sense, but why one from ten years before that sequence started? Is it an anniversary of some sort? I think it must be.

I decide to go back another ten years to 1994. The paper's look is very different. More words, fewer photographs. Much more packed into each page and so more difficult to pick anything out. There's a huge airlift of emergency aid to Rwanda as reports of genocide emerge. The Space Shuttle Columbia lands after a record stay in space. I read as carefully as I can, but nothing jumps out as being relevant.

1984. A report says the nuclear plant at Sellafield isn't connected to clusters of leukaemia locally. Vanessa Williams, the first African-American Miss America, has resigned after it's revealed she'd posed nude. There's a fatal car crash in Paisley, three dead, and a manhunt after three men robbed a Post Office in Thornwood, clubbing the postmistress in the process. On and on but nothing fits.

One more try, then I need to get out of here and get some fresh air. 1974. The military government in Greece has collapsed and democracy is supposedly on its way back in. It's two days after Turkey invaded Cyprus. There are stories about IRA bombings and talk of a second general election that year. Then my eyes are caught by a Glasgow story on page 5. *Two Die in Glasgow Gang Fights*. Two youths, said to be seventeen and eighteen, fatally stabbed in a gang fight involving up to twenty people. Then I see page 11.

Ten years on, no answer to Bute missing person mystery

The headline is enough but, with a thudding realisation, the date is too. July 1964. The old newspaper that was wrapped around the framed photograph taken on Bute was dated August '64. My heart misses a beat, and the store cupboard is suddenly smaller as the air is sucked out of it. I read on quickly.

Ten minutes later and I don't know what to think. I'm sitting on the floor, cross-legged, the volume of old papers in front of me. My mouth is open, my heart is banging at my ribcage, and my mind is jogged by something Doug Christie said earlier.

I leave the 1964 volume and go back towards the door where the boxes are jumbled. This might take time but in the end it will be quicker. I need to find one I've already seen.

Missing Persons#3 doesn't have the information I need but it gives me the help to find what I'm looking for. Another five minutes of scrambling around and I have it. Eleanor of the Cuttings turns out to be just the legend she was made out to be.

I have to go by the editorial department on the way out and I'm hoping to slip by unseen. I don't make it. I'm two steps beyond the door when it opens behind me. I know it's Doug without turning to look.

'How did you get on, Grace?'

I think, *I don't know. Ask me tomorrow once I've made sense of it. But no, don't ask. I don't want to tell.*

I say, 'Fine. Thanks. I'm going now.'

'Did you find the family history things you were looking for?'

I say, 'What?'

I think, *Family history, you idiot. Family history.*

I say, 'Oh yes. I did. Thanks a lot for helping, Doug. I've got to go. I need to feed the cat.'

I turn slowly so that the cuttings won't fall out from inside my jacket, praying the pieces of paper will stay where I've hidden them. I walk away from him with my hand pressed to my stomach to keep the articles in place and make my way down the stairs and onto the street.

I walk back the way I came, Central Station ahead of me, looming large and imposing, and I know I'm going to go in and stand on the concourse where the trains left – and still leave – for Wemyss Bay and the ferry to Bute.

Chapter 18

Funeral days should always be like this one. Dark skies threatening to burst and wind on the rise, all the elements conspiring together to remind us that nature's in charge. Biblical, that's what weather should be on funeral days.

Bob Meechan is being laid to rest at Cathcart Cemetery, following a service at Shawlands Kirk. I'm going. I can't not go.

Harry Blair told me that the police traced some relatives, a son that lived in London with his family, including Meechan's two grandchildren, a nephew in Kilmarnock, and a couple of cousins who live locally. Not local enough to stop the man lying undiscovered for two weeks, clearly.

I've cleaned the flat, handed in my report and the keys to the Fiscal, and declared it fit for human habitation. The clean is a science; clinical, regulated, precise. Getting rid of stains and pathogens is the easy bit. Cleansing a home of memories, emotions, and all the ghosts of guilt, is much harder. Thankfully, that's not my job because I'm hopeless at it.

Shawlands Kirk is a handsome blond gothic building on the corner of Moss-Side Road and Pollokshaws Road. I'm sheltering against the outer wall of the

Granary pub across the way, with a clear view of those passing through the church's broad red doors. It's clearly a busier affair than Tommy Agnew's, a few family groups are inside already, and I've seen people of various ages make their way in. Most of them are older, but there are a few younger ones that might be neighbours or relatives.

A taxi arrives and I see someone struggling to get out of the far side of it. I sense who it is before I see him. The cab pulls away, leaving the stocky figure in a black suit to pass through the black, wrought-iron gates and hobble towards the front doors. Jackie Stevenson is leaning heavily on his stick and something is leaning heavily on his shoulders. His progress is slow and laboured against the wind.

There's no sign of the only other mourner I've been on the lookout for. No fifty-something man with cropped dark hair. No tall, intense stranger in a tailored suit.

There's only a couple of minutes left before the service is due to start. I better go in if I'm going. I cross the road quickly, hurry down the path and through red doors that are faded through years of staring into the afternoon sun. There are maybe thirty people inside, dotted around in clusters of mourning.

It's an old and theatrical church, the altar like a stage with its red-walled backdrop. To the sides, tall pillars curve together into extravagant arches that frame gallery seating above us. I sit at the back, wary of turning to find someone sitting behind me again.

Jackie Stevenson is two rows from the front. I see a couple of people come up and talk to him, commiserations offered, or acquaintances renewed. His back is broad, his hair grey and sparse. He's staring forward where Meechan's oak coffin sits on a wooden stand.

There's a shuffle of feet and more people appear in the aisle, heading for the front row. There's a tall man, a woman on his arm, two sullen teenagers behind them. They're followed by a woman in her seventies and another couple, heads bowed, who might be around fifty.

Part of me wants to shout out. Tell them what I know. Tell them that Meechan's death was no accident. That him dying so soon after Tommy Agnew was no coincidence. They deserve to know.

I don't. Instead, I sit and wait and watch. I let them have their ceremony undisturbed, let their moment of duty and contemplation pass without being invaded by a harsh reality. There are two main reasons that I say nothing. First, that the idea of making a public announcement in front of strangers is terrifying. Second, that I don't want to interrupt the one moment of communal guilt that they're likely to allow themselves.

I'm hoping that they're enjoying some remorse right now. That they have the good grace to admit to themselves that they should have looked in on him, that they should have at least phoned or emailed or even just wondered why they hadn't heard from him. I want them to be suffering from that right now and have no intention of letting them off the hook by telling them that the truth is even worse than they're imagining.

The minister comes in, a grey man with a serious face. I think he practises this look in front of the mirror. Maybe he has a different face for weddings and christenings. He delivers his sermon, a much more personal effort than Father McKenzie's was for Agnew. The son has clearly written a lot of this or at least given the information. I learn lots of things I didn't know.

The only child of Robert and Jean Meechan, he was born in Dennistoun in 1946 and brought up in Partick. He worked as a welder in the shipyards, doing his time with the Fairfield yard in Govan. After five years, he graduated to the office and into management.

He met Margaret and they married in 1969, being blessed with the birth of Richard in 1971. Family was hugely important to Bob and he was never happier than when spending time with them. In years to come, Richard and his wife Jennifer presented Bob and Margaret with two grandsons, Iain and Fraser.

Bob's life changed for ever when Margaret passed after complications from a car accident in 1997. He never remarried and considered himself still in a lifelong relationship with his wife.

Unfortunately, Bob had suffered from ill health in recent years but bore it with good humour and little complaint. He had been diagnosed with lung cancer and although the prognosis was without hope, he chose not to share his bad news to protect those who cared for him.

I'm wondering who he was really saving by not telling them how ill he was. Not anyone who cared enough to know he'd died.

What's worse, I wonder? A man who had three mourners at his funeral and whose death went undiscovered, or someone whose death wasn't noticed by thirty?

We listen, we pray, we sing, we pray again. The minister nods sombrely and six men emerge from the pews and move forward. The son, the grandsons, Jackie Stevenson, and two other older men. One is taller than Stevenson, heavier too, breathing hard as he and the others heft Meechan's coffin onto their shoulders. The sixth man is ashen-faced and poker slim, and I think the weight of the coffin might snap him in two.

They make their way slowly down the aisle, Stevenson working hard to support himself on his stick. As they get near the back of the church, he sees me, and his face darkens. He glares at me, eyes like slits, until they pass and exit the church.

I'm a bit shaken by the ferocity of his stare. Even in carrying his friend's coffin he had time to look at me like that, and it doesn't make me feel good at all.

I let the rest of the mourners file down the aisle and make their way to the front doors, tagging on to the end of the line and looking around to see I'm the only person left in the body of the kirk. Until something catches my eye.

I look up to the gallery above, seeing someone just disappearing from view. A man. Dark-haired. I can't swear to any more than that. But it rattles me. I step back for a better look but see nothing.

The front door is crowded with people, all milling around and seemingly reluctant to leave. As I get to the back of the throng, I can hear why. Rain is hurling itself at the ground. I can glimpse it over their heads. It's biblical.

It's still hammering down as I get to Cathcart Cemetery. My windscreen wipers are working furiously yet I can only just make out the old gatehouse leading into the cemetery grounds. I park and manage to push out an umbrella and walk under it to the graveside.

Around half of those from the church have made the effort to see Meechan placed into the ground. The son and the grandsons are there of course, standing dutifully by the open grave. I think all those that were in the front row are here, including the two men who helped carry the coffin. Stevenson is propped up on his walking stick, his face darker than the sky and just as thunderous.

I give up on the umbrella. It's fighting to turn itself inside out and barely keeping the rain off anyway. I clasp it in two hands and hug it close to me. All around me is a wavering sea of black, wet and wild and quivering in the wind. I'm wondering how many of them will end up in that hole along with Meechan.

The son is standing tall, securing his wife under one wing and his sons under another. I feel for him. Losing a parent you love is one of life's most testing chapters. You're never too old to become an orphan.

The minister isn't hanging about. He races through platitudes and prayers then asks for cords to be taken.

Jackie Stevenson edges forward and accepts one. Bob Meechan is lowered slowly, hand over hand, into the sodden earth. The men throw handfuls of wet dirt onto other wet dirt and carefully retreat from the edge.

I join a line of people who are forming a muddy queue in a thunderstorm to shake the hand of a man I've never met. Richard Meechan doesn't ask who I am or how I knew his father, he just takes my hand and thanks me for coming. His suit is soaked, his hair dishevelled, and his hands are cold. Rain or tears or both are running down his face. I tell him how sorry I am, and leave.

I've taken no more than a few steps when I hear gravel crunching behind me and the laboured sound of heavy, unhealthy breathing. I know it's Jackie Stevenson before he calls out, his voice almost deserting him because of his efforts in trying to catch up with me.

'You. Wait there. I want to talk to you.'

I turn to face him.

I think, *Good, because I want to talk to you too.*

I say, 'How are you, Jackie?'

'Don't fucking Jackie me, you lying little bitch.' He looks around and drops the volume a notch or two as he takes me by the elbow and leads me off the path. 'What's your fucking game?'

'What do you mean?'

'You lied to me. To me and Bob. That day at Tommy Agnew's funeral. You told us you were Tommy's niece. You said your name was Cathleen.'

'I …'

His head is close to mine now and I can feel his breath on me. 'I read the fucking newspaper. Grace McGill. That's you. You're some … freak. Cleaning dead people's houses. You *lied* to us.'

'I just didn't want to tell you my name …' I hear how pathetic it sounds.

'I read the newspaper,' he repeats. 'I saw the photograph. I know it was Tommy's room that you made that freaky model of. I *know*.'

He's still got hold of my elbow, rag-dolling me by the sleeve. His face is getting redder and people are staring at us. The two other men, the ones who helped carry the coffin, are coming towards us.

'What are you up to?' he demands, losing control of his volume again.

'How could you be sure it was Tommy's flat?' I ask.

'*What*?' The response is as much snarl as word.

'How are you so sure it was Tommy Agnew's flat? You let me think you hadn't seen him in years.'

'Think you're smart? With your creepy model thing. Think you can just do something like that, and no one will notice? Well, I noticed. That photograph on the dresser? That's the one you asked us about. The one you said you'd only seen when you were a wee girl. Lying bitch.'

'You recognised that photo from seeing it in the newspaper?'

'Aye, I did!' The other two men are with us now, looking confused, and the larger one is reaching out an arm to Stevenson's shoulder. I'm surrounded and nervous. 'You okay, Jackie?' he asks.

'Aye. Just talking to this lying bitch who said she was Tommy Agnew's great-niece. Lied to me and Bob.'

The men's faces melt into anger. The skinny one tilts his head to the side and for a moment I wonder if rain will run out of the lower ear.

'How could you be so sure that's what that photograph was?' I ask Stevenson.

'What?'

'It was a copy of it, but only a tiny copy. Only someone who knew it could possibly recognise it.'

His faces squashes in towards his mouth, all concertinaing towards a scowl, his skin turning puce with rage. 'Are you telling me I don't know what I can see with my own eyes?'

'I'm not the only one who lied am I? You and Bob, you lied to me about Bute.'

I can see the reaction on his face. On the other men's too. Eyes widen, faces contort. I keep going.

'You told me you didn't remember Tommy ever going to Bute. *Never* went there that's what you said. You said I'd know more about the photo than you or Bob. That you couldn't tell me anything about it.'

Stevenson glowers at me and struggles for words and breath. The bigger man leans in aggressively and I'm scared he's going to hit me. 'Why don't you fuck off before there's trouble?'

'She's a liar,' Stevenson says. 'A mental case too. Fucking Walter Mitty. I've no idea what she's talking about.' He jabs a fat finger at me. 'Why are you even here? Who asked you to come?'

I think, *I don't need to be asked. It's a funeral, I don't need a ticket. And why are you getting so unravelled by what I'm asking?*

I say, 'I lied about my name. You lied about Bute. And about that photograph.'

He's rocking back and forward, losing it and getting angrier and angrier. Maybe I should stop. All my survival instincts are telling me I should run. I can hear thunder booming not far away.

'You're a lying, nosy little bitch.' The skinny man has a hand on Stevenson's arm, trying to calm him. It's not working. 'This is the man's funeral. Have you got no respect, no decency? Coming here lying, asking questions.'

'What about Valerie Moodie?' I ask.

For a moment everything stops. Stevenson doesn't speak. I'm not sure he breathes either. The other two men just look at me, mouths slightly open. The fatter guy is staring at me as if he can't work out what I am. The world is frozen.

Then it bursts.

Stevenson lunges forward, all noise and fury, his hands clawing the air towards me, reaching for my face. The two others grab at him, to stop him or to hold him up, I don't know which because it all happens at once. Stevenson's face is an explosion of purple and then it's sinking below my eye level, disappearing out of sight.

He's on his knees in the muddy turf, his hands clutching at his chest, not at me. His eyes are bulging, and he can't find a breath. He's having a heart attack.

The bigger man drops to his knees alongside Stevenson, mouth wide, tending to his friend. There must be more noise, but I can't hear it. Can't hear anything. The skinny old man pushes an arm at me, forcing me back, I can see him shouting at me to go. People are approaching from around us, surging past me. I'm outside the circle. Some are staring at me; most are staring at Stevenson.

I stagger back and suddenly the noise pours in like it's come over the top of a waterfall and is landing right on top of me. Screams, shouts for an ambulance, anger, thunder, rain and more rain.

I need to get out of here.

I hurry back, sloshing through the gravel, fire the car door open with the remote and jump inside. I turn the ignition on and sit with the engine running, windscreen wipers flying. At every pass, the deluge disappears, and I can see the scrum in the distance, the people in black bending over the man on the ground.

And all I can think of is the name that broke him and put him on his knees.

Valerie Moodie.

Chapter 19

The Scottish Standard, Monday, July 27, 1964

POLICE FEARS FOR MISSING TEEN. LAST SEEN IN ROTHESAY.

Police are urgently appealing for information about the whereabouts of a young woman amid increasing fears for her safety.

Valerie Moodie, seventeen, from Royston, has not been seen by her family since leaving with friends to visit Rothesay on the Isle of Bute on Friday. Valerie's parents, Thomas and Jeanette Moodie, are pleading with her to come home as they are desperately worried for her safety.

Valerie, a shop assistant with Woolworths on Argyle Street, travelled to the popular Glasgow Fair destination with friends but became separated from them. Police have not been able to ascertain if she took the return crossing. Her parents raised the alarm when she hadn't returned home by the next day as planned.

Valerie is described as being five feet three inches tall, with long fair hair and green eyes. She is of slim build and was last seen wearing a white cotton dress with red and black detailing and a red belt. She was carrying a red handbag.

Rothesay is currently home to hundreds of holidaymakers from Glasgow, as is common during the Fair Fortnight.

Officers from Renfrew and Bute Constabulary have been joined by colleagues from City of Glasgow Police and are interviewing everyone on the island as well as conducting a thorough search.

Anyone with information relating to Valerie Moodie's whereabouts are asked to contact their nearest police station.

The Buteman, Friday, August 14, 1964

Police searching for missing teenager Valerie Moodie are investigating reports that fishermen saw a body in the Firth of Clyde on the day the teenager disappeared.

Sources say that the two men were fishing in the Firth on the evening of July 24 when they saw a large white object floating on the surface around 100 yards from their boat.

The men are believed to have told acquaintances in local public houses what happened, and Rothesay is rife with rumour that they saw Valerie Moodie's body.

One of the two men is said to have told several people he's been struck with regret since the incident and wishes he and his companion had pursued the object rather than letting the tide take it away from them. The man is said to be convinced he saw the body of Valerie Moodie in a white dress.

Full story on pages 2 and 3.

The Scottish Standard, Monday, July 23, 1984

A heartbroken mother yesterday made an emotional appeal in an attempt to finally solve one of Scotland's strangest – and sadly forgotten – missing persons cases.

Twenty years ago today, Valerie Moodie left Glasgow and took a steamship from Wemyss Bay to Rothesay along with hundreds of other Fair Fortnight holidaymakers and day-trippers. She was never seen again.

What happened to Valerie remains a mystery but her mother, Jeanette Cook, says she's never given up hope of being reunited with her daughter, and yesterday she called for anyone with information to come forward.

Miss Moodie travelled to Bute with two friends from the shop where she worked. Marion Millar and Dorothy Harrower became separated from Valerie later in the day and raised the alarm after not being able to find her the next day.

Jeanette Cook says she's not given up hope that someone will one day let her know what happened that day twenty years ago. 'People don't just disappear, not without someone knowing. I've no doubt that someone out there has information that they still haven't given to the police. It's not too late. Please come forward now. And Valerie, if you are out there, if you ran off for some reason, just let me know. I don't need to know where you are, just that you're okay.'

When asked if the twentieth anniversary of Valerie's disappearance was a particularly difficult time, Mrs Cook disagreed.

'Anniversaries are for other people. I miss my daughter every day.'

Chapter 20

There weren't many cuttings to be found about Valerie Moodie, and precious few after the first week or so. The national newspapers covered the story until they got fed up with it, the locals kept it going a bit longer and then they too moved on to something else.

A young woman gone missing. Devastating for her family but after that, who cares enough to keep reading about it? There was no sign of her being hurt, little to suggest she'd been kidnapped, nothing juicy enough to titillate the tabloids. Someone they don't know has disappeared to do something they don't care about, so what?

The only newspaper that continued to have any indepth coverage after that first week was the local paper, *The Buteman*. It was a weekly, published every Friday, and ran front-page stories for two weeks with another two pages inside. But, annoyingly, all the cuttings had to offer for the second week was page one with a promise of 'Full story on pages 2 and 3'. And they, of course, were missing.

I'm sitting at my kitchen table, the pieces of newsprint spread out in front of me, George sleeping on my lap, Jackie Stevenson's heart attack reaction to the girl's name playing on my mind. To my right is an unfinished diorama, one I've been working on for a long time, and I find my eyes being drawn to it as if I'm going to find Valerie Moodie hiding under its lonely single bed.

The same photograph of her is used in two of the articles. It's black and white, of course, and shows its age. Valerie's a pretty girl, fair-haired and smiley in a floral dress. There's inevitably something tragic about seeing a photograph of someone when you know something bad happened to them. It's just one second, a snapshot in time, but that's the way the world will always see them. Valerie will for ever be summer and smiles.

There's another photograph, in the 1984 article. In colour, and presumably taken that week. *Fifty-eight-year-old Jeanette Cook, pictured by the pier at Wemyss Bay, where her daughter Valerie set sail on the ferry for Rothesay but never returned.* Mrs Cook looks like she hadn't had a single night's good sleep since July 1964.

The Buteman has photographs of holidaymakers on the front at Rothesay, gazing at the camera and telling the reporter the little they knew about the missing girl. There's something very familiar about them, like so many other old holiday pictures, seaside and sun, and everyone looking sort of the same.

They remind me of photographs, doubtless lying in a drawer somewhere, of my parents in settings like this. Some in Rothesay for sure, before I came along, others in Largs or Anstruther or Millport. Short sleeves and summer dresses. I remember again how my mum used to say they appreciated a photograph more back then, took more care over it, because each shot had to mean something.

Today, people take pictures of their dinner and fire off frame after frame of their kids doing nothing at all. They lazily button-push in the knowledge that they have limitless goes at getting it right because their phone's camera will always let them try again. I can hear my mum saying 'in her day' every photograph was a prisoner, twelve shots to a spool, twenty-four if you were really lucky, and they couldn't be wasted. She'd laugh like she was describing another world, and it felt that way a bit to me as she talked about how they'd have no idea if the shot was any good until they got home and waited for it to be developed at the chemists.

Photographs were prized. She told me they'd all be dated, names written on the back, put in frames or folders or just the packets from Boots, all kept safe like the family silverware, treasure for another generation rather than just a gigabyte of never-seen phone frippery.

I stop. My hand frozen where it was rubbing behind George's ear. My mind working overtime. A thought that should have occurred to me long before now.

'Sorry, George. Mum needs to get up.'

I lift the grumbling cat from my lap, place him gently onto the floor, and go to get the box that holds Tommy Agnew's mementoes. I bring it back to the table, the plastic bag of newspapers on the top, the other treasures underneath.

The photograph from Bute is familiar now. Six inches by four. Faded by time and technology. Those five young men, shirtless and carefree, sunny and smiling, caught in a moment, captured for ever. Tommy and his ears, his musketeers on either side. Quiet boy; freckles boy; Tommy boy; grinning boy; fat boy.

The frame is old and black and boring, just four functional pieces of wood pinned together. I've already got rid of the broken glass in case it did any more damage. There's a shake in my hands as I turn it over, a nervous excitement. Four little rusty metal tabs hold the print in place, a piece of card behind it, pressing it to the glass for over fifty years. I ease each tab back with a fingernail, each one feeling like a lock picked.

When the last one is pulled back, the print and the cardholder are free but still sitting in the frame, like pardoned prisoners wary of leaving a cell. I take a knife and slide it gently under the card and the print until they ease up and out, blinking into the light.

The photo still has its picture side to me, still hiding its secrets if it has any. I turn it; gently, respectfully, fearfully, hopefully. And there, written in pencil, is all that I hoped and feared to find.

Bob. Mick. Tommy. Jackie. Norrie.
July 1964

Chapter 21

I've taken to staring down on Glasgow while I think. Maybe it's helping me to see people when I'm struggling to understand them. It started with Tommy Agnew, his daisy, his newspapers and his wrapped-up photograph. Every layer that's been unwrapped has just made me understand less.

So, I'm at the window, George in my arms, seeing Glasgow wander back and forth on the street below. I'm keeping an eye out too. Looking for anyone looking for me, on watch for the man on the corner gazing up.

George knows I'm rattled, and he doesn't like it. The bad vibes flow through me to him and he's restless in my grasp. He keeps looking at me, desperate to know what's wrong.

I think, *My head's a mess, Georgie. I can't stop thinking about daisies and funerals.*

I say, 'It's okay, George. Mummy's fine.'

I'm not fine though. I'm obsessing over islands and lost girls. Lost girls and bad boys.

Quiet boy; freckles boy; Tommy boy; grinning boy; fat boy.

Bob. Mick. Tommy. Jackie. Norrie.

Valerie.

I should go back to the police. Make them listen. Tell them everything this time. That's what I'm going to do.

Ping. My phone signals a text, breaking my vigil and my thoughts, and making me jump out my skin. It's a message from my father.

I've nothing in for dinner. And I'm out of beer.

I almost laugh at his cheek, but I don't have the heart for it. The lack of beer I could ignore easily but I'll have to get him food. Maybe doing something routine like being my father's servant is what I need to take my mind off things that are scaring me.

The car is in one of the parking permit bays nearby, city centre gold dust, and this time it's not far from my front door. I press the fob to open it and am reaching for the handle when I spot a light-coloured line that shouldn't be there.

There's a vicious silver streak running along the driver's door towards the lock. Some bastard has keyed my paintwork.

I kneel to examine it, taking a wary look around over my shoulder before I do so. It's been dug in deep. No casual, accidental scratch, more like aggressively gouged.

It's only when I'm kneeling by the front tyre that I see that it's flat.

There's a gash in the tyre sidewall, maybe two inches across and a quarter-inch wide. Even if I hadn't already seen the jagged scratch along the door, I'd have thought the puncture was deliberate. The cut in the tyre is too neat not to be. It was done with a knife, nothing surer.

I jump to my feet and look around, no real idea what I'm expecting to see. Anger, adrenaline and fear coursing through me. Something or someone disappears from view at the corner with Wilson Street. My brain's scrambling to make sense of it but I think there was someone there and they slipped away as I looked around.

I'm running. Almost before my brain catches up with my legs, before fear has a chance to take a grip, I'm haring towards the corner in a fury, arms pistoning. I nearly crash into an old lady and need to career around her wildly, catching a few choice words that leave no doubt she isn't best pleased.

I'm still apologising to her as I look down the street, heart pounding, neck stretching in the hope or expectation of seeing a man in a black leather jacket with dark close-cropped hair. My breath is hard and fast and all I can see are bodies, in ones, two and threes, all shades and shapes, but no glimpse of the man I thought I'd see. Maybe he was never there.

People are looking at me, no doubt seeing the wildness in my eyes and the steam coming out my ears. I'm suddenly self-conscious about the attention, and need to get away. Also, as my temper ebbs, worry washes over me. I put my head down and retreat to my car.

I first text my father.

> Sorry. Car problems. Will need to get a taxi. Be there as soon as I can.

The answer is immediate, terse, and typically unsympathetic.

I'll change the tyre myself but I'm not doing it tonight, not here with daylight about to fade. My phone rings in my pocket and I assume it's him, impatient for an answer and for food. It isn't.

My heart stops when I see the name on screen. I'd saved the number the last time it called. No name, I've just listed it as Threatening Caller.

My hand is shaking and I'm scared to answer it. I'm also scared not to.

Swallowing, I hit the green button and wait for him to speak.

The voice is thick and hoarse, and dripping with malice.

'I said you had to be careful.'

'Who are you?' I can hear the tremble in my voice.

'Just be careful. Won't be your car next time.'

The line goes dead and I'm standing in the street with the phone hot in my hand and my mouth open stupidly.

I should phone the police. I know I should.

I should be careful.

I'm not going to be careful.

Chapter 22

It's two weeks since I stole the cuttings from the *Standard*. Two weeks since I stood on the platform at Glasgow Central and thought of Valerie Moodie. Now, I'm back here, on platform 14 and waiting for the train to Wemyss Bay.

Central Station is basically as it was in 1964, and as it was fifty years before that. The famous station clock that hangs from the roof is the same one that Valerie would have walked under. Maybe it was here that she arranged to meet Marion and Dorothy, the friends she journeyed to Bute with, the same arrangement that hundreds of thousands of Glaswegians have made over the years. It's hard not to see her there, slim, with long fair hair, the white cotton dress, the red belt and handbag. She's coming on the train with me.

I can't quite believe I'm doing this but I'm not sure I had much choice. I was on Team Tommy and now it seems I'm on Team Valerie. And I'm on my way to Rothesay.

What's that thing they say about it being better to travel hopefully than to arrive? I'm travelling more in hope than expectation, and fearful of what I might find when I get there. Hoping for answers, knowing something awful has happened and needing to know what it is. I want to be where Valerie was.

It's been half my life since I was on this line. I think I was maybe seventeen the last time we did it. Valerie's age. Back when Mum was still alive, and we were pretending to play happy families. Glasgow Central to Wemyss Bay, through Hillington and Paisley, by Langbank and Port Glasgow, the Clyde on our right all the way, past places I've only ever known from the train – Whinhill, Drumfochar and Branchton – till the hundreds of white hulls and masts of the marina at Inverkip are signalling we're almost there. It's the same line, the same trip, probably the same stops she made. A trip of memories and futures, of postcard-perfect views and neglected towns, of hopes and fears.

We're nearing Wemyss Bay and my stomach is in knots. My mind floods with the memory of a bitter shouting match between my parents, me wanting the ground to open up and swallow me. Me and Mum sitting at one end of the ferry, him on the other. The longest week of my life as it felt at the time.

The train pulls into the station and everyone gets off. I'm last and reluctant, but my anxiety is forgotten for a moment as I look around. I'd completely forgotten this place, or else just didn't notice, in the way teenagers don't. The station at Wemyss Bay is inside the ferry terminal and is a vast Victorian masterpiece. It's jaw-droppingly stunning, a huge circular glass roof with beams sprouting out of a central rotunda. It's freaking me out to realise this place hasn't changed since I came here as a kid. Or since Valerie did.

It's a short stroll under the covered walkway to the pier, a couple of dozen people ahead of me in the queue. Looking to my left, I see twenty or thirty cars parked up and ready to board. No going back now.

Once underway, I climb to the top deck, enjoying the views and a stiff, autumnal breeze in my hair. Seagulls swoop and squawk overhead, the sea sparkles dark, and the views are breathtaking – headlands dotted with white cottages, lush green mountains crowded together, their tops swirled in mist. There's shouting from my left and I wander over to see people pointing excitedly into the sea. I follow their stare and my heart flutters excitedly at seeing a pod of dolphins.

They're following the ferry like they're racing us, putting on a show by skimming the waves and surging through the wake, their bodies grey, glistening and powerful. A little blonde girl is watching, wide-eyed and open-mouthed, wrapped in a sense of wonder that's infectious. I feel like a teenager again, with both Bob Meechan's funeral and Jackie Stevenson's heart attack left behind in Glasgow.

When the show is over, the dolphins seemingly tired of the game, I feel deflated. Without the distraction, I'm left only with the confusing reality of my trip. I decide a coffee will help and turn to go back downstairs to the cafeteria. The stairs are steep and narrow, and I'm not happy to see someone coming up as I descend. He's tall and broad so I'm forced to squeeze uncomfortably to the side to avoid him, his shoulder still brushing against mine.

I'm at the bottom of the stairs before I can turn and look back up. He's just disappearing out of sight, a baseball cap tight to his head and I barely glimpse his face. It's more a feeling than anything else, something primal that runs down my spine and makes me shiver.

I think, *It's probably nothing. Just some random stranger passing by.*

I think, *Just because I'm paranoid doesn't mean they're not out to get me.*

There's a shake in my hand as I cradle my coffee in the cafeteria. I'm either being hunted or I'm crazy, and neither makes me feel good. I've positioned myself into a corner so I can see without being seen and I'm not moving from here until we dock in Rothesay.

When the announcement is made for drivers to go to their cars, people begin to funnel downstairs. Those on foot, like me, can wait a bit longer and I'm waiting till last. Me and Valerie.

I shuffle, finally, onto the end of the queue to disembark. The man on the stairs, whether he's the freak who's been following me or not, is tall, so I'm sure I'll see him if he's ahead of me, but I can't. I look back anxiously, just in case, but there's no one there. The ship docks, ropes are thrown, the gangway comes down and metal clangs. People begin to move.

I step off the iron trampoline that is the gangway and onto the island for the first time in eighteen years. Then I hear heavy footsteps on metal behind me.

My blood freezes but my feet don't, they keep moving and my brain goes into overdrive. My mind weighs it up, rationale over fear. If I'm sure it's him, I don't need to turn around. If it's him, I can't be sure who he is anyway. If it's not him, I'm losing my shit for no reason. Either way I look ahead and just keep walking.

There are footsteps behind me for five paces, then ten. I'm on the point of turning or running when I realise they've gone. Whoever it was has stopped or, more likely, turned off in a different direction. I'm breathing easier, reassured by paranoia – the acceptance that I'm crazy.

The front at Rothesay looks like Rothesay has done for a long time. Putting greens and palm trees, rising hills, a sweeping bay in a near perfect semicircle, and a seafront lined with shops. I turn back to the sea and stop to stare. I count eight, no nine, summits on the mainland across the shimmering bay, all in different shades of green and brown depending on how the light has caught them. Jesus, it's beautiful. I'm sure they weren't there when I was seventeen.

I turn right, past Guildford Square, past the Victoria Hotel, the Winter Gardens and the putting greens, in and out of memories. Another hundred yards and I'm there. The Bannatyne Guest House.

It's out of season so it isn't at all busy and I'm able to get the room I ask for. The owner is surprised I have a preference, but she shrugs, checks her book and says I'm in luck. Room 4 is available. She's leading me upstairs when a thought occurs to me.

I think, *Wait. What if they've changed it?*

I say, 'The rooms haven't had their order changed over the years, have they?'

She looks at me as if I'm mad. 'I don't think so ... Anyway, Room 4 is the only one that sleeps three people so if it was that one before, it's still that one now.'

That's the one.

I drop my bag inside and close the door behind her as she leaves. Three single beds and a view to die for.

Would three teenage girls really have spent this much time looking out at the bay and the mountains beyond, at the curve of buildings and greenery back to the town centre and the hills above with their tobacco-baron mansions? Or would they have been sprawling on these beds, giggling and giddy at the prospect of the fun that lay ahead?

I walk, as they would have done, back into town. Following the details in the newspaper cuttings, following in their footsteps in the hope of answers.

Some of the shopfronts are faded; poor relations of those the girls strolled by in the monied glory days of the sixties when Glasgow flocked here en masse, pockets bulging with holiday cash. There's a boarded-up jewellers and a second-hand furniture shop, then Zavaroni's. It's my first stop because one newspaper report said it was theirs.

Most people in west and central Scotland have heard of Zavaroni's. Ice cream and fish and chips and a singer named Lena who was a household name before I was

167

born. A waif-like child prodigy with a big voice and a short life. It seems an appropriate place to start.

There's three Zavaroni shops in Rothesay – Café Zavaroni, Zavaroni's Café, and Zavaroni's – all within half a mile of each other along the same seafront stretch. This one was where the girls bought ice cream and ate it as they walked and chatted and laughed. Inside, it's small and busy, and another trip back in time: onyx and Formica; stacks of cones; a tall, glass-fronted drinks fridge that whispers of forgotten summers; boxes of Tunnock's Tea Cakes and Caramel Logs; ice cream, sweeties and ghosts.

I catch sight of my reflection and stare long enough to wonder if I'm from the past or the present, or maybe not quite either. I look distracted and lost and although my hair is pulled back, multiple strands of it have escaped the clutches of the hair tie. My waterproof walking jacket is zipped to my neck in shades of dark grey and pink, and I look tired. I always look tired.

Something in the way the woman behind the counter speaks tells me she's had to repeat herself before I've heard her.

'A cone, please,' I tell her. 'Vanilla. Two scoops. Please.'

She's cheery but also smart enough to realise I'm not a talker. She hands me the wafer cone with two creamy rounds of joy and lets me be. I look at it and it makes me happy for a while. I taste it and it makes me smile.

I follow the girls down the road, the town centre in front of us, the sea rippling on my left and a breeze catching my hair. I've got ice cream and a sense of purpose; maybe things are looking up.

I'm heading for the library. I know it's behind Rothesay Castle and I remember that's off the right-hand corner of Guildford Square, past the amusements where I spent so much time as a kid, and up a short hill. The castle is a semi-ruin with a perfect moat around it. I stop for a moment, press my head into the bars and imagine myself inside. It might be my ideal home. Pull up the drawbridge, fill the moat with alligators instead of ducks, and tell the world to stay the fuck away. If only.

The library is a two-storey white-fronted building, very 1970s-looking. Inside, I'm directed to what they tell me is a microfiche reader, which lets me see all the pages of old copies of *The Buteman*, including the frustratingly absent pages two and three in the week after Valerie's disappearance.

They had three reporters working on it, detailing Valerie's known movements right up to the point where she vanished from the face of the earth. They'd been much more thorough than the nationals because it meant more. Throw a rock in the ocean and it barely makes a splash. Drop a pebble in a pond and watch the waves.

I read through it, make notes and underline bits. New nuggets of information, missed or ignored by the national papers, jump out at me. How the three girls took a trip out to Ettrick Bay and how they supposedly were talking to *a group of young men* there. A short interview with a box office worker at the Winter Gardens who thinks she sold Valerie a ticket for the variety show on the night she disappeared. Sightings of the girls in cafés and pubs.

I don't have all the answers by any means, but I have a map of the island now, footsteps to follow. The library also directs me next door, to Bute Museum where I'm told the curator, a lady named Anne Speirs, is the authority on all things Bute.

It's not going to be me that goes in though. Me barging in anywhere unannounced and speaking to strangers is never likely to end well, if it happens at all. I've decided who I'm going to be. I just hope I get away with it.

The museum doesn't look that big from the outside but as I go in, I see there's a theatre-style hall in front of me and the corridor I'm standing in leads left and right to two larger rooms. I choose right and find myself in a bright hall with a confusion of exhibits. There are objects in glass cases, terrifying taxidermy, a penny farthing, skulls and weapons, and who knows what. I've never seen anything like it. Moving along, I find myself in front of a model of a woman's head next to an ornate black collar-type necklace.

The necklace is beautiful, but I'm transfixed by the face. It's incredibly life-like, nuanced and bewitching. She's young and proud, defiant, challenging me to look at her, daring me to look away. She might be more beautiful than the necklace.

'She's the Queen of the Inch,' a voice says from behind me, 'and the necklace was hers.'

I turn and see a cheery, fair-haired woman walking towards me. 'They were buried together on the island of Inchmarnock in the Sound of Bute. She's hard to turn away from, isn't she?'

I think, *I spend my life working with death and never know how to look away.*

I say, 'Yes, she is.'

'She was dug up from a shallow grave by a farmer ploughing a field. We're sure she was a queen or chieftain of some sort. The necklace is Whitby jet.'

I think, *Shallow grave.*

I say, 'When did she …' I know this is a dumb question. 'She didn't die in the 1960s. Did she?'

She laughs. With me, not at me, I'm sure, but I still feel daft. 'Oh God no. Far from it, she's over four thousand years old. She was found in the 1950s. Bone analysis later found she died around 2000 BC.'

'And the face?'

'It's modelled on her skull. A forensic anthropologist at Dundee University, Dr Caroline Wilkinson, did a reconstruction for us. Her usual area of expertise is doing facial reconstructions of murder victims.'

That freaks me out and I need to change the subject. 'Hi.' I offer her my hand. 'I'm Lorraine Chalmers. I'm a reporter with the *Standard* in Glasgow. I'm looking for Anne Speirs.'

Her eyebrows rise in surprise, but she recovers quickly. 'Am I in trouble? It's not Brad Pitt complaining again, is it? I've told him it's over, but he just won't listen.'

'Eh, no. Not this time. I'm doing a feature on the disappearance of Valerie Moodie in the sixties and hoped you might be able to help. I'm trying to get an idea of how the island viewed it then and now. Readers love a mystery.'

'Really? It's been a long time since anyone asked about that. I thought the rest of the country had forgotten. But why now? There isn't an anniversary coming up. Not a significant one, anyway.'

I think, *I thought you might ask me that.*

Lorraine Chalmers says, 'Valerie Moodie's mother Jeanette said that anniversaries are for other people and that she missed her daughter every day. So, we felt that the timing wasn't as important as looking at it again and seeing it with fresh eyes.'

She tilts her head slightly in puzzlement. It doesn't sound quite as convincing when I say it out loud as it did in my head. But it seems there's just enough sense that she doesn't question me further.

'Okay,' she begins. 'You're young, so you might not realise just how huge the Fair Fortnight was here. Glasgow would virtually empty for the second two weeks in July and head for the seaside. Largs, Millport, Dunoon, Ayr, they'd all be busy, but Rothesay would be overwhelmed. Every boat would bring hundreds of people. The line at Wemyss Bay would go round the block. Some would be here for the full two weeks, hundreds more would be day-trippers. Valerie Moodie was a needle in a very big, very busy haystack.

'So, when she was reported missing, there was just confusion. With so many strangers on the island, it was almost impossible for anyone to have been sure if they'd seen her or not. All the guest houses were full, all the hotels booked up. The police – it was the Renfrew and Bute Constabulary at the time – had their hands full trying to work out who was here and what they might know. City of Glasgow Police were called in and everyone who got on or off a steamer was interviewed.'

'And no one was ever sure if she left again?'

'No. She got separated from her friends and they thought she got a boat home. There were reports of sightings of her on return steamers and in other places along the Clyde coast, but none of those were ever confirmed.'

'What was the reaction among people here?'

'Well, I was just a girl myself, so I was only vaguely aware of it. But I know that it varied a lot. At first some thought she'd got drunk or lost or ran off with some boy. Then there were stories that someone had been seen in difficulty in the sea and that someone had fallen off a steamer. But the idea that she might have been killed here, that really left a cloud over the island. It scared people of course and left a stain on Bute for a long time.

'One of her friends, Marion Millar, moved to Lancashire, and the other, Dorothy Harrower, emigrated to Canada in the eighties. Her name is … let me think … Denton, that's it. She's Dorothy Denton now and lives in Toronto.'

'So, what do people think happened to her?'

'Och, there are all sorts of stories. People who swear they saw her after she was reported missing, some say they saw her go in a car late that night, others say they saw her back in Wemyss Bay heading for Glasgow. There were the stories of her being in Largs, that she'd been kidnapped. As you can imagine, with a story like that in a place this size, people talk. Some of them might know the truth, but lots have just been listening to too much gossip.'

I think, *Tell me the truth. Tell me the gossip.*

I say, 'How do I know which is which?'

Her eyes narrow and I think she can see me. Her voice is sterner. 'Well, that's your job isn't it?'

'Right … right. There were reports of two fishermen who were supposed to have seen a body floating. Do you know who they were?'

She sighs and I know I'm testing her patience. 'I'm sure it wouldn't take a reporter long to find it out, but I don't think I should help you with that.'

I realise I'm getting nothing more from her, say my thanks and goodbyes, and get out before she sees through my lies.

I walk back down the hill until I'm on Montague Street. Marion Millar told *The Buteman* they headed there from the guest house. It was the main shopping street in Rothesay and in the summer, it thronged with people from all over. I've got a photocopy of a cutting with a photograph of it in the sixties and it's far removed from the much quieter street I find today. In the photo, there's well over a hundred people in view, the women in summer frocks, the men in white shirts, sleeves rolled up, everyone more formally dressed than today. Not a

T-shirt or pair of shorts in sight, no trainers, and quite a few of the men in suits. Among the host of shops, there's a drysalter, a tobacconist, a coffee bar, and a household bazaar. It was the world of yesterday that Valerie disappeared into, and maybe she's still there.

The Buteman said that she, Marion and Dorothy took a bus out to Ettrick Bay, so I go to Guildford Square and do the same. I nearly ask for four tickets but stop myself in time. The bus takes us out along the coast, past Zavaroni's, past the guest house, on by the Pavilion and on until we round the point and Rothesay is out of sight. Before Port Bannatyne, the road forks and we turn inland and are soon on the other side of the island, the west coast, in Ettrick Bay.

It's a cold October day but the sun is shining, and a beach is a beach, irresistible. The tide is out, and this beach is huge, so I do what I know Valerie did. I slip off my shoes and walk alone on the sands, feeling the cold grains of it squeeze between my toes. It's so flat here that I have to walk and walk until I get to the sea's edge and then walk and walk some more before the freezing water even comes halfway up my shins. I turn slowly through 360 degrees, taking it all in, feeling small and alone. There are five hundred yards between me and the sea wall, a mile from one end of the beach to the other. It's an enormous stretch of sand and I'm the only person on it. I look across the Kyles of Bute to Arran and don't see a single boat. I close my eyes and hear nothing other than a whisper of breeze and the gentlest lapping of sea on sand.

I stay like that for an age; hearing little, seeing nothing, feeling separate from the world. For a while, even my mind is at peace.

A gull disturbs my dreaming, flying within inches of my head and squawking furiously. The spell is broken, my feet are cold, and my jeans are wet. I'm going to the tea room, to be where the girls were, to be where the newspaper said they met a group of boys.

Ettrick Bay Tea Room is a time capsule, a haven for chips and cakes and cups of tea that's stood on the fringe of the beach since the sixties and before. According to the library cuttings, Marion and Dorothy told the police they were here with Valerie, having lunch and strolling on the sand. Reporters followed it up and *The Buteman* had an interview with a waitress from the tea room.

I take a table at the back so that no one can see over my shoulder, and order a slice of cake and a pot of tea. The tea room's windows are wide, with a view directly onto the sea and it's so much like sitting in the dining room of a ship that I'd swear we're moving. Steadying myself with one hand on the table, I take the cuttings from my bag with the other and carefully place them on the table to reread.

The local paper quoted a waitress named Margaret Sutherland who remembered serving the girls, saying they'd been lovely, no trouble at all, very polite she said. They'd all had fish and chips, two of them had cakes, but she couldn't remember which. And they'd got talking with a group of young guys at the next table. She didn't think they came in together but couldn't be sure.

Dennis Hayman, a holidaymaker from Carlisle, said he and his wife saw Valerie and her friends. He remembered them because they got loud and giggly when talking to a group of four or five lads. He had to tell the lads to quiet down and one of them gave him some cheek. He said the girls came in after the boys did and were still there after they'd gone.

I think of the photograph of Agnew and the others. *Four or five*. My guess is five.

It was just a chance encounter, limited to no more than half an hour in the tea room. No reason to think any more of it. The police wouldn't have tried too hard to find the boys, if they tried at all. It would be pushing it to imagine they had anything to do with Valerie's disappearance. Unless you knew what I knew.

We all get on the bus back to Rothesay, the girls laughing and chatting. Me deep in thought. Both Marion and Dorothy told the police and the press that they'd gone to Ettrick Bay, but in nothing that I've found did either of them mention their encounter with the young men at the next table.

My thoughts are spinning and I'm going to head back to the guest house for a rest and then freshen up to go out at night. That's how it was in 1964, just before everything went wrong.

Chapter 23

Putting on make-up is alien to me. I do own some, but rarely have a reason to use it. I wear a mask to clean the homes of dead people and my cat loves me or doesn't depending on his mood, not on whether I wear lip gloss. This evening is different. Dorothy Harrower said the three of them got dolled up before they headed into town for the night. That's why I'm warily applying lipstick, powder, and paint, and trying not to end up looking like a ventriloquist's dummy.

When it's done, I can barely recognise myself in the mirror. Maybe that's the point.

According to *The Buteman*, Valerie, Marion and Dorothy went to the Royal Hotel on Albert Place for dinner, no doubt feeling all grown up in their summer dresses and lippy. The paper says the hotel confirmed the girls had a booking for 7 p.m. and that they believe the group left by 8.30.

Eating in the Royal isn't an option for me. The hotel closed years ago, and the building now sits semi-derelict facing the seafront on Albert Place. As it's no longer in the itinerary, I've decided to skip food and go to their next stop, the Taverna Bar, in search of gossip.

The Taverna is where the three girls went after dinner and where they split. I'm just getting ahead of schedule.

The bar sits on the corner of West Princes Street and Guildford Square, a door on each side, its walls painted blood red with a thick black stripe along the top, looking like the funnels on a steamer. Deep breath and I go in.

My only hope on the rare occasions I go into a pub is that no one notices me, that I can hide in the crowd or the corner and observe unobserved. When I pull back the door of the Taverna and walk inside, every pair of eyes in the place turns to look at me.

There are a few smiles and heads raised in greeting. A couple of people say hi as I go to the bar, and the barman greets me cheerfully. This is hell.

I need to be Lorraine Chalmers, girl-reporter, and she needs to up her game for us both to get through this. I order a Diet Coke, stand at the bar looking around. Inside I'm squirming.

I still can't quite bring myself to just go talk to someone, so I take a seat near the window and hope they come to me. It takes some cola sipping and airily looking around, but it happens. The woman at the table next to me turns and asks if I'm all right. I tell her that I am.

'Are you on your own, hen? Come sit with us if you want.'

There's four of them, all women, all in their fifties or sixties, happy, chatting loudly over a table littered with glasses they're drinking from; along with refills waiting to be had.

I think, *No way. That's my idea of a nightmare.*

Lorraine says, 'Oh thanks, but I wouldn't want to bother you all. Anyway, I'm working. Shouldn't really start drinking.'

She looks at me, confused. 'You're working?'

'I'm a reporter. Just over for the day covering a story.'

She lights up and her voice lowers, her friends are suddenly interested. 'Oooh. What's happening? I'm Maria, by the way.'

'I'm here doing a piece on Valerie Moodie.'

The excitement fades fast from Maria's face. 'The wee lassie who went missing in the sixties? I've heard all sorts hen, but I couldn't honestly tell you what's true and what isn't. Sorry.'

One of the other women, the oldest of the group, glares at me, gets up without saying a word and takes a seat at the far end of the bar, her eyes fixed on me, still scowling. She's a peroxide blonde in her late sixties, silver spectacles perched on her nose.

'Don't mind Sheena,' Maria says quietly. 'She's always had a thing about the disappearance of that wee lassie. She gets like that when anyone from off the island comes to talk about it.'

'Why? Did she see Valerie that day?'

I get a weary shake of the head. 'She was only young herself. Couldn't have been any more than ten or twelve. She doesn't know anything, whatever she says.'

I'm interested. 'So, what *does* she say?'

Maria sighs. 'Best left alone, trust me. It's not that folk don't care what happened to her, they do, but they mostly forgot it a long time ago and are fed up of

Rothesay being associated with it. I was only four when it happened but most of the older ones are certain it was a visitor that did it. And whatever happened, she's not on Bute. She'd have been found by now if she was, dead or alive.'

I think, *It is probably best left alone. I know you're right*.

Lorraine says, 'Okay, thanks. Can I ask one more thing? There was a story that two local fishermen were supposed to have seen a body floating in the sea when Valerie disappeared. Do you know who they were?'

She purses her mouth unhappily, looks around, then lowers her voice. 'That was Malky McTeer and Alec Thomson. Some days they'd say they saw that and some days they'd say it was all nonsense.'

'Are they still around?'

'Alec Thomson died about ten years ago now. Lung cancer. Malky McTeer is still on the island though.'

That makes my breath catch. 'Any idea where I could find him?'

She lowers her voice further. 'You could try the Golfers. If you find him soon, he might still be sober. If he isn't, stay away. Malky's bad news with a drink in him.'

That last bit of news shouldn't make me happy, but it does. Malky being bad news makes him interesting. Anyway, my father's made sure I've no shortage of experience in dealing with ugly drunks.

I leave the last of my cola and say goodbye, suddenly aware that this is where the story gets blurred, where accounts start to diverge. It's the point where Valerie went one way, and her friends the other.

Marion and Dorothy told the police that Valerie was tired and wanted to go home. They never saw her again. Standing outside the Taverna I take a deep breath and go left, suddenly feeling more alone as the ghosts of Marion and Dorothy leave us. It's just me and Valerie in the dark.

I get no more than a few paces when someone steps out of the other door to the bar and blocks my path. It's Sheena, a few glasses of vodka to the good and a mist in her eyes. Her voice has a slur to it.

'So, you want to know about Valerie Moodie? Well I can tell you something.'

This I didn't expect, and it makes me nervous. I can't think of anything to say other than, 'Yes, please.'

'So, if you know about Valerie then you'll know she was in here with those two friends of hers. And that Valerie left to go home on her own.'

'Yes.'

'Well that's the story and everyone believes that's how it was. But it wasn't.'

'No?'

Sheena looks pleased with herself. 'No. I keep telling people this and they don't believe me. Those lassies had a row, that's why the Valerie one went off. The other two were with fellas and she didn't want to get involved and rushed out. I know that for a fact because my mother was in the pub and saw it with her own eyes. She wouldn't have said that if it wasn't true. So, stick that in your paper.'

'Um. Right. How many men were they with?'

'What?' She looks deflated as if disappointed what she's told me isn't enough. 'I don't know how many. More than two though. More than just one each for that Marion and Dorothy. I've told people this and they don't believe me. And they say even if it was right it wouldn't matter. But I think it's important.'

I think, *Me too.*

I say, 'Thanks. I believe you and I'm sure it's important. Do you know anything else?'

Just then the door to the pub swings open and Maria's head pops out. 'Sheena for pity's sake. Leave the lassie alone. She doesn't want to hear your stories. Come away in.'

Sheena looks apologetic and angry and a bit drunk. She does what she's told and the door to the Taverna swings closed. I look ahead to the end of the street and see the Golfers. It's my next stop.

The Golfers is what my father would call a proper pub. Wood floor, huge old-style gantry, art nouveau fittings, and short stools for falling off. It's a busy place, most of the seats taken and people standing around the bar.

The barman approaches and asks what I'd like. I get the notion that the cola isn't a good cover and I should have something alcoholic. The only problem is I don't know what. 'Vodka and Coke, please.' I hear myself say it and realise it's what Lorraine the reporter drinks.

When he brings the drink, I ask him quietly if Malky McTeer is in. He nods to the far end of the bar where a man is standing alone with a glass to his mouth.

He's weather-beaten and lean, in faded denims and a checked shirt under a blue V-neck jumper, the sleeves rolled towards his elbows. He looks like a man who's spent his life at sea and can't get used to the land not moving from side to side. His left arm is firmly planted on the bar and his right hand is gripping a glass of whisky like it's anchoring him to the room.

He must be in his mid-seventies but he's wiry and strong, no fat on him. Years at sea would do that I guess, plus doing more drinking than eating.

He turns when he sees me approaching and smiles when he realises I'm going to speak to him. 'Hello darling, what can I do for you?'

His voice is gravelly, the sound of someone who's smoked forty a day for a lifetime but smoothed out with a coating of old man sleaze. He's had enough to drink that he's forgotten thirty of his years and thinks I'm interested. I swallow back down the thing that just died inside me and decide to make use of his leching. I smile.

'Are you Malky?'

'The one and only, darling. What can I do for you?'

'I wanted to ask you some questions about fishing. I was told you'd be the best person to talk to.'

'Sure thing, doll. You've come to the right place. Can I get you a drink?'

'I've already got one, thanks.'

He grins. 'That won't last you long. Hey Peter ...' the barman looks over, '... a drink for the lady. Make it a double.'

Peter the barman looks at me and I shrug. I suppose so.

McTeer picks up his drink and mine and nods at me to follow him. We're in what old pubs call 'the snug', in this case red leather seating, etched windows, partition walls, and privacy. I'm not sure it's a good idea but it's where I am.

I've decided not to go right to it, worried that if I start by asking about what he and his pal saw in the sea that night he'll just pull the plug on the conversation. If I can get him talking then maybe he'll be more receptive to it when I get there.

'I'm told you've been fishing these waters a long time, Mr McTeer.'

'*Mister McTeer*. Don't make me feel old. Please, it's Malky. But aye, I've been fishing round here since before you were born. What is you want to know? And what's your name?'

I ask about the type of fish found around the island, about how fish stocks have grown or shrunk, how prices have gone up or down, anything I can think of to warm him up and delay the point when I need to mention Valerie. It takes long enough that he's bought another round of drinks and I can feel the vodka working on me.

He's enjoying showing off, smiling at me far too much and boring the arse off me with drivel about fishing. It's a tough game apparently. Too tough for the young guys who give it up far too easily and want everything handed to them on a plate. You've got to know what you're doing, according to Malky.

'So, do you fish on your own these days?' I ask.

'Sometimes. Sometimes I'll take someone on for a bit. Can't get any of the young ones to stick at it for long though. I had a partner for years, but he's gone now.'

'Was that Alec Thomson?'

'Aye.' There's an edge of wariness to his voice. 'How did you know that?'

'I was asking around. I wanted to know who'd fished around here for the longest, and someone mentioned you and Alec.'

'Right. Okay. Aye, Alec was a good lad, salt of the earth. Gone ten years now.'

'Is it right that you and Alec saw a body floating when you were out fishing? Back when Valerie Moodie disappeared from here.'

It's like I've flicked a switch. His glass stops before his lips. '*What?*'

'That was the story I'd heard. That you and Alec saw what looked like a body in a white dress. Must have been a shock that.'

'Who the fuck told you that?'

'I can't remember.'

I think, *God, that sounds weak.*

I say, 'It seemed that everyone knew about it.'

'Aye? Well people know fuck all. What else did they tell you?'

I think, *This isn't what I planned. He's way angrier than I expected.*

I say, 'Just that. That you and Alec said you saw what looked like a body the night that Valerie Moodie disappeared. And then that you denied it when the newspapers came sniffing around.'

'The newspapers? Who the fuck are you and why're you here? No more of your shite. The truth. Why are you asking about that lassie?'

He's closer to me now, his boozy breath in my face and his hand gripping my elbow. He's strong and I can't pull away from him. I'm not going to tell him I'm Lorraine the reporter, mainly because I'm not any more. I'm just me, scared and clueless, and wishing I was home with George.

'I'm just … interested. That's all. From what I'd been told, you might know something about it. It's just one of those cases people are curious about, you know? Because no one knows what happened.'

'Aye? Well I don't know what happened either. You got that? It was nothing to do with me whatever it was.'

He's awfully angry and anxious for someone who had nothing to do with it. He's squeezing my elbow tighter and it's hurting. I reach for my glass with my other hand and knock it over. The vodka and Coke spills out over the table towards McTeer, startling him enough that he releases his grip on me.

I take the chance while I can, stand up and hurry out of the snug into the main bar. He's right at my back but the pub is busy, and people are watching the commotion. He calls me a fucking bitch just loud enough for people to hear, and goes back to his station at the end of the bar. I can hear the barman pulling him up for speaking to me like that, but I'm not fussed. I'm just glad to be away from him.

I'm next to a table of women, carbon copies of the ones in the Taverna, and they almost drag me into a seat in their rush to comfort me and satisfy their nosiness. *What was that all about? He's got a terrible temper on him that one. What did you say to upset him?*

The good news is it leads easily into a discussion of Valerie Moodie. My distressed state softens their attitude to me, and they gossip like sweetie wives. They're not telling me much I don't already know, but I can see it's annoying the fuck out of Malky McTeer and right now I'll settle for that.

It's pitch black as I fall out of the pub, my legs unsure and unsteady. I'm not used to alcohol and it's showing. I cross the road best I can, my head a mess of music and stories, all swirling and swaying between my ears. I feel vulnerable. There's a wind on the street and it confuses me, shuffling noises around so I don't know where they're coming from. I stumble on the kerb in front of a bookshop and have to take a bigger step to keep my balance. It feels weird and jumbly and I don't like it.

I try to walk very deliberately, following an invisible straight line and concentrating on putting one foot in front of the other, but my weight takes me to my right, and I follow, crossing the narrow street involuntarily. I run my hand along the wall to keep my balance and to keep me from crashing into it. I can feel concrete, cold but reassuringly solid. My hand runs over the rough iron of a downpipe, then the wood of a door, and the cool slide of what might be marble. Then the wall disappears.

It takes me by surprise, and I fall to my right where the wall should be, where there's just fetid air and two feet of nothing. It's a doorway or a trick, but either way I stumble into it and sink down on one knee. I'm halfway up again when there's an eruption of pain under my ribcage and every bit of breath I have bursts out of me as if I've been cut open.

I'm struggling to think and to breathe, but the pain burns, and I realise I've been struck by something. In the same instant that message works its way through to my dizzied brain, I gasp as I receive another blow to my stomach. I'm being kicked hard. There's a fist at my back and my hair's been grabbed. My senses are tumbling over each other in a rush of fear, pain and confusion.

I hear the voice and recognise it. Slurred and raspy, cigarette-rough, thick with menace.

'Fucking bitch. Sticking your fucking nose in.'

My hair is yanked back and my head with it. I'm gulping for air.

'Asking me questions like you've got some fucking right. *No right*. Nothing to do with me what happened to that lassie.'

I'm facing up, seeing the ceiling of the doorway swaying. His head is just out of view, his boozy breath filling my nostrils. I'm hurting.

'Saw the way you looked at me though. Like older guys, don't you?'

There's a hand on my left breast, squeezing it roughly. I want to scream. I want to vomit. I want to run. I kick at the ground to try to push up and away but he's too strong. His face is by mine and his breath is at my ear. I feel his wet tongue on my neck, slimy, slithery, squirmy. I throw my head from side to side, but he laughs, and I want to kill him. He's grabbing lower, hands scrabbling through my clothes. I try to push him off and I can't.

He makes a noise. Strange groaning, moaning. I can't make sense of it, but his grip loosens on me. He groans again and my head can't decipher if it's sexual or painful. I can't feel him on me, don't know if that's good or bad, and curl into a ball to protect myself. The noises above me are violent and my heart pounds, adrenaline flooding me. Then it's quiet and that scares me more. I'm waiting for the punch, the kick, the grab. They don't come and I curl tighter.

I don't know how long I'm like that. Seconds, minutes, the times spirals and stretches, my nerves spiking, my mind rolling like the deck of the ferry, and everything is in shades of black. It slowly winds down to something approaching an even keel and I dare to open my eyes and turn my head.

He's lying on the ground. Malky McTeer. His arm is twisted into a shape that doesn't quite make sense and there's blood at his temple. He's unconscious. Or dead.

I edge towards him on my knees, weirdly wondering if I did this but knowing that I didn't, and put my hand on his shoulder. I push at his bone and flesh and he recoils, a gasp of fear escaping from inside him.

I scramble to my feet and look around, seeing no one and nothing, just the blur of lights inside the Golfers and the blackness above. Backing away, I keep my eyes on McTeer long enough to be sure he's not going to get to his feet and follow me. I turn and run, huffing, wobbling, until I'm out of West Princes Street, bursting into the open expanse of Guildford Square and breathing deep.

One last look over my shoulder, and seeing no one, I slow to a hurried, anxious walk, nerve ends jangling. The guest house seems much further away than it did on my way into town, street lights blurry, the waves throwing themselves noisily at the shore to my right. Senses overloaded.

This is the return journey that Valerie Moodie never made.

My head's a mess of wondering. It seems a long time since I began walking into town with a Zavaroni's ice cream and Valerie by my side. I walked with her till I lost her, and now I'm walking back alone. Or am I?

Chapter 24

I wake to find two large yellowing patches of pain between my hip and ribs. I try to touch them but even a dab with the tip of a finger makes me squeal. My right elbow and knee are both scuffed, and there's a dull pain in the middle of my back. None of it hurts like my head though. Part hangover, part trauma, it's darkly depressed.

Dragging myself out of the guest-house bed, I head to the bathroom and pee. Then, staring at myself in the mirror above the sink, I wonder who the fuck I'm looking at. It's not just that my hair is even more of a mess than normal, straggly and tangled and writhing with snakes, not just that my eyes are dark-ringed and red-tinged, not just that I look worn out and pale. I don't recognise the person who is here, the hungover Miss Marple, the crazed obsessive. I look at myself and begin to cry.

I shower, dress, and pack my bag, all done at a funereal rate. I'm in no hurry to do anything or be anything. Breakfast restores some of me, grudgingly working my way through a fry-up while sitting at a table overlooking the sea. I'm still struggling though. A fog of memories and imaginations are messing with my mind, what-ifs tripping over whys.

My head, or at least my conscious head, still doesn't know where it's going when I leave the Bannatyne and walk into the town centre. My feet do though. They lead, I follow, and within a few minutes, I'm crossing Guildford Square and am on West Princes Street. *The scene of the crime.*

Being here nudges memories, sorts out the nasty reality from the horrible dreams that plagued me all night. I find the doorway that I tumbled into and that stops me in my tracks and makes my breath leave me. I realise that it's the back of the abandoned Royal Hotel, the place Valerie, Marion and Dorothy had dinner on the night it happened.

I can see it was probably inevitable that I fell into the doorway given that I was working my way along the wall of the building, it holding me up as much as anything. The doorway is painted in a muddy brown, fallen into dark disrepair, pocked with flaking paint and graffiti. Above head height is an old grill, maybe an extractor fan, that looks like it harbours a million germs.

I look up and down the street, seeking help that wasn't there last night and probably isn't here now. On the other side of the street, there's a dentist, and a charity shop that looks closed. The best bet is Print Point, the bookshop on the corner, facing the Golfers. *Books-Stationery-Art & Crafts-Copy-Print*, it proclaims on a sign that runs the length of the shop. I sigh, breathe deep and go for it.

The door has a bell on it, announcing my arrival, making it harder to sneak out again. There are two people inside, a female customer skimming through books, and a woman behind the counter. I can't do this while there's anyone else in the shop, so I go to a shelf and pick up the first book I come to and pretend to flick through it. I can't help but eye the room, flicking from the pages to the other customer, and out onto the street where the empty doorway is winking at me.

Movement inside the shop drags me back and I see the woman customer with two books in her hand ready to pay. 'Thanks, Sandra,' the woman behind the counter says. 'See you later.'

I go over, the book still in my hand even though I don't know what it is. I hold it out lamely and the shop worker goes to take it from me but is puzzled to find I'm still holding onto it. She smiles, brows furrowed. 'Is everything okay?'

I think, *Is it? I don't know but I doubt it.*

I say, 'Yes. I mean … Yes.'

She can see it's not okay, that I'm not okay. There's concern in her eyes and I know she's reaching out to me. 'We do coffee,' she tells me. 'Can I get you one?'

'Yes. Please.'

She nods quietly and reaches for a mug. 'I'm Karen. If you want to take a seat with your book, I'll bring this over to you.'

I'm fiddling with the book, idly looking at the back cover, when she returns. The coffee mug is hot and reassuring in my hand and the smell calms me. I feel comfortable enough with her that I'm sure I can do this. I'm busily working out a way to ask when another part of my brain just blurts it out.

'Do you have CCTV?'

It surprises her. Worries her too. She's probably been guessing at what's wrong with me, but my question has made her raise the bar as to what it might be.

'Yes, we have it. A camera in the shop and one onto the street. *Why?*'

'I … just …'

I think, *I don't have words. I'm not Cathleen the niece or Lorraine the reporter. I'm me, and have no one else to speak for me. Maybe all I have is a version of the truth.*

I say, 'I was in the street last night. Late. And I … Nothing really happened but someone … Someone attacked me out there.'

Her mouth falls open. '*What?*'

I start again but fail and settle for just nodding. 'Wait there,' she tells me.

She locks the shop door and guides me gently behind the counter to a computer monitor. 'What time was this?'

I shrug awkwardly. 'I'm not sure. I don't drink. Usually. But I was in the pub across the road. I'm really not used to it and …'

'It's fine,' she tells me calmly. 'You don't have to explain. What time would it have been?'

'About 11, I think.'

She works her way through the video, the time stamp flying past us as we watch shadows come and go along West Princes Street, ghosts in the machine flitting by. As it gets nearer to 11, she slows the pace and we watch nothing, nothing, nothing … then me.

I'm embarrassed to see myself staggering into view, first on the right of the screen and then lurching to the left. My head is low, and I've got an arm outstretched to the wall for support. I look at Karen to see if she's judging me, but she's fixed on the screen. Turning back, I see myself tumble into the doorway and my stomach tightens. If it happened as I remember, then here it comes.

She gasps when she sees him and so do I. I'm sure she recognises him. A place this size it would be surprising if she didn't. Her mouth opens again but clamps shut, and I see anger burning. We watch him kick me, punch my back, grab my hair, fondle me. I'm turning red and my stomach is in knots.

He's grabbing at my crotch, and I can almost *feel* his hand on me, when another man strides into view. It's a blur of movement as he seizes the attacker by the collar and drags him off me. Malky McTeer stands and tries to fight back but an arm shoots out and sends him crashing into the wall, his head hitting it. The single punch, and the impact against the wall, flattens him. My mouth drops open as we see the newcomer stand over me briefly then walk away.

It's less than a minute before I move, much less time than I'd thought. We watch me crawl to the man on the ground and check if he's alive before getting up and running raggedly away. When she stops the video, me and my new friend continue to stare at the screen, trying to make sense of it. For me, it's mostly as I remember it, some significant gaps filled in, and much more in focus than it had been the night before. For her, I realise, it's a big shitty shock that I've dropped on her from a great height.

She turns to me and I know what she's going to say. 'You've got to go to the police.'

I think, *I can't do that. You don't understand. I can't. I'm scared.*

I say, 'I don't want to make a fuss. I didn't get hurt and I'd rather just leave it.'

She looks like she can't quite believe what she's hearing. 'You've got to. You need to report this guy.'

'No, I just want to leave it.'

'You can't leave it. What if he attacks someone else? You've *got* to report it. If not for your sake, then for the people that live here.'

I think, *She's not going to give up on this easily. She's angry and determined.*

I say, 'Okay. I will. I'll go to the police.'

I think, *I won't.*

She stares at me, deliberating. Then she nods, accepting. 'The guy who attacked you is Malky McTeer. He's a bit of a bam with a drink in him, but I didn't think he'd … That's got to be stopped.'

'I'm going to the police,' I lie.

'Okay. I don't recognise the man who pulled McTeer off you. I don't think he's local.'

I think, *Oh, I'm sure he's not. He was on the same boat over as I was and I'm betting he'll be on the same boat going back.*

I say, 'He saved me.'

I think, *He saved me and I don't understand. I thought he was the one I had to be afraid of. The man who's been following me since Tommy Agnew's funeral. The tall, broad man with close-cropped dark hair. My stalker. My saviour.*

I stumble out of the bookshop in a haze, questioning every decision I've ever made and wondering what the hell I'm supposed to do next. The only thing I can think of is right in front of me. I need to get on the next ferry and get out of here.

I'm not looking when I cross the road to the ferry terminal, and a car has to brake sharply as I weave across. I wave a hand in apology and keep walking until I can hold myself up on the railing overlooking the marina.

I stare out to sea and realise everything's different from the day before. The hills that were various shades of green and brown, of light and dark, now all glower blackly. And the sea that shimmered in yesterday's sunshine is churning ominously.

The ferry is pitching in the wind and there's rain in the air under a thickening sky.

I hide myself on the lower deck, watching the windows fog and Rothesay slip away into the gloom. I made the trip across sure that I'd done so in the company of Valerie Moodie, but I'm equally certain I've left her behind on Bute. Taking a seat by the window, I pull my feet off the floor and my knees up to my neck, hugging myself despite the pain thats shoot through me, and stare at the rain. Rothesay has disappeared, swallowed up along with its secrets.

I can't be glad I went, but I'm not sorry I did either. I heard a voice and followed it, and if caring makes me crazy then lock me up now.

Chapter 25

I'm home. My head still full of Bute and Valerie, Tommy Agnew and Bob Meechan. Of the man who attacked me and the one who saved me. I'm sitting next to my phone and I'm fretting.

I hate making phone calls. I always get nervy beforehand, overthinking what I'm going to say and making it worse. I'm like that even if it's nothing important, phoning about a job or calling a taxi, so now that I'm about to phone Valerie Moodie's friend Dorothy, I'm shitting myself.

I got her number from the internet. It was an easy bit of detection involving the few Dentons in the Toronto phone book and cross-checking with a search on Whitepages. I did the same for Marion Millar but can't find her anywhere; so, I'm guessing she's moved, remarried or died. Any and all are possible.

Tracking Dorothy down was simple enough, but making the call is proving much more difficult. I've picked my phone up twice, dialled the number once, and still haven't found the courage to do it. Instead, I've tried to lose myself in the diorama. I've been working on this one for what feels like a lifetime, but I want to get it right. I *always* want to get it right, and that search for perfection is my curse. Or part of it.

It's a simple room, nothing in the way of flourishes, just a lonely single bed, one chest of drawers, one wardrobe. Having little in it doesn't necessarily make it easier to make though. In many ways, replicating a room is simpler when it's busier, when you can make copies of all the component parts. But whether it's more or it's less, you have to put feeling into it. That I can do.

I've been painting the walls for the past hour; anything to avoid the phone call. It's a pale, uninteresting yellow, a lazy disinterested choice. But as I finish the final corner of the third wall, carefully filling in the last bit of space with the tip of my smallest brush, I know I've run out of distractions and can't put it off any longer. I'm going to do it quickly before I get the chance to change my mind again.

The dial tone has that muted sound that you get long distance. They're five hours behind us so it's six in the evening over there. Prime time for her to be home.

'Hello?' Her voice has that transatlantic mix that probably makes Canadians think she sounds Scottish, and Scots sure that she's American.

'Hi, is that Dorothy Denton?'

'Speaking.'

'Mrs Denton, my name is … my name is Grace McGill. I'm sorry to call out of the blue but I wanted to talk to you about Valerie Moodie.'

The silence is lengthy. It's long enough that I'm not sure if she's hung up. There's a buzz on the line and little else. I don't want to push her in case she's still there and I put her off. I wait. And wait. Then finally.

'Why are you calling me? This is not something I want to talk about any more.'

She sounds surprised, annoyed, nervous and weary, all at once.

I think, *She's probably had more calls like this over the years than she'd like*.

I say, 'I think I might know something about what happened to Valerie. Well, I'm not sure but—'

She doesn't let me say anything else.

'Well, if you know something then you know more than I do, and you should go to the police. This all happened a very long time ago and I don't want to think about it. This is nothing to do with me.'

There's a click and silence and it takes me a few moments to realise she's hung up. I don't know what I expected her to tell me that she hadn't told the police, but I'd hoped for something. Something more than that.

I wanted to tell her about Bob, Mick, Tommy, Jackie, and Norrie. I wanted her to tell me that it was fine, that those boys had spoken to the police and they'd nothing to do with it. I wanted her to say it was all okay even though I know full fucking well that it's not okay. I wanted her to care enough to talk to me.

This is nothing to do with me.

She was your best friend. Even though it was a lifetime ago, surely it still hurts, surely you want to know what happened to her? I know I do.

I bought a notebook and have written VM on the cover. Inside I've jotted down dates and names and the little I've been able to glean from the newspaper cuttings and the internet. The page open before me has DOROTHY DENTON written in capital letters.

I've just underlined it. Twice.

It's taken me an age to fall asleep. My head is full of the call with Dorothy and her reluctance to talk about what happened. A head full of doubts and worries isn't one that sleeps easily. I may have drifted off a couple of times, into that strange middle ground where you might be dreaming you're awake, consciously unconscious, asleep but still thinking through all that's bothering you. In fact, I only realise I've been dreaming when I'm rudely woken from it.

I sit up, disorientated and alarmed, seeing by the clock that it's 2.30, and aware that my phone is ringing. I grab at it in a panic, sure that only the direst emergency is on the line at this time. My eyes make sense of the screen and my breath catches. It's him. The anonymous caller.

I hit decline and fall back onto the pillow. My heart is beating loudly in my chest and it's the only sound in a room of dark silence. *Bastard.*

I'll never sleep now, not with my nerves like this. And yet, somehow, at some point, I do. I only know this because I'm woken again.

It's not as surprising this time, perhaps part of me has been waiting for it, but it's still a shock when it comes. The time is 3.30. Exactly one more hour since he last called.

I look at the phone and consider answering, confronting him, but I don't have the nerve. I'm not going to decline either though, not going to give him the satisfaction of that. I turn the ringer off and slide the phone under my pillow.

I'm still awake when 4.30 comes around. My head swimming with anticipation and worry, thoughts tripping over each other in the dark. The phone is still under the pillow, still silent, but as I watch the clock hit the half-hour, I feel the mobile vibrate beneath my head.

I slide it out, take a deep breath, hit answer, and wait for him to speak.

And I wait.

The silence is louder now, crawling over my skin, and I try not to make a noise as I swallow. He's there, I know he is, but he's saying nothing and driving me crazy. I stand it as long as I can. Then I can't stand it any longer.

'What do you want?'

He laughs. Deep, hoarse and malicious, pleased with himself.

He's still laughing when I end the call and throw the phone across the room.

Chapter 26

I'm going to visit Jackie Stevenson at the Royal. It seemed the most likely place for him to have been taken after the heart attack at the funeral but a phone call, full of little lies, confirmed it. Yes, I assured them, I was a relative. They told me he'd been critical but stable, and now is merely serious but stable.

I've thought about it, debated the risks, and I'm going. I haven't worked out what I'm going to say, what I'm hoping to achieve, but I'm going.

The Royal Infirmary doesn't hold good memories for me. Too many visits to see my mother there. Too many tearful walks along endless, gloomy corridors. I can close my eyes and smell it; waxed floors, disinfectant, and bleach. I can reach into my memories and feel it; hope, fear, anguish, misery.

There was the time she was kept in for three nights with a fractured skull. I still remember how slowly I walked along the corridor to her ward. My feet trudged, trying to delay finding out how she was, expecting the worst, not wanting to see her face. The reality was worse than I'd prepared for. Not so much the swathe of bandages that held her head together, or the tube that fed her liquids, nor even the machine that spewed out her data. The worst thing was her demeanour.

She was upbeat and cheerful. For me. She didn't want me to worry, said she'd be as right as rain in no time, and laughingly said it was her own fault for being so clumsy. That would teach her to look where she was going, she told me.

I vividly remember opening my mouth to argue, but she silenced me with a raised hand and a look. She wouldn't hear anything other than her truth. She tripped. She fell. She hit her head on the side of the coffee table. Hard.

That's what she'd told the doctors. That's what she'd told the ambulance crew.

I had to go pick her up once after she broke her arm. Another trip. Careless woman, my mother. She fell on the stairs and put her arm out to brace herself, she said. The doctor asked how the break could be above the elbow and she explained she rolled as she landed.

She'd spent two hours waiting in A&E before I got the call. Another two before she was X-rayed and put in plaster. All the way home in the car she sat looking straight ahead, not catching my eye, saying nothing.

The worst though was when she had her illness. She was in and out of the Royal for months, including one eight-week stretch in the winter of 2007. It took about ten days before I stopped getting lost and learned to find my way to her ward deep in the bowels of that overgrown Victorian monstrosity.

Knowing where to go was only half of it though. Hour after hour sitting by her bedside, her often asleep or drugged to the eyeballs, probably not knowing I was there, but nowhere else for me to be. It was draining. Physically, emotionally, mentally. Bad for me, worse for her.

The Royal is old and haunted, and I hate it.

Just the sight of its weather-blackened stone as I approach along Cathedral Street is enough to turn my stomach over. Towers and turrets, all Gothic menace. The cathedral peeking out behind it and the Necropolis, the cemetery, hidden behind that, the city of the dead. It's like it's saying that prayers are all that stand between the hospital and the grave. And I know prayers don't work.

I go through the main entrance and immediately the memories climb on my back. It's the smell and the walls; the long, tight corridors smothering me, the sound of my heels on the floor. I want to turn and run but I won't. I want to talk to Stevenson.

He's been moved from the Coronary Care Unit into a general ward on the fifth floor, and I know I have to take the lift even though I'm already feeling claustrophobic. Just as the doors open two other people arrive, an older man and woman, and they get in as I do. There isn't room for three of us, not when one of them is me and my head is messed. I hold my breath until they get out on floor four, glancing sideways at me as they go.

One more floor and I burst out of the lift doors and go in search of his ward, counting off numbers as I walk, hoping it will keep other thoughts at bay. Twenty-one. Twenty-two. My plan is to go in as if I'm supposed to be there, as if I've been there before.

Twenty-three. Don't ask for directions. Don't ask if I can see him. Twenty-four. Just go in, own the place, be confident. Twenty-five.

I won't know which bed he's in, don't know how many beds there will be. One would be good, but that's unlikely. Be confident, look without looking lost.

I see straight away that there are six beds. An old man asleep. A younger guy reading a book. Two visitors at bed three. There. In the corner, by the window. Sleeping. Jackie Stevenson.

I go straight over, no hesitation, no waiting for permission or giving anyone the chance to ask who I am. There's a chair by the bed and I sit on it, but I'm immediately back on my feet again as I get bold and draw the curtain around the bed.

He's incredibly pale. Deathly white with just a hint of rose to his cheeks. His moustache lies limp against his skin and his jowls sag. There's a vein to the side of his head that throbs as a signal that he's still alive, if not quite kicking.

The last time I saw him, he was on his knees, violently clutching at his chest, eyes bulging. He had one foot in the Necropolis, and they pulled him back. His heart giving up at the mention of Valerie Moodie.

The area around his bed is stark, with few home comforts or personal effects. No get-well-soon cards, no flowers. The cabinet by his bed is bare but for a half-empty glass of water, a book, and a pair of spectacles.

I want to prod him. Jab a finger into his chest. Wake him and have him shaking with fright at finding me sitting by his bed. I can't think of a good reason not to. Then he stirs by himself, making me jump, and the need and the opportunity is gone.

His eyes ease open, seeing only the ceiling and not seemingly making much sense of it. He doesn't have focus or much idea of where he is. His eyes crease in discomfort and they float shut again. He's going to drift back to sleep, so I cough.

This time his eyes open with a start and his head swivels left. He doesn't recognise me or know where to place me. And then he does. He looks alarmed and confused and angry all at once.

'What are you doing here?'

His voice is thin and rusty but still riddled with resentment. I'm glad he doesn't have the strength to be heard any further than where I sit.

I think, *I want to know what you did to Valerie Moodie.*

I say, 'I wanted to see how you are.'

He makes a noise. Something guttural and dismissive that rises in his throat but doesn't get as far as his lips. There's loathing in his eyes, but I don't mind that.

'They say your condition was critical.'

'I know.'

'Severe myocardial infarction, they told me. That's a massive heart attack.'

'I fucking know. What do you want?'

Maybe I'm doing him some good. There's colour flushing in his cheeks and more bone in his voice.

'I told you. I wanted to see how you are. When you went down, I thought you were dying.'

His eyes narrow. His mind wants to fight me more than his body does. 'Sorry to disappoint you. Not dead yet.'

I think, *Maybe I do wish you were dead. Tell me what you did.*

I say, 'You were okay till I mentioned her name. At the funeral.'

He says nothing. Just stares back.

'But as soon as I mentioned her name, you collapsed. As soon as I said Valerie Moodie.'

He tries to push himself up off the bed, but he can't. Even that little effort causes him to sink deeper into the mattress and his mouth falls open in search of more air. He settles and swallows, breathing out hard.

'Why did it have such an effect on you? Her name.'

He stares at the ceiling, so I say it again. 'Valerie Moodie.'

I can see it crease his face. See it make the corners of his eyes tighten. I get out of the chair and move closer, lowering my voice, only a whisper now. 'Tell me about Valerie.'

'Leave me alone.' He breathes slowly. 'I'm ill.'

'I only want to talk to you. I want to know what happened.'

He lets his head fall to one side so that he's looking at me. He's trying to convince me by looking me straight in the eye. 'I don't know what you're talking about.'

'Then let me explain it.'

He faces the ceiling again and closes his eyes.

'You, Tommy Agnew and Bob Meechan and your other two pals. The five of you on holiday in Rothesay.'

I see the reaction. The vein on his temple throbs, his lips part, and his skin tightens.

'Is it ringing any bells yet, Jackie? July 1964.'

His eyes squeeze tighter. His mouth contracts. I think he's trying to shut off his ears and keep me out of them. That's not how it works.

'Five lads *doon the watter*. Just having fun, right Jackie? A few beers, a bit of sun.'

He doesn't open his eyes, but he speaks. 'I'll call for a nurse. You shouldn't be in here.'

The words are laboured, more breath than voice. He can't call for a nurse even if he wants to.

'You were there, Jackie. Weren't you? Are you going to deny it?'

'Leave me alone.'

'I've seen the photograph. I *have* the photograph. It's you. It's Tommy. And Bob. You were there.'

His jaw clenches and he can't help himself. 'Half of fucking Glasgow was there. That's just the way it was back then.'

Something quickens inside me. Heart, pulse, breath.

'So, you were there?'

He lets loose a heavy sigh. 'I went to Rothesay, yes.'

'But you went with Agnew and Meechan and the other two, Norrie and Mick.'

He says nothing but his face tightens. It's as good as another admission.

'Why weren't they at Tommy's funeral? The other two. You were obviously all friends since you were kids. They went to Bob Meechan's funeral. So why not Tommy's?'

'It's none of your business but they fell out. Happens all the time.'

'But you were all there the weekend Valerie disappeared?'

He turns and glares, his lips closing to form what I know is the start of a shout.

I clamp a hand over his mouth.

His eyes widen. Probably in shock, possibly in fear. He reaches for my arm, grabs it just above the wrist but he doesn't have the power to shake me off. It doesn't take much to stop him shouting. Just holding it there is enough. I leave it till he gets the message, lifting my eyebrows in question until he nods slightly in acquiescence.

It takes him a moment to find enough breath to talk. 'What do you *want?*'

'I want to know what happened to Valerie Moodie.'

'I don't know.'

I think, *You're a liar. You're a liar.*

I say, 'Then tell me what you *do* know.'

His mouth opens and closes. He's thinking, debating. Letting go secrets held for nearly sixty years can't be an easy thing. I need to make it simpler for him.

'Were you in Rothesay with Meechan and the others?'

He sighs like it's the last bit of breath he has. 'Yes.'

'And you were there on the 23rd of July 1964? The day Valerie Moodie disappeared.'

'Yes.'

'Why don't you just tell me everything, Jackie? Make it easier on yourself. Can't have been easy keeping this hidden for so long.'

He's agitated. His breathing is shallower, quicker too. I can see the thoughts racing through his head. The words are still locked away though, still prisoners.

'Did you meet Valerie and her friends?'

Nothing.

'Come on, Jackie. You may as well tell me. I know that you did. I spoke to Dorothy Harrower. She's Dorothy Denton now.'

His eyes widen at that. I imagine if Jackie was wired up to a machine then I'd be seeing his heart rate soar. His secrets are squeezing his heart. It's on his face too. More strain, more effort, more pressure.

'Tell me, Jackie. Get it off your chest while you still can. What happened to Valerie?'

'I can't.'

'You *can*. That girl's mother died not knowing what happened to her, but she's still got family out there. People who'll never properly rest until they know. And you can help them, Jackie. What have you got to lose now?'

'It wasn't me.'

It comes out in a hoarse, breathy whisper and I have to lean closer and ask him to repeat it.

'It wasn't me. I didn't want anything to do with it. I tried to stop it.'

'Stop what? Tell me what happened, Jackie.'

His eyes are wide and wet, but he slowly shakes his head. 'I tried.'

He's feeling sorry for himself, and the self-pity enrages me. 'But you didn't stop it, did you? I don't think you could have tried very hard.'

Something changes in his eyes. I think he's had enough. I can see that he's struggling to swallow, his colour changing. His mouth has two attempts at what he's about to say. Opening, closing. It's on his lips. He forces it out.

'Fuck you.'

He's wasted his last bit of effort on that. He'll give me no more; I can see that now. There's a curl of satisfaction on the corner of his mouth. A lick of spittle and a hint of a sneer. *Fuck you*.

His skin is flushed red, a final defiant roar against the grey. I'm sure his heart is creaking that little bit more at the effort of spiting me.

I move closer, right up to him until my head is by his. It's unnerving him, I can see that. I whisper.

'I know you're not happy, Jackie. It must be tough being on your own and having all that guilt to deal with for so long. You're lonely, aren't you? No one to share your burden with. I knew you weren't a happy person from the first time I saw you. It's all over your face, Jackie. The outside always reflects the inside after a while. Your face gives you away.'

His eyes are wary and wide. He's confused and not a little afraid.

'I know you're not going to tell me what happened. You're going to let it eat you from the inside, slowly killing you, slowly destroying you. You don't need to live like that, miserable and guilty and lonely. I can help you.'

I reach towards his head and he flinches, but he's misread what I'm doing. As he leans forward to avoid my hand, he helps my real intent. I slip one of the pillows away from behind him and place it softly over his face.

He struggles, of course, but he hasn't the strength for the fight. I can easily fend off his hands, and his anxiety – at being unable to breathe – is just putting more and more effort on his heart. This time it's going to explode. If there was a monitor, I'd be able to watch the numbers spiral, see the graph spike.

His hands are just waving at air, his heart racing at a speed it can't sustain. There's a bend in the road ahead, and it's going far too fast to stay on the road. His hands are forming claws, the knuckles of his fingers chalk white. They waver maniacally and then fall. There's no struggle beneath my hand, no life beneath the pillow.

I lift it from his face, take a tissue from the box by the bed, wipe the damp spot that's flecked with his final breath, and place the pillow back behind his head.

He looks like he's sleeping. At peace at last, all his demons drifting away.

I say a quiet prayer, for him and for me, then reach across to the cabinet by his bed and pick up the pair of spectacles, slipping them into my pocket. I straighten the pillow and am ready to leave. I'll soon re-emerge from behind the curtain, take a moment to stop and wave goodbye, then turn and walk out as confidently as I walked in.

My legs won't move though, they keep me rooted to the spot in front of him. I stare, and fight to control my breathing. I've one more thing to do. I reach into my other pocket and bring out a small plastic bag containing a daisy.

I place it carefully on his pillow. Now I can leave.

Chapter 27

My legs don't start shaking until I'm home and the front door is closed behind me.

It's always like this. A strange kind of calm that I don't really like, a pretence that I can carry off but that also feels like it's going to shatter at any minute. And then it does. I'm a beach ball held under water. A tightrope walker over a swimming pool of sharks.

I can walk and walk and walk. And then I buckle at the knees.

It's just twenty minutes on foot from the Royal to my flat. In that time, I passed thirty-seven people on the pavements. I counted them. Thirty-seven normal, breathing, mostly law-abiding people who couldn't see me, certainly couldn't see what I was or guess what I'd done.

The closest was a young mum with a buggy and two kids near to Cathedral Square. She gave me a look that I couldn't explain other than to think she could smell it on me. She reached out to the boy walking next to the buggy, put an arm on his shoulder, and pulled him closer to her as I passed them. Some part of her knew.

The four smokers outside the Old College Bar didn't have a clue. *Awrite, darling? Geeza smile.* They couldn't see what was in front of them, too full of drink and nonsense to be able to recognise someone who had just killed.

There was another old man, probably not as old as he looked but close enough to make me stop and stare. He was sitting on the pavement with his back to the wall at the traffic lights on the corner of Ingram Street, a skinny black-and-white dog lying beside him and an upturned flat cap on the ground. He held my gaze for an age, knowing a mark when he saw one. I put a tenner in his cap and hurried on, hearing his surprised laughter in my wake.

There were two cops on the other side of the street as I passed the Italian Kitchen. They were just strolling and chatting, hi-vis visible, no urgency, no all-points bulletin. I don't think they even looked at me. I couldn't be sure because I just stared ahead with as much casual indifference as I could muster. That was easy enough. Resisting the temptation to turn around a hundred yards later to see if they were looking at me, that was much harder.

I could feel my legs start to go as I got to Brunswick Street, felt them twitch as I got inside the building, and sag as I was in the lift. But it's only when I fall back against the inside of my own door that they collapse. I slide to the carpet in a clumsy heap, my head in my hands and my mind a muddle.

There are tears streaming down my face and I'm aware that I'm talking but even I don't know what I'm saying. I'm mumbling, rambling, random words and names, apologies and excuses. It's just noise. Noise and fear. I clasp my hands tight behind my head and push my elbows together hard; silent screaming as loud as I can. I didn't plan to do this, be this. Fuck. *Fuckety fuck. Fuck.*

My eyes are screwed shut but I can still see Jackie Stevenson lying sleeping, not sleeping, on his hospital bed. I pull my elbows closer, squeeze my head and my eyes harder, but he's still dead, still and still and still.

I feel a weight step onto my thighs then work its way up my chest. George has come to see what's wrong with me. If only I knew, I'd tell him. He pushes his way past my hands and headbutts me. Then does it again in case I somehow missed it.

For such small creatures, cats have extremely hard skulls. Or at least they are when they smash into your nose or chin. I let him butt me till it hurts.

'Hey kit cat. It's okay. I'm okay. Mum's okay.' My words burble out in tears and snot.

He doesn't believe me, nuzzling his head harder into mine. Showing love can be complicated for George. He's a west of Scotland male so even his caring side is aggressive. And he's a very bad judge of character; he loves me.

I ease my head back so I can see him properly, my damp hair unlicking from my face. I wipe at my eyes and cheeks, straightening myself up so he doesn't worry so much, and reach for the spot behind his ears that he likes best. His head tilts up in contentment and he lets me transfer the emotional spotlight onto him. I rub a finger firmly until he gets bored, his jaws snapping at me just slow enough that I can evade the bite. He jumps off and calmly walks away, job done.

I sit for a few minutes longer, my head still mush and my eyes focusing on nothing more than my lap before I struggle to my feet, absentmindedly take off my coat and hang it on the nearest peg.

The next thing I'm aware of is being in the kitchen with an open tin of cat food in my hand, just no memory of the steps in between. I spoon it onto George's plate, him talking loudly and urging me to hurry up.

Weaving my way into the living room, I fall into my chair, but I'm back on my feet again almost immediately. I walk across the room in a daze until I'm standing before the shelf of ornaments and knick-knacks. I stare at it stupidly for an age, my mouth goldfish-like, before I pick up the little statue of an old man with a fishing pole in his hands.

It's a silly little thing. The man is dressed in a brown suit and has a hat on his head. No way to be dressed to go fishing. It has a charm about it though. The man's moustache and his plump cheeks make him likeable. He's someone who doesn't take life too seriously. I dust his head with my finger, wiping a month of world from his face. I like to think Helen McCrorie would appreciate me looking after the old boy.

Her name in my head makes me remember what I got up to do and I return to the hall and reach into the jacket I'd hung on the wall, bringing out Jackie Stevenson's spectacles. I know I'm looking at them as if I've never seen them before, as if someone else took them from his bedside cabinet and put them in my pocket. In some ways, I think someone else did.

As I walk back to the living room, back to the shelf on the wall, I see a single grey hair caught in the joint behind the left lens. A solitary strand of Jackie Stevenson's DNA.

I nudge a couple of the objects aside, edging Edward Connarty's little carriage clock a few inches to the right and Graeme Holmes's glass paperweight to the left, and place the spectacles in the space I've created. A pair of glasses are maybe a bit incongruous, but I didn't have the range of choice I normally would, and it had to be that or the book.

They look okay there though. Something personal. Something uniquely his.

Each of the things has its own story. You could call them reminders or mementoes, souvenirs even, although I don't like that so much. Not trophies though, that's a step too far and not what they are at all. They're all rescued strays, like me and George.

Eddie Connarty used to work in an asbestos factory. That's not what they called it but that's what it was. When he started, there were no masks, no health and safety, no chance of avoiding breathing in at least some of the fibres that swirled around him on the shop floor. Forty years of that, even one solitary particle a week, will sooner or later sign your death certificate.

They gave him a clock for his forty years. A little carriage clock worth fifty quid, and malignant mesothelioma.

Eddie was a good guy, not one for complaining about things, even though he had more right to than most. He used to tell me how he was lucky, that he had outlived a lot of his mates. He'd tell me about this guy who'd died at forty, or another who left a wife and three kids before he was fifty. Eddie was sixty-five and he reckoned that equated to a good innings.

He'd been divorced when he was in his late thirties and never got hitched again. He explained it as having made a mess of one marriage and he wasn't going to put anyone else through the same thing. He enjoyed his own company and reckoned he just wasn't cut out for compromising. And that was fine until he got ill.

He'd had a cough for years but put that down to smoking. His breathing hadn't been great either, but he thought he was maybe just overweight. Then about a year before I met him, the cough became constant, his breathing got shorter and shorter, his chest burned, and he got stabbing pains in his abdomen. He couldn't sleep, couldn't walk the length of himself, and he was constantly bloated.

By the time I knew him, he suffered from night sweats, had fluid on the lungs, and couldn't get out of a chair without help. He couldn't breathe on his own. He wheezed every second he was awake and a fair few of those when he was sleeping. He once told me that every breath was like coughing broken glass. There was so little oxygen getting to his fingertips that they were black.

Eddie faced another nine months of that. No more, possibly less, but less would have been a blessing. No cure, no respite, no chance.

He said that the things he missed weren't important, but he missed them anyway. He couldn't walk to the bookies and put a fiver on the two horses he'd pick out each day. He couldn't blether to his mates when he was there. He couldn't argue about football or politics when he couldn't bump into anyone. He couldn't go for a pint, couldn't go for a walk or cut his grass. None of it mattered much, but it was all he had. Instead, he had to sit and wheeze at the TV, coughing on bits of glass.

Eddie had a brother that lived in Aberdeen. A nephew that lived there too, and one in New Zealand. They all sent Christmas cards and the occasional Facebook message. The real people in his life had been in the pub and the bookies and the bowling club. He couldn't see any of them any more.

So, I quadrupled his morphine dose.

I didn't ask him if I wanted me to do it because he'd have said no to keep me from getting into trouble. That's the way Eddie was. I think he knew though, when I handed him the plastic beaker. It should have been 20mg in 1ml of liquid, but I gave him 80mg in 2ml. He looked at it, then at me, then swallowed the lot.

It might have taken one minute, maybe two, but he was soon telling me he was sleepy and needed to nap. I helped him into his comfy chair and slipped his shoes off and his slippers on. I watched.

You can't tell, not really. A person goes to sleep then goes deeper, then deeper again till there's no way back. You can't tell from watching when they go over the line. They can't tell inside either, and that's the blessing. It's a sleep with pain that goes to a sleep with no pain. Who wouldn't want that?

I tidied Eddie's flat, leaving it the way he'd like it. I did the dishes and put them away, took the empty glasses from the side of his bed, emptied his bin and took the black bag with me. I wanted to make sure whoever found him wouldn't think badly of him. He deserved better than that.

It was a week before they found him. That was longer than I'd expected, but he'd stopped hurting and that was more important than how long he sat in that chair. The nurse had been there in the morning on the day I helped him, and it was another week before she was due back. When she couldn't get an answer at the door, she tried phoning and eventually called the police. Poor old Eddie in his favourite chair. Nobody blamed him for taking the overdose.

I don't know if it all played out exactly that way, but I imagine it was pretty close to it. It was a week, that was sure, and it was the nurse that found him. Better that way. A professional.

Helen McCrorie suffered from the same curse that afflicted many Scottish women, although to some it was also a blessing. It was a play on an old joke about husbands. Can't live with them, always outlive them. Her husband, John, had been dead for thirty-six years, yet she was still going strong.

And that was the problem. Sure, he'd been a lazy so and so around the house, was too fond of a drink and could be a crabbit sod when things didn't go his way, but he was her lazy so and so, her crabbit sod. And she missed him every day that she breathed.

That was far from the end of Helen's misfortunes. She and Jock had a son and a daughter. Charlie died in a car crash when he was in his twenties and Susan passed from cancer at fifty-four. Helen outlived them all and hated herself for it every day. It's maybe hard to understand someone feeling guilty for nothing more than not dying, but that's how Helen was, and it crippled her.

She was eighty-four, no heart problems, still walked without a stick, and only needed glasses for reading. Her blood pressure was normal, her cholesterol as it should be, her waterworks were as reliable as ever, and her joints were all her own. Her doctor thought she could live to be a hundred. And, worst of all, her mind and her memory were both as sharp as a tack.

She remembered meeting Jock at a dance in the church hall. She'd never forget Susan's first smile. Or the look on Charlie's face when he got picked for the school football team. She could picture, clear as day, Susan in her wedding dress, happiest bride in the world, standing next to the biggest waste of space you could imagine. She remembered Jock squeezing her hand as he lay dying in the hospital. She recalled every moment, whether happy or sad, funny or infuriating, and whether she liked it or not. Another reason for her continual, clawing guilt was that she knew people with Alzheimer's and, just sometimes, she envied them.

Helen McCrorie was alone, unhappy, and not ready to live till she was a hundred.

She had friends and neighbours that she'd spend time with, she'd go shopping or walk in the park, but every day she'd come home to a house full of memories. It was just her and the television and a lifetime of things she couldn't forget.

You can't imagine how longs days are when you don't want them to be. They drag. They spool out endlessly, yawning with nothing to do except be swallowed up in the thoughts that torture you.

I made sure Helen didn't have to endure any more of that. I made sure she didn't suffer the pain of seeing her hundredth birthday. I made sure she was able to stop remembering. I made sure she was at peace.

Graeme Holmes was a thirty-two-year-old orphan. Both his parents had died in a car crash the year before, spinning off a wet stretch of midnight motorway and careering down an embankment. Graeme was supposed to have driven them that night, but had ducked out to be with friends instead, forcing his dad to take the car. He'd only had one glass of wine according to reports, two at the most, but he'd never have been behind the wheel if Graeme had done what he'd agreed to.

People told him it wasn't his fault, but he knew different.

Within a month, he'd split with his girlfriend. When you hate yourself enough, you start to hate those who seem to be too stupid not to hate you too. He sold his flat and moved into his parents' house, making it all worse by drowning himself in memories, surrounding himself with constant reminders of what he'd done.

He began working from home, then he started not to leave it. He refused invitations to meet friends, slowly cut all ties to his old social life; he ordered food online, alcohol too, and the little communication he had with the world was through a fibre-optic cable. He was a thoroughly modern hermit living with the person he detested most in the world: himself.

It was just him and his parents' house. Just him and the growing realisation that if he died there, nobody would know. He didn't die, but hope did. Depression came to the funeral and never left.

It wasn't long before he made the transition from realising no one would notice his death to wishing for death to come. He didn't have the guts to do it, so he went online, looking for answers, looking for people who felt like he did, looking for a way to get what he wanted.

He found the same Facebook group that Eddie and Helen had. A group called A Lonely Place. The name is oddly ironic because it's got over a thousand members and is constantly busy, a small corner of the internet thronged with people who are very much on their own. There's all sorts in there. The newly lonely, maybe divorced or widowed and thinking they understand what loneliness is all about, or the long-term, the long-suffering, who do actually know.

Graeme found the group and, like Eddie and Helen, he found me. We talked, he opened up, he told me he'd come to the end of the road, that there was nothing else to live for. I did try to persuade him differently, to give it another chance or to move house and make a fresh start somewhere else. It was too late for that though, the loneliness was in his bones, the depression was in his heart.

Graeme bothered me for a long time. He'd only been thirty-two and it was possible he could have turned it around, that he'd have had time to grow and change, to develop the new friendships he needed to thrive, to gain the confidence to stick two fingers up to the world and survive.

But the longer he lay undiscovered, the more my doubts faded. It was two months later that I read about the young man's body being found in a flat in the east end, decomposed and almost unrecognisable. Two months proved me right.

If anyone had cared enough to have given him a chance in life, then they'd have noticed his death long before they did. The quotes of shock in the newspaper from his relatives, the Facebook messages of sympathy from his old friends, the fake moralising from his anonymous neighbours, they all proved I was right.

The only person that had cared enough was me. And I'd cared enough to kill him.

Chapter 28

I killed Eddie Connarty, Helen McCrorie, and Graeme Holmes. I killed them all, I saved them all, but they weren't the first. Margaret Gilmour was the first.

Nothing was planned or intended, not to begin with. In fact I'm sure that if, before any of this happened, you'd told me that someone had done what I had, then I'd have been horrified. I'd have been all morally indignant and told anyone who'd listen that it was wrong. Life is sacred, right? No matter how bad things are, decisions to end a life must be made by a doctor or by your god if you have one. I'd have called it murder.

But, like most people, I didn't understand. I hadn't walked a mile in their shoes, I hadn't lived under their skin. I didn't get it.

Margaret Gilmour changed that.

She taught me that life is only sacred if life is worth living. Like everyone else, I'd heard the phrase 'quality of life' and thought I knew what it meant. I didn't. I knew what quality of life was to me, but I'd zero understanding of what it could be like for other people.

Margaret used to say she was unlucky. That she fell out of the unlucky tree and hit every branch on the way down. Branch after branch after branch.

She married an abuser. A man who started out fine, a bit rough around the edges and with a bit of a temper, but nothing that he couldn't grow out of. Except he didn't, he grew worse. Where he'd snapped, he shouted. Where he'd shouted, he roared. Where he'd been picky, he criticised. Where he'd criticised, he'd tear her to the ground. Where he'd occasionally lash out, he punched.

She got in too deep. Loved him when he was salvageable and then couldn't do the rescue job. Like it was her fault. Some people can't be saved, shouldn't be saved. Her abuser was one of those. A weapons-grade arsehole.

The first time he hit her, properly hit her, she was shocked. He was too, or so it seemed. So apologetic, would never do it again, just a reaction. She forgave him, blamed herself, knew it wouldn't be repeated. Until it was. He convinced her that was her fault too. She provoked him, was deliberately doing the things that annoyed him, not his fault, he didn't want to react like that, but she made him.

The first time she landed in hospital, that's when she should have known. Instead she lied. She lied to the doctor, to the nurse, and to herself. She told them she fell. That she'd been unlucky. She told herself it wouldn't happen again.

This was all before he started drinking seriously. That's when her luck took a turn for the worse.

The first time the police were involved. The first time she was kept in hospital overnight. Her first breakdown. Just a little one. The first sign that her body would pay the price for what her mind couldn't handle. The first indication that her mind would suffer for what her body endured.

It took her another eight years before she left him. People probably wonder what's wrong with someone who puts up with that kind of shit for so long. I know I wondered. But then I didn't have to live with the fear or the guilt or the shame. I simply couldn't understand because I hadn't been there.

She found enough courage one day to walk to Women's Aid. They took her in, found her a place, and kept the bad wolf from the door. She was safe, at last. He wouldn't be able to hurt her any more, but she still had to live with the damage done.

She thought she was unlucky when she developed fibromyalgia, but doctors told her that people who suffered abuse trauma were three times as likely to get it. They said it was something to do with the way the central nervous system processes the pain messages that are carried around the body. The triggers are physical abuse and psychological stress.

The same went for her irritable bowel syndrome and chronic fatigue. And for the stroke she had when she was just forty-four. All of that contributed to her depression.

She'd lived with it for two years before I found her. A withered soul and crushed spirit, a broken body living in fear. And she lived with it alone. She'd had her fill of people, and she preferred the agonies of loneliness to the possibility of it all happening again.

I learned a lot from her. All my preconceived, church-bought ideas about life went out of the window and were replaced by a sober reality. Better no life than a shit life. Better that than a life wracked with constant pain.

Doctors say 'chronic' means lasting a long time, and they're right, but it's more than that. It goes deeper. Chronic pain goes into your bones, into how you live your life, how you think, how you feel. It changes how you face getting out of bed in the morning and how you crawl back into bed at night. Sometimes it makes you crawl in there in the afternoon because sleep, if you can find it, is the only escape.

Chronic pain means you only ever see the world through a fog. Painkillers make sure your mind is always dampened, your senses dulled, that *you* are never quite there. And even paying that price, it still hurts. Always. She told me that it was like having the worst toothache you'd ever experienced but times ten or twenty, and have it happening twenty-four hours a day for a year. And then for another year.

I'd sit with her, maybe help her do a crossword or watch television. I'd bring her flowers, daisies were her favourite, or cook her a meal. I'd read to her and she'd listen, never saying much. I visited as often as I could, given I had to work and that I lived on the other side of the city, but it would never have been enough anyway. The problem with visitors is that they go home.

She started asking me to help her. I said no. Then she began to beg. She'd be in tears, saying she couldn't bear the pain, that she'd no reason to live and no desire to.

Every moment of every day was a trial that she didn't want to go through any more.

It took maybe four months before I agreed. Or before I found the courage – I couldn't honestly say which it was. Maybe it was just an act of weakness on my part as I couldn't stand to see her suffer for any longer. Either way, better or worse, I said yes, and together we made a plan.

When the day came, I helped her have a bath, then dressed her in her favourite nightdress. I brushed her hair and read the last of the book she'd chosen. We sat together, me by the side of the bed and her lying on top of it, as the golden light of a summer's evening filtered through the window, casting the room in a warm, comforting glow.

I doubled the dose of the duloxetine she was prescribed for the fibromyalgia, and she took it. It wasn't enough to kill her, but it would ensure she went into a deep sleep, deep enough that she wouldn't be aware of what happened next.

I talked to her as she drifted off, holding her hand, making sure she knew someone was with her. I let her sink deeper, sounder, in case something instinctive in her made her struggle. That wouldn't have been helpful to either of us.

When I was sure she was in a place that she wouldn't know, wouldn't feel, wouldn't fight, I placed the pillow over her face. Without resistance, I couldn't be sure when it would be done, so I held it there for ten minutes, with just enough pressure to be certain that she'd be deprived of oxygen.

I took a tissue and wiped the inside of her nostrils, dried my tears, kissed her cheek, placed a daisy – her favourite flower – on her pillow, said my goodbyes, and closed the door behind me.

It felt shameful to leave her for someone else to find, but that was what we'd agreed, and we'd timed it to leave the maximum possible gap before anyone else was due to visit. Decomposition was to be our cover, *my cover*, because her main concern was that no blame attached to me and, like a coward, I agreed.

They say you never forget your first, but there was never any chance that I'd forget mine.

Margaret Gilmour was my mother.

Chapter 29

It's late. My nerves are still jangling, trying to come to terms with my day, with what I've done and who I am. None of that is easy to deal with and all of it is my own fault. My head is full of Jackie Stevenson and the others, and all I want to do is go to bed and sleep, but there's fat chance of that.

I take my phone from my bag and see six texts and a voicemail. Three of the texts are from my father, inevitably getting more irate and more abusive with each message. There's a text and a voicemail from Harry Blair about an undiscovered that needs to be cleaned. All that, and George. Gorgeous, noisy, needy, hungry George.

He is, as always, my number one. He gets a cuddle and some time in my arms before wriggling to get down and be fed. I open a tin and spoon some of this week's favourite into his dish. From behind me, I hear the phone ping and know that there's a new text before I've had the chance to answer any of the previous ones. My dad, demanding and drunk.

It's too much. My head is spinning, and I've got to prioritise, or I'll get nothing done. George I've dealt with. Then it needs to be a cup of tea for me. Harry's message said to call whatever the time was, so I'll do that while the kettle is boiling. The other one, the paternal demand for food and company, stops short of life and death and it can wait till tomorrow.

I stand by the kettle, my hand on the lid, my eyes closed, and buy myself a moment of peace. I like the darkness behind my eyes and float in it for as long as I can until my jangling nerves settle enough to make the call.

'Hi Grace, I've got one for you.'

I've never been sure how to take this news. Pleased that I've got work, depressed that someone has been so alone that they've lain dead and undiscovered, relieved that I'm the one handling it and at least their home and their things will be treated with respect. I settle for sounding neutral.

'Okay, Harry. Give me the details.'

'It's an elderly lady. Catherine O'Halloran. We think she was in her nineties. Neighbours say she'd lived in the same flat for longer than anyone can remember. At least since the 1970s it seems, so forty years plus.'

'And how long since she died?'

He hesitates, and it makes my skin tingle. I know Harry, and the pause means it's a bad one.

'Maybe six months. The decomp is so bad they can't tell, but that seems to be the last time anyone saw her. She was at a church fundraiser and then never seen till the police knocked the door in.'

'And no one thought to go look for her?'

'Doesn't look like it. Do you want to take it, Grace? You can say no. Word from the scene is it's rancid.'

'I'll do it. Someone has to, and it may as well be me. I'll be there first thing in the morning.'

I wake early, the clock showing just a few minutes after seven, and I think I've barely slept. I feed George, pour myself a coffee, make some toast and manage to eat half of it. It's still too early to go to the job, so I work on the diorama until it's time to go.

Tommy Agnew had a mirror on his bedroom wall. A frameless, bevelled-edge mirror, sort of vintage, that hung on a chain. It's taken me ages to find something close enough to satisfy my obsessive-compulsive needs, but I eventually sourced a company that cuts mirrored glass to custom-made specifications. Their email made it clear they'd never had a request for a piece this small before. Appropriately, it cost a small fortune too, but if something's worth doing, it's worth doing right.

I've pasted a wooden back to it, the same as on the Agnews' mirror, and I've bought a tiny chain link that I'm about to fix to the wood. It's fiddly, and my fingers seem too big for the job. My shredded nerves aren't helping either. I think I've almost got it, finally, when my landline rings and makes me jump, the links slipping from my grasp.

I start towards the phone, instinctively about to do what you're supposed to do, but I stop myself. It won't be Harry, the job's already arranged and he's much more likely to call my mobile. My father's as likely to call the mobile as the landline but either way, I don't want to know.

The answer phone kicks in and I hear the voice over the speaker. The nasal tone is familiar, and I think my subconscious must recognise it before I do because it triggers a nervousness – my heart racing faster. It's not till he says his name that I know for sure where I've heard it before.

'Ms McGill, it's DC Murray Phelan from Stewart Street police station. I'm following up on your visit to us and would like to speak to you as soon as it's convenient. There's been a ... a development regarding the information you gave us, and we'd like to discuss it with you.

'If you could call the station as soon as it's convenient and ask for myself or my colleague DS Carsewell.'

He leaves a number. I'm not going to call it.

They've found Stevenson. They must have found the daisy. They couldn't have overlooked it again. Not now that they know there's a link to what I told them.

I need to go to work.

Ms O'Halloran lived in a tenement flat in the West End, one of the upmarket ones up the hill from Byres Road. Another house to clean, another life to put in order, and a welcome distraction from my memories and my conscience.

This is a beautiful part of the city, but parking is a nightmare. Narrow, winding, climbing streets of white sandstone gentility, perfect for a horse and carriage but not much use when there are more cars than homes. I manage to bag a spot on Saltoun Street and humph my cleaning cases up the steep hill to the flat on Athole Gardens. The street is lucky enough to overlook and have access to one of the few green spots in the West End, where gardens are rarer than parking spaces. I'm halfway up the hill, the backs of my legs beginning to tighten and ache, the cases getting heavier in my hands. I stop, rest the equipment on the pavement, and take a breather, looking back down the hill.

It takes me a moment to recognise the figure walking up, perhaps a hundred yards behind me. I realise who it is just as he sees me looking, walks into the next building and is gone. It was him though, I'm sure of it. The man from St Simon's church, the man from Bute, the tall, close-cropped stalker and saviour.

I'm scared. Scared of him, and suddenly scared that he also followed me to the Royal last night. That he'll be able to join the dots and connect my visit there to Jackie Stevenson's death. I turn, hurry up the hill and quickly unlock the entrance to the old woman's building, hoping he won't have been able to see which one I've gone into. Inside, I stand and breathe, my head swirling.

The woman's flat stinks. I haven't been this bothered by the smell in a property in a long time, maybe since my first clean. As soon as I'm inside the door, it hits me and sickens me, the stench rolling over me in waves. I thought I'd become hardened to the smell of death, but it seems I was wrong.

Her home is a time capsule. A floral, faded, over-stuffed cushion of a house. Full of fire-hazard furniture, heavy curtains, paintings and more paintings, cabinetry and china. The ornate rug under my feet has a deep pile, thick with fibres hiding blood, body fluids and potentially lethal pathogens.

I don't have the energy or the inclination to do anything other than clean. No prayer, no collecting mementoes, no ordering of a chaotic life. I will make the flat safe and habitable, I will remove and soak, disinfect and dispose, I will decontaminate, I will wash my hands, and I will try not to think.

It's done in little over a handful of hours, a sloppy, half-arsed job that I'm not proud of, but it's done. I take one final look out from the living room onto the vast square of well-tended fenced gardens below, the poor, forgotten spinster's window on the world, and I remember to feel a pang of sympathy for her months of undiscovered neglect. I pack my equipment away and leave.

I open the front doors of the building, and he's there. Waiting, blocking my exit, and staring right at me. I back up instinctively, but the door has closed behind me and I've nowhere to go.

'I don't mean you any harm. I just want to talk to you. Okay?'

He's got an English accent. I didn't expect that. I think it's from around Manchester somewhere, definitely northern. And he's not the person who's been phoning me. That's both a relief and a worry.

I think, *No, it's not okay. Not okay at all.*

I say, 'Who are you? Why are you following me?'

'I'll explain if you let me. Can we go somewhere to talk?'

My brain's scrambled, my heart rising to my throat, and I don't know what to say or do. I can't get past him, can't run away from him, and I can't call the police. I've got the keys for the house and they include keys for the garden opposite. At least it's open and overlooked, so relatively safe.

'We can go in there,' I tell him. 'I've got an alarm in my bag. If you try anything, I'll set it off. Understand?'

'I do. And I won't. I just want to talk to you.'

We go into the gardens and choose a bench. I sit as far to one end of it as the armrest will allow. Close up, I can see he's in his mid-fifties, fit and lean, skin lightly tanned, with startling light blue eyes.

I think, *Who are you? What do you know? Did you follow me last night?*

I say, 'Why have you been following me?'

It sounds braver than I feel. It's also more direct and more stupid than I'd intended. And I've no real idea of what my next move is, whatever he says, so I ask another question before he can answer.

'Give me one good reason why I shouldn't just go to the police.'

He looks away, blankly gazing at the trees, before giving a short, unhappy laugh and turning back to face me.

'You won't go to the police. You didn't tell them about what happened to you in Rothesay. And I think you don't want them to know what you've been doing.'

I think, *Shit. Shit. Shit.*

I say, 'And what have I been doing?'

He stares at me like a poker player trying to work out if I've got aces or twos. 'I don't know. Not for sure. But I know you're doing something you'd rather people didn't know about.'

I just nod. I don't even know what that nod means. Sort of yes but I'm not telling you any more than that. I want to ask what he thinks he knows, but I don't dare.

'My name is Phil Canning.' He's looking at me keenly as he says it, as if his name might mean something to me. It doesn't. 'And I really don't mean you any harm. That's not why I've been tracking you. Are you okay? That guy gave you a bad kicking the other night.' There's concern in his voice and I'm confused. I'm sure it's some kind of trick.

'I'm okay. Bit bruised but okay. Thank you. For stepping in, I mean.'

'It's okay. I couldn't stand back and let it happen. I followed you back to your hotel to make sure you were okay. Do you know who the guy is who attacked you?'

243

'No. I don't.' I move on before he can question my lie. 'Where are you from and why are you here?'

He considers the question long enough that I'm not sure I'm going to believe his answer.

'I'm from a village called Warton, near Preston in Lancashire. I'm retired so I've got time on my hands. I'm up here to do some family history research.'

None of that quite rings true. 'You look very young to be retired. And … you say you're doing family research but you're following *me*? We're not related. Are we?'

He looks away again, his fingers rapping on the arm of the bench. 'I wondered if maybe we were, for a while. But, from what I know of you, no we're not. I've been following you because I want to know more about Thomas Agnew. You went to his funeral when only three people did, you held a wake for him, you went to the house of one of his oldest friends after the old friend died.'

He knows too much. And he's looking inside me like he's reading every line and every page. I need to get away. And yet … I want to know more.

'Why didn't you speak to me at Tommy's funeral? And why the hell did you follow me and not the others?'

He sighs and forces half a smile. 'I wanted answers, but I didn't know who I could trust to tell me the truth. I needed to know more before I risked talking to anyone. But you … you seemed agitated. Anxious. I got the feeling you had something to hide.'

I think, *Oh man. I hope you don't know just how much I've got to hide.*

I say, 'So why are you so interested in Tommy Agnew?'

He pauses, thinking, deliberating, deciding.

'Because he's my father.'

Chapter 30

I know that my mouth has bobbed open and I close it firmly, quickly, but the damage has been done. It's told Phil Canning what he wanted to know.

My mind is full of the photographs that lined Tommy Agnew's dresser. Photos of him and Elizabeth, ageing together, no children, not even one. Every photograph hiding the truth. Tommy Agnew the liar.

'Five years ago, my father, Jim Canning, developed chronic kidney disease. Dialysis wasn't treating it and the only solution was a transplant. I offered to donate one, of course, but he wouldn't hear of it. He said he was too old for it to be worth damaging the rest of my life, and I couldn't talk him into it. My mother agreed with him, she was adamant about it, and so I relented, and we waited for a donor.

'Six months went by, my dad getting steadily worse, and there was no sign of a matching donor. I couldn't take it any more and insisted I was donating a kidney and they'd just have to accept it. My mother took me aside, clearly distressed, and said she needed to talk to me alone. She was shaking like a leaf, tears streaming down her face, and explained to me that I couldn't donate a kidney because Jim wasn't my biological father.

'Their pact was always that I'd never find out, no matter what. She said it would break his heart if he found out that I knew. She wouldn't answer any of my questions, said it wasn't the important thing, it was all about my dad.'

He's struggling to tell me this, and I believe him. It's too raw and too painful not to be true.

'It was still all about my dad when he died three months later, no suitable donor found. I did what my mother wanted, but I did it for him. It was only after he passed that I really began questioning who I was and where I'd come from. It was like I'd been doubly orphaned.'

I think, *I know exactly what you mean.*

I say, 'How did you find out about Tommy? Your mother told you?'

'No. She never would have. I ordered one of those genealogy DNA kits, the kind that tell you where in the world your ancestors come from. It told me I was seventy-nine per cent Scottish, meaning my dad was a Scot as well as my mum.'

He's taking a breath before he goes on and I sense we're getting to it.

'The other thing these genealogy tests do is tell you who you're related to. There's a database of other people who've had tests done, and if you have partial matches then it shows up. I found matches to people in Glasgow, Stirling, Aberdeen, with what they call a small percentage of relatedness, so maybe second cousins, or cousins once or twice removed. But there was a match to a Catherine

Durham in Melbourne, Australia that was high – high enough to be first cousins. I contacted her, she knew her family tree, had no uncles or aunts on her father's side and just one uncle on her mother's …'

My mind had already joined the dots. The great-nephew with no interest in his relative's belongings, his parents who'd emigrated to Australia. Kevin Durham, son of Catherine.

'… and that was Thomas Agnew. She had photographs of him, and …'

It's been whispering at me for the past five minutes, but now, with thoughts of photographs of Agnew and his wife in their fifties big in my mind, there's no question. I can see the truth with my own eyes.

'You look like him.'

'Yes. I've seen a photograph of him, and I see the likeness every time I look in the mirror. I probably can't prove it, but I've no doubt about it.'

I think, *I can probably prove it. I have enough of Tommy Agnew's things that there must be DNA there.*

I say, 'Did you ask your mother about Tommy?'

'Yes. I didn't say I'd done the research, didn't tell her why I was asking. I just sat her down and asked her who Thomas Agnew was. I saw the truth in her face. Any doubt I had vanished. She was horrified to hear his name, appalled that I knew. She fell to pieces in front of me, then ran off to her room and flat refused to talk to me about it. It was as if something terrible had been dug up.'

I think, *Yes, that's exactly what it's like.*

I say, 'So she never admitted it?'

'She begged me to promise I'd leave it alone, for her sake. And I did. Even when she died, I kept my promise.'

'When did she die?'

'Three years ago. Of breast cancer. I've felt very alone since then. I'm divorced, two grown-up kids who're off doing their own thing. So, it's just been me and my thoughts, and a man in Glasgow that I didn't know. It was Catherine Durham who told me Tommy had died. Her son Kevin was contacted by the police, and then someone brought Agnew's belongings to his door. I think the worst thing is he wasn't found right away. He lay in his flat for five months before his death was discovered.'

'That's terrible. Really awful.' I mean it.

'It really got to me. Not just that he was there for so long like that, but that there was no one to notice he'd gone. I didn't know him, but it broke my heart to think he'd nobody in his life, no one to care enough to miss him. What kind of society lets that happen?'

I think, *He understands*.

I say, 'We're supposed to look after older people, not leave them to fend for themselves. And not just older people, we're all meant to look after each other, but most people are too busy in their own lives to notice others are struggling.'

He's looking at me curiously and I wonder if I've been weird. I probably have.

'What …' I'm wary of asking the question and scared of the answer. 'What was your mother's name?'

'She was Mary Chadwick.'

He's still talking but I feel a strange sense of disappointment that the name Valerie Moodie didn't come out of his mouth. I don't know if I expected it to be, but I certainly wondered.

'She'd lived in England since she was young. I was born in Preston in 1965 but I guess I'd never thought how long she'd lived there before I was born. It was only when I had to sort things after her death that I found her birth certificate and discovered her full name wasn't Mary but Marion.'

Something tumbles deep into the pit of my stomach and rises again. I swallow it and don't say anything.

'Her birth name was Marion Millar.'

I'm silent but I'm aware of how closely he's watching me, looking for a reaction. I feel trapped.

'I did more research once I knew that, but it didn't take me too far. I tried looking for connections between Marion Millar and Thomas Agnew but got nothing. The nearest I got were old news reports of a Marion Millar whose friend went missing in the 1960s. I didn't know whether there was anything in that, seemed a bit of a stretch to think it was my mum. And it stayed like that until I saw you boarding the train for Wemyss Bay.'

Shit.

'I didn't know where Wemyss Bay was, had never heard of it, and didn't know if you were planning to get off at a stop before there. But your demeanour told me it was important. You were anxious, disturbed even. I grabbed one of the station staff and asked him where the train was going. He told me it was the ferry terminal for Bute and the stuff I'd read about Valerie Moodie and Rothesay came flooding back. I knew that's where my answer was and, more than that, I'd no doubt you knew it.'

I still say nothing but I'm shaking. He's reeled me in and caught me. There's a harder edge to his voice.

'Grace, I gave you a chance to tell me what was happening, and you didn't tell me the truth. Are you ready to tell me now?'

I think, *Am I? Do I even know what the truth is?*

I sigh. I say, 'Yes. I am.'

Chapter 31

I tell him the truth. Some of it.

About the photograph. The five young men on holiday. About Bob and Jackie's lies. About Valerie and Bute. About his mother and Dorothy and how Dorothy refuses to talk to me.

I admit I know the man who attacked me, that his name is Malky McTeer. The fisherman who said he saw a body then denied it. I tell him how I'm sure McTeer knows more than he's telling.

I tell him that Jackie Stevenson has died of a heart attack and watch his face for a reaction. I don't get one beyond surprise, and I'm both relieved and disappointed. I tell him there are two others. One large, fat and ruddy-faced, one skelf-thin and flinty-cheeked.

I admit I have no idea what happened to Valerie Moodie.

I don't tell him the whole truth, of course. I don't tell him I killed his father.

I don't tell him who I am.

Chapter 32

I drive back to the Merchant City, leave the cases in the boot of the car and make the short walk home to my apartment block on Brunswick Street. My shoulders are heavy with worry, and I'm mentally exhausted after opening up to Phil Canning. Talking like that isn't something I'm used to, and I'm drained by the effort of it.

As I punch my number into the entry system, I hear footsteps approaching, heavy and purposeful, and – paranoid or not – I know they're coming directly towards me. When my name is called out, I nearly drop dead on the spot.

'Grace McGill?'

The voice is familiar, but I can't place it, other than a distinct sense of associating it with something bad. I desperately try to enter the numbers to get inside the building but mess them up, pushing at the door and nothing happening. The footsteps are closer, the voice louder, and adrenaline is flooding through my body.

'Ms McGill?'

I steady myself enough to get the entry code correct and yank the door handle open. Someone is right behind me and I can feel their breath on my neck.

'Ms McGill. It's DC Phelan from Stewart Street. I've been trying to call you.'

I freeze, not sure if this is good news or bad but flooded with relief that I'm not in physical danger. I fix my face before I turn, aiming for a show of surprise rather than fear. Sure enough, it's the fair-haired cop Phelan staring at me. A stride behind him is the detective sergeant, Carsewell, all stern-faced, dark bushy eyebrows and hair shrinking back from the middle of his forehead.

I think, *I must have guilt written all over me.*

I say, 'You made me jump.'

'Sorry.' Phelan doesn't sound sorry at all. 'We need to talk to you and as you didn't return my call, we'd no option but to come to you.'

Carsewell is studying me over Phelan's shoulder, saying nothing but watching for a reaction. Phelan still hasn't said why they need to talk to me and I'm guessing he's being vague in the hope I'll tell him something he doesn't know.

I say, 'Right. Sorry. I've been busy.'

'Cleaning houses?' Phelan asks, his expression not changing.

I think, *What do you mean by that? What do you know?*

I say, 'Yes. You said in your message there'd been a development?'

His eyes burrow into me and he holds the look for a beat too long before replying. 'Yes. It's concerning John Stevenson, known as Jackie, the man you mentioned when you were at the station. He's died. Did you know that?'

I think, *Yes. Yes, I knew it.*

I say, 'No, but I knew he'd been very ill. What happened?'

DS Carswell coughs and I know he's not just clearing his throat. Phelan gets the message.

'It's probably not a good idea to continue this conversation on the street, Ms McGill. May we come in? It will be more private in your flat.'

I think, *Do you have a warrant? Of course you don't. I really don't want you in my home but if I say no it will look suspicious. I can't afford to look suspicious.*

I say, 'Sure. Come on up.'

I lead them upstairs, nerves jangling, my head working overtime, trying to think if there's anything I need to move or hide. *My shelf.* My shelf of rescued things. It's going to be right there in front of them and there's nothing I can do about it.

At my front door, I quickly say a silent prayer, one of the good Buddhist ones, and let them inside. I am as polite as I need to be, offering them tea or coffee that they don't want and showing them to chairs in my living room.

Phelan is still doing all the work, like he's on his driving test and Carswell is the silent, stony-faced examiner. Phelan's making sure I keep my eyes on the road, my attention on him, while Carswell studies me and the room. It feels like he's sitting on my shoulder, staring at me and daring me to look.

I'm walking a tightrope. One slip and I'm dead.

Phelan tells me how Jackie Stevenson was found dead in his hospital bed. I say that's terrible. He again asks me for details of the daisies I saw at Agnew's and Meechan's. I see Carsewell's eyes roll, and he gets to his feet and wanders out of my eyeline. I instinctively turn to see where he's going, but DC Phelan drags me back to him with another question. I answer with as little as I can, no new information, nothing to trip me up.

I hear muttering from behind and to my right and realise Carsewell must be near to my shelf of stuff. I need to look.

He's standing in front of it, examining each item in turn. Phelan is talking to me but I'm only hearing sounds, not words. Carsewell is holding Helen Mc-Crorie's ornament, the old man with the fishing pole. I want to tell him to put it down, but I can't.

He works his way along the shelf, every step of scrutiny taking a year off my life, every curious stare tightening the ratchet on my heart. The glass paperweight from Graeme Holmes. Eddie Connarty's carriage clock. The cross that hung on Tommy Agnew's wall. My silly, vain collection of rescued memorabilia, my stolen relics.

Carsewell pauses before the blue glass candle holder. My mother's candle holder. A shout is forming in my throat. I can feel it coiled there, ready to uncurl and unleash. If he picks the candle holder up, I'm going to have to scream at him to put it down.

He passes it by. He stares at the hand-painted vase from Bob Meechan's mantlepiece but lets that go too. He's got his eye on something else, and now I'm scared that my heart is going to burst out of my chest it's beating so fast. He's picked up Jackie Stevenson's spectacles and is holding them close, studying them. He looks confused and glances back at me.

I remember the strand of Stevenson's hair trapped in the joint next to the left lens. A solitary strand of grey hair. He's wondering why it's grey when my hair is still the same shade of brown it's always been. He's confused and I sense he's teetering on the edge of a conclusion.

Me having Jackie Stevenson's glasses is probably what they call circumstantial evidence, but it would be a thread they'd pull until the whole thing unravels.

At last, after what seems an age, Carsewell wanders away from the shelf and I have to fight the urge to let loose a sigh of relief.

I realise I'd barely been listening to Phelan and have to tune back in to hear what he's saying to me.

'Please tell us again about Robert Meechan. How did you come to clean out his flat after his death?'

I begin to explain in as little detail as I can but manage only a few words before I'm interrupted.

'So, this …' from behind me, Carsewell speaks for the first time and it sounds like he's tasting something nasty. I turn to see him standing by the diorama, and my stomach churns, 'This is one of those models? The things that were in the paper?'

Things. I've never really thought of them as art or therapy or any of the highfalutin words that Harry Blair puts on them, but calling them *things* is annoying me. I know I should be worried about what Carsewell sees or thinks, but instead I'm furious at what he's said.

'Yes.'

'Why do you make them?'

He's hanging over it, his head closer to the model room than it should be, a fat finger hovering in the air over the miniature bed. If he touches it, I don't know what I'll do. Ten years probably.

I say, 'It relaxes me. It's my way of working through what I do. For a living.'

I think, *Did they hear that? The pause before 'For a living.' Why did I add it? I need to calm the fuck down.*

I say, 'I'm sure your job's even more stressful. You know what it's like. You need something to help you unwind.'

Carsewell's face creases unhappily. His expression is saying 'not like this'.

He continues to bend over it, his breath fogging the little mirror on Tommy Agnew's wall, his head shaking slowly side to side in wonder or disgust or both. Then he abruptly straightens up, brows knitted, and turns to face me.

'There's a daisy. On the pillow.'

I think, *And it's still too big.*

I say, 'Yes. Everything's as it was in his flat. The daisy was on his pillow.'

'And the same at Meechan's house?'

I think, *Get out of my room.*

I say, 'Yes. I told you. It was on the floor. By the chair where he fell.'

I think, *You would not listen. You did not know how.*

I say, 'I showed you it.'

Carsewell sighs unhappily. Here it comes. Here it comes.

'The thing is, Ms McGill, we have a situation here which, I don't mind admitting, I don't completely understand. And I need you to help me with that.'

He picks up a chair from next to the table, carries it over to where I'm sitting, and positions himself directly across from me. If I reach out, I could slap him.

'You say that you found a dried-out daisy in Mr Agnew's house,' he's speaking slowly, oh so deliberately. 'And you say you found a dried-out daisy at Mr Meechan's house. But where it's become confusing is that there was a daisy, freshly cut, lying on Mr Stevenson's pillow in the hospital.'

He pauses. Stares. Looks for a reaction. I don't know *how* to react. I open my mouth slightly and let my eyes widen. Is that how it should be? I say nothing.

I say nothing for long enough that Carsewell has no choice but to speak again.

'The hospital reports nothing suspicious about Mr Stevenson's death. He'd been admitted after a massive heart attack and the staff attending him had no reason to think anything else had happened other than him having another one. But ... then there's the daisy. A pretty weird coincidence, wouldn't you say?'

I think, *I tried to tell you. I did tell you. Before it got to this.*

I say, 'Yes.'

'Now ...' he laughs like he can't believe what he's going to say next, 'the Royal, like most hospitals, don't allow visitors to bring in flowers these days because of the infection risk. It's possible one of his family brought them in, but the staff say they're sure they'd have noticed right away and removed them. So, help me out here, Grace. What's going on?'

I hope my hands aren't shaking. I think they might be, but I daren't look because that will make them either start, or shake more. I'm desperately trying to contain everything, but it feels like I'm at the wheel of a runaway train.

'All I know is what I told you. I came to the station because I thought there was something you should know. That the deaths were connected. You thought I was crazy.'

Carsewell makes a face and tilts his head to one side. It's a look that says he still thinks I'm crazy but even a stopped clock is right twice a day. I want to tell him that stopped clocks are never right, but I don't think it would help me.

'What was the connection between Mr Agnew, Mr Meechan and Mr Stevenson? You said they were friends, possibly many years ago?'

I think, *I don't want to go there. I don't want you to go there. To Rothesay. The police had their chance to find out what happened to Valerie and they blew it.*

I say, 'I don't really know. Jackie Stevenson was at Tommy Agnew's funeral. He said they were old friends. I think they knew each other when they were in their teens.'

Carsewell's face crumples. This hasn't made him any happier. He rubs at his forehead and I wonder if that's what made his hair disappear there.

'Did Mr Meechan or Mr Stevenson talk about anyone else, a mutual friend, maybe? Anyone else that connected them?'

'Not that I know of.'

'So …' he pauses, and I know he's doing it for effect, 'it looks like the only person that links them is you.'

I think, *I don't know what to say.*

I say nothing.

And he laughs in my face.

I'm confused and scared, my mouth bobbing open of its own accord and words are lost to me. I think it's better to say nothing and appear guilty than to speak and confirm it.

'Ms McGill, why were daisies left by the side of three old people who've died, two of them after meeting you?'

All I can think to do is shrug my shoulders. 'I don't know.'

'Of course you don't.'

At first, I hear that as being sarcastic, but then I realise he means if he doesn't know then there's no chance of me knowing. Or does he?

'What?' I play along, taking no chances.

'I'm sorry, I shouldn't have joked.'

I don't think he was joking. I've no idea whether he was joking.

'I need you to tell me everything you know about Jackie Stevenson, Ms McGill. Okay?'

I say yes but I don't mean it. I tell him what I want. Just enough to keep me safe and him guessing. Just an old man with an old friend at another old friend's funeral.

'What about other clean-up scenes?' he asks. 'I know it might be a daft question, but have you ever seen a dried daisy on another job, in another old person's home?'

'No.'

As soon as the word is out of my mouth, I remember the photograph in the paper of my diorama of Mrs McCrorie's house. The tiny daisy on the edge of the little bath. I wonder if it could be made out from Doug Christie's photograph in the *Standard*. I wonder if I've been trapped. Or if I've trapped myself.

Detective Sergeant Carsewell holds my stare, taking note of my thoughts, and nods as if he's heard all he needs. With a look to his DC, he passes the baton back to Phelan for the closing words.

'We'll keep in touch, Ms McGill,' the younger cop tells me, looking as serious as he can. 'If you remember anything else, anything at all, please contact us.'

The two men turn to leave, interview done, for now at least.

I think, *They're almost out the door. Almost gone. All I need to do is say nothing for one more minute.*

I say, 'It's a crime.'

Carsewell turns and looks at me sharply, trying to make sense of it. 'What do you mean?'

'Old people not being cared for. Not being missed when they're dead. Don't you think?'

I can see him wondering, debating, wheels slowly turning. He's no choice but to agree.

'Yes. You're right. It's criminal.'

They say goodbye and they're gone.

Chapter 33

The visit from Carsewell and Phelan has left my nerves shattered. They're gone but I'm sure as hell they haven't forgotten. It doesn't mean the hospital hasn't flagged it up as a suspicious death. It doesn't mean nurses or doctors didn't mention seeing a woman behaving oddly, visiting Stevenson behind a drawn curtain just before his death. It doesn't mean there isn't someone somewhere going through hospital CCTV looking for a sighting of me.

Every time my phone rings, I jump. I think it's the police or Phil, or the police about Phil, or it's my father and all that brings. None of it is good. I've turned down two jobs for no good reason, I can't settle, and I can't stop seeing Stevenson's face. I've slept no more than a few hours in the three nights since it happened. Since I did it.

Jackie Stevenson wasn't like the others. There was a reason for the others, and it was for them, this time it was for me. And I'm scared I'll be caught.

I'm mad at myself too for getting nothing useful out of him. I keep thinking that if I'd given him more time, if I'd let him speak, let him live, then he could have told me what happened to Valerie. At the time I was sure he wouldn't, my gut instinct told me he wouldn't. But what if I was wrong?

I keep checking the papers, keep googling his name, together with the Royal. And I keep getting nothing. I could ask at the Fiscal's Office, but I'd be as well going in with my hands out asking them to arrest me.

Three days and I've barely left home. Just one brief visit to my father in the newly repaired car, dropping off food, making his dinner and my excuses, then leaving. He wasn't happy but that didn't worry me much.

It's just been George and me, holed up at home, looking out of the window at Glasgow down below. Window watching and online surfing. All the world we need to see on the other side of the glass.

Sometimes I'll hold him, and we'll look out together. Others he'll jump onto the window seat at my side, stretch his front paws up onto the ledge and stare, king of all he surveys. I'd love to know what he makes of it, if he's sure it's the same streets that he used to walk. I don't think he misses being out there.

I do, though. Sort of.

I have this big window onto the world, and it tortures me sometimes. I see the buildings and the rooftops; I see beyond them to the hills. I can see Glasgow. All of it. All of *them*. I'm surrounded by people yet can't reach out to any of them.

It's not so bad during the week, when the evening streets aren't as busy. Then there might just be couples walking hand in hand, small groups of friends. I still have society envy, but it's manageable. But at the weekend, when the streets throng and people go from pub to pub, restaurant to night club, good time to good time, I can't stand it. I stare out of the window and never feel more alone.

Being alone and surrounded by people is suffocating. It took me a long time to realise that it wasn't quite that I wanted to be with them, it was more that I wanted to be the kind of person who wanted to be with them.

At night, when they've been drinking, the noise increases, drifting up to my window on the breeze. Laughter. Singing. *Together noises*. I look down at them and imagine they're all happy. I convince myself they're having the time of their lives. I let myself believe that being out there with people, among them, is how it *should* be. Every happy person means an unhappy me, reminds me of my own failure. I watch them and a bit of me dies.

It's day four when I find the obituary notice online. The days of them being in newspapers are largely gone and now there are specialist websites set up where families can post obits with funeral details and people can leave messages of condolence. Inevitably, I know them all because of my job.

The one I find him on is probably the most popular site. I count twenty-five listings for this month alone, then page after page of months and people gone by.

John Fraser STEVENSON. March 1945 to October 2022. Funeral Glasgow.

There's a photograph of him, a close-up of his face. I click on the link that says View Obituary.

In loving memory of John, known to all as Jackie, who passed peacefully in Glasgow Royal Infirmary after a short illness. Father to John and Brian, father-in-law to Hazel and Caroline, grandad to Luke, Caitlin, Aaron and Jess. Great grandad to Kimberley and Josh. A loving brother, uncle and a great friend to many.

Funeral to be held at the Linn Crematorium on Tuesday, November 22 at 11 a.m.

Peacefully. It's the only word I take in on first reading. *Peacefully.* Then I see the date of the funeral and know it means no post-mortem, no suspicious death. The body has been released because he didn't die at home and there's no need for the police to investigate. I'm relieved and ashamed all at once.

Below, there are messages and virtual candles.

Thoughts and prayers from the McFarlane family. We'll remember good times and Jackie's sense of humour. RIP.

God rest your soul Jackie. Your mum and dad will be waiting for you in heaven. John and Brian are both in my prayers. RIP. Mary T.

Gone but never forgotten. Love you Dad. John and Hazel, Brian and Caz.

David Breslin had lit a candle and there was an illustration of one to prove it. The Young family had done the same. So had Anne Collins.

A true gentleman. Always in our thoughts. Iain and Margaret Black.

Rest in Peace Jackie. One of the best. Our heartfelt condolences to the Stevenson family from all at Mansfield Park FC.

Gerry McEwan lit a candle. Christopher MacDonald lit a candle.

Always in our thoughts Jackie. At the going down of the sun and in the morning, we will remember you. NC and MB

Cath Gillies lit a candle. The Andrews family lit a candle. Michael Brennan lit a candle. Peter Geir lit a candle.

RIP Jackie, one of the good guys. Thoughts and prayers. Jim and Francis Auld.

The candles go on and on. George Barrett. Sandra Kerrigan. Mary Taylor. The Andersons. Harry and Ann Todd. The Reynolds family. I didn't imagine Jackie Stevenson would be so popular, but death can make hypocrites out of us all.

I go back and read them again. Mansfield Park FC. The same football club that Tommy Agnew was involved with. I remember the name of the secretary that I came across online and know that I need to speak to him.

Stevenson's funeral is at the Linn on Tuesday. Going would be risky. And stupid. It makes no real sense. I'll probably go.

I get obsessive about things. Sometimes I'm aware of it and sometimes not, but I know I get that way.

When I clean a flat, I can't leave as much as a particle. I'm openly OCD about it, but that's doing my job, and going for anything less than a perfect clean wouldn't be doing it right. Each flat probably takes me longer than it should do but I make sure they get value for money. I make sure I do it right. Other things are more difficult to explain.

I'll get hooked on something to eat, maybe some super-food that cleans your arteries and boosts your immune system. I'll get into a new fitness thing or a series of books or a band or a meditation technique. Or a person.

I'm bad for getting obsessed with people, and now, I'm obsessed with Valerie. It's not like want-to-know-the-answer-to-the-mystery type obsessed. It's caring-about-her type obsessed. It's kindred-spirit type obsessed. That could have been me on that trip to Rothesay, me left alone with no friends, me lost and lonely for the past fifty-five years.

That's why I know I'll go to Stevenson's funeral. Why I can't not go.

I'll go because I need to know what happened to her. I need to know if *they* will turn up. The other two. I'm sure they will, they won't be able to stay away. Just like me. Just like Valerie.

Chapter 34

I'm at Mansfield Park, the football club, in search of Agnew and Stevenson and whatever other answers I can find. I haven't told Phil where I'm going because I'm sure he wouldn't approve and would probably try to stop me.

We've spoken a lot in these last few days, more than I've spoken to any other human being since my mum died. He's asking around, trying to find someone who knows someone, trying to make sense of the history before his history, wondering what he came from.

He's gone from being an orphan to having a father to losing him and inheriting an historical mess instead. We have a bond of sorts, him and me, just that neither of us knows quite what it is.

I'm not sure what I expected a football 'clubhouse' to be like but something bigger than this for sure. It's a garage with a lace-curtained window and a front door. I knock and immediately get a shout to enter.

Inside, it's like an office. A small computer screen sits on a large teak-effect desk. The walls are lined with pennants and photographs, team line-ups in various shirt designs of red and white. Most of them are hung at distressing angles and I have to resist the urge to straighten them.

The voice that called me in belongs to a short man, as round as he's tall, in his forties with a goatee beard and cropped hair. He walks towards me with a pronounced limp. 'Hi. I'm Davie Shaw. Lauren, is it?'

He starts to offer me a handshake and then awkwardly morphs it into a waved invitation to come further inside. Some men still don't know how to greet a woman they haven't met before and it's still funny.

'Thanks for meeting me,' I tell him. 'It was good of you to take the time.'

'Not at all. Glad to help if I can. Your message said you wanted to know about Mansfield Park's history?'

I think, *Yes, that was the story before I thought of a better one.*

I say, 'Yes, my grandad used to play for Mansfield, and he died recently. We're putting a few things together for a memorial service and I thought it would be nice if we had something from his football days. I was hoping you could help us.'

It's probably too late to start worrying about how well I can lie when I'm being someone else.

'Oh, I'm sorry to hear that.' He sounds like he means it too. 'Listen, if I can do anything at all to help then I will. Who was your grandad?'

'Jackie Stevenson. I think he played here in the mid-sixties.'

'Oh right, right. I'm sorry for your loss. I didn't know Jackie well, I only met him a couple of times, but others in the club did and they always spoke well of him.'

Again I think, *Death can make hypocrites out of us all.*

271

I say, 'Thanks.'

'Come on, let's have a look,' Davie says. 'I'm sure we'll be able to find something.'

He leads me to a tall, metal storage cupboard at the back of the room and pulls the doors back. It's a mess of books, ledgers, boxes, and framed photographs stacked on top of each other. 'There's only so much space on the walls so a lot of the older stuff gets shoved in here. We're always meaning to sort it out, but you know how it is. Let me see, mid-sixties …'

He works his way through a pile of ledgers, stacking them on the floors as he searches, wiping away dust as he goes. He finally holds one up that pleases him. 'This is from season 64–65. If your grandad played for us around that time, then he's probably in here. Do you want to take a look and I'll see if I can find a team photograph from around then?'

I take the book from him and open it halfway through. I see the names immediately. *T. Agnew*. *J. Stevenson*. I turn the pages and two matches later I see *R. Meechan*. I flick on through it and match after match the three men are listed. My mind jumps to the photograph, five young men in black and white on Rothesay pier. That band of brothers, comfortable on each other's skin. Teammates.

'Ah, got one!' I'm torn away from the names by a triumphal shout from Davie Shaw. I look up to see him brandishing a black-and-white photograph in a gold-coloured frame. 'This is from May 1965. The year we won the Balfour Cup according to this. Is your grandad in this?'

I take it from him with a slight tremble in my hand. I recognise Tommy Agnew right away. In the middle of the back row, tall and skinny with sticky-out ears. To his right Bob Meechan, smiling shyly. And there's Grandad Jackie in the front, stocky and grinning.

I scan the rest of the line-up, no doubt in my mind now that they will be here. The other two. *There*. Freckles, pale skin, and a manic grin. And kneeling in the front row, the chubby, cheery, dark-haired boy.

'Is he there?' Davie Shaw is asking me.

I think, *Yes, they are*.

I say, 'Yes. He's here.'

'Well that's great!' he smiles. 'You must be thrilled.'

I am. It's like they've brought the band back together. My famous five. The ones I found and the ones I'm looking for. My heart is pounding.

'This is him,' I point at the picture. 'Do you know any of the others?'

He frowns. 'I doubt it. Unless … is that Tommy Agnew? He was secretary here before me. He passed away quite recently too.'

'Oh, that's really sad. So close together. But you wouldn't know the others?'

'Sorry, no.'

'Could I get a copy of this?' I ask. 'The family would love to see it.'

He shrugs. 'Don't see why not. I can take it into …'

I interrupt. 'That's okay, I've got an app on my phone that does copies of old photos. If you can take it out of the glass that's all I'd need.'

'Sure. No problem.'

He fiddles with the frame, eases the photograph out, and hands it to me. I hold it up and take a closer look before flipping it. *Bingo*. The names are all written on the back.

'Oh wow, look, his teammates,' I'm sounding as girlishly enthusiastic as I can. 'I think some of his pals will be on here.' I don't ask if I can photograph the back as well. I do it and he doesn't object.

'Do you know any of these names?' I read them out to him and get mainly shrugs or a no. There's a shake in my hand and I'm trying desperately to control it.

Davie is keen to try to find me other bits from his history collection, but I assure him that I'm delighted with his find and that the family will be happy to see the photograph. It's just what I'm looking for, I tell him.

I sit in my car and make myself breathe slowly. It's not going to help to be flustered or whatever the hell it is I'm feeling right now. Breathe.

My phone is hot in my hand though and I can't hold it off any longer. I need to stare at them.

I get the team photograph up on my phone, enlarging the screen and closing in on the faces I need to see. Agnew. Meechan. Stevenson. The other two. I've got a copy of the Rothesay photo on here, but I don't need to look at it. Those images are engrained on my memory and, now, so too are the positions in which they're standing in the team line-up.

I flick the screen on to the next image, the photo of the back of the print. The names are handwritten but clear enough, particularly as I've seen them before. Middle of the back row Tommy Agnew. Back row third right, Bobby Meechan. Front row, second left, Jackie Stevenson. All the names where they should be. Back row second left, Mick Brennan. Front row right, Norrie Caldow.

The names come back to me from the obituary website. Jackie Stevenson's page.

Always in our thoughts Jackie. At the going down of the sun and in the morning, we will remember you. NC and MB

Michael Brennan lit a candle.

The names on the back of Agnew's Rothesay photograph. *Bob. Mick. Tommy. Jackie. Norrie.*

The two faces aggressively pushing at mine when Stevenson collapsed at Meechan's funeral. The heavy-set man shouting at me was Caldow, the skinnier one with flinty cheeks and wide eyes was Brennan.

It hadn't occurred to me till now, but it's just hit me with such crashing obviousness that I'm shocked at how stupid I am. They're the last two. *And they know it.*

Five of them went to Rothesay in 1964. Five of them were involved in that terrible thing. For five decades they've lived with it, thought they'd got away with it, had it on whatever scrap of conscience they have. And now, all these years later, it's catching up with them.

They probably thought nothing of it when Agnew died. Hardly a surprise given his age and health. They must have wondered when Meechan followed him, but probably dismissed it as a coincidence. Stevenson would have been one too many though. When he died, they knew, they must have.

And they must think that whoever is doing it, knows everything. Their secret. Their lies.

And … fuck, of course … they haven't been able to tell anyone. They can hardly go to the police and explain the connection. So, what are they doing?

The phone calls. The voice, thick and hoarse. I think back to Caldow shouting at me at Meechan's funeral and join the dots. The calls that have come to a stop.

With a creeping dread, I jump to what seems a reasonable, paranoid, terrifying conclusion. Brennan and Caldow have to protect themselves. They have to keep their secret from coming out.

They must think that I'm coming for them, that I've picked them off one by one.

Now I fear they're going to come for me.

Chapter 35

The day of Jackie Stevenson's funeral dawns cold and still. My breath fogs in front of me as I make my way to my car but there's barely a whisper of wind. The weather people call it crisp, but I think of it as lifeless and chilling.

My plan, such as it is, is to be first to the crematorium and last into the service. To see but not be seen, and to avoid confrontation at all costs. That's the extent of my thinking and I'm well aware it's light on detail and heavy on hope.

I try to work on the plan as I drive across the river and head due south, but all I can think of is the pillow I placed on Stevenson's face and the breathing that ceased beneath it. The closer I get to the crem, the more the image looms in my mind, so that by the time I get to the gates, I can barely see where I'm going.

I'm wondering too about Brennan and Caldow, sure that they'll be there and fearful of what they might do.

It's not yet ten o'clock and although I'm sure I must be the first arrival for the Stevenson funeral, I'm far from the first to get to the Linn. The small car park is already full as I roll in, and I have to park on the drive. I sit, squirrelled in my seat, eyes patrolling left and right for half an hour before a better location becomes available. A funeral party leaves and one of the mourners vacates a spot where I'll have a clear view of the entrance. I grab it before anyone else can and settle down to wait.

More cars arrive, more bodies, all in funeral uniforms of blacks and greys. I'm back in black too; black trousers, black leather jacket over a black blouse, black flats and a dark cloud hanging over me.

People begin filing inside, fifteen minutes to go, no sign of the two I'm looking for. A limo pulls up, another behind it. *Family*. Jackie Stevenson's family.

They stagger out in ones and twos then assemble in front of the crem. Two men in their fifties, their wives and children, and children's children. They make a mournful throng and I have just enough time to work out who's who before they're swallowed up in a wave of well-wishers. Their names come back to me from the funeral notice.

> *Father to John and Brian, father-in-law to Hazel and Caroline, grandad to Luke, Caitlin, Aaron and Jess. Great grandad to Kimberley and Josh.*

Stevenson's sons, both in their fifties, are doing their best to hold it together but even from fifty yards away I can see they're distressed. Wives comforting husbands, grandchildren awkwardly hugging mothers. They're a mess of hugs and tears that moves into the chapel as a single, winding mass.

I wait, and watch, and wait. Five minutes to go. The last of the black suits have gone inside, so it's time for me to do the same. Two older men greet me at the door, hymn books in hand and a disapproving look on their faces. I make an apologetic tilt of my head and duck past them into the chapel, taking a seat in the back row.

It's a familiar view. The long, narrow 1960s simplicity of St Mungo's Chapel with its wooden pews on parquet flooring. It's sparse and calming, with light flooding in through the high windows on either side at the front. The only thing coming close to being showy is the beautiful white marble stand that the coffin will soon rest on. It's called a catafalque and this one's inscribed with a cross and two Greek letters, alpha and omega. The beginning and the end.

In front of me are rows of heads. Some bowed, many grey, all filled with their own thoughts and memories. I can only guess at their content, wonder at their memories of Stevenson, knowing only that they didn't know him as well as they think. *Good times. A true gentleman. One of the best.*

Maybe they're not thinking about him at all. Funerals inevitably make you dwell on your own losses, unlocking doors in your mind that you'd closed for self-preservation, and forcing you to remember good times and bad. I wonder how many of the people with their backs to me are here out of duty, showing face for old Jackie but thinking about their own. Knowing what I know, that would be a better choice.

I'm in my seat less than two minutes when music starts up and the sound of feet drags me from my thoughts. I turn in time to see the slow march of men in black, the dark wooden coffin on their shoulders, as they make their way to the front. Stevenson's men. His supporters.

They rest him gently on the catafalque, bow and retreat, taking their places in the pews. There's a large printed photograph of Jackie to the left, propped up on an easel for all to see. He's smiling. The same benign, happy face that was on the obituary website and a world away from the one he wore when I met him. This is a face for his grandchildren.

The minister appears. He's one of the younger ones, all new and shiny, not yet worn down by the grind of tending to the needs of non-believers. Maybe I'm just getting old, but more and more of them seem to be social media ministers these days, good-looking Insta-generation happy clappers fresh out of God school. He'll be a good talker; all the young ones are.

When he gets to the eulogy, he proves me right. Saying it likes he means it, showing off that he's done his homework and delivering it like he should be on TV. And Jackie Stevenson comes off sounding like quite the guy.

He adored his grandchildren. He was besotted with his great-grandchildren. He was so proud of his sons, so fond of his daughters-in-law. There was nothing he wouldn't do for his family.

I think, *Including keeping his true self hidden from them.*

I see heads nodding, endorsing Jackie's goodness, and I want to shout to them. *You don't know this guy. You don't know what he's done.*

The minster talks warmly and gratefully about Jackie's work with the church, how he volunteered to take meals to those who couldn't get out, dropped in to check that those older than him were okay, how he'd always be there when they were running charity events, always first to put his hand in his pocket or give up his time. Some man.

He talks about Jackie's gruff humour. The gruff bit I remember. He waxes lyrical about how Jackie was quick with a joke, had a wide knowledge, and was always keen to offer advice. I read this as taking the piss out of people, thought he knew everything and would readily tell you that you were wrong.

The minister's sincerity mode deepens a notch and I know from experience that something serious is coming next. I'm not wrong. He recalls in ever-more hushed tones how Jackie's grandson Luke needed a kidney transplant and would have died without it. His dad Brian couldn't give him one of his because of illness, but Jackie had no hesitation in offering a kidney to save his grandson. Everyone who knew him knew he'd have gladly given both if that's what was needed. *Oh for fucksake*.

That, of course, induces sobbing and ever more head nodding from the seats in front. Saint Jackie is being canonised in front of our eyes and I'm aware I'm getting more agitated with every word. *I know*. I know that he played a part in what happened to Valerie Moodie, that he either did it or did nothing to stop it. If he did that, what else did he do?

Jackie's son John gets up to speak, then his grandson, the kidney-carrying Luke. They both cry, both lose their voices and struggle through it. Luke wouldn't be standing here today, he says, if not for his papa. He owes him his life and he'll never forget him. This sparks a small scream that I suspect comes from Luke's mother, and there's a flurry of comfort in the front row.

I realise I'm angry at them and furious with myself. I'm full of righteous indignation that they're full of love for the man that died. *The man that I killed*. That says more about me than them and I feel small; curling up awkwardly inside and squirming in my seat.

Maybe I'm the one that's wrong. Maybe Jackie Stevenson should be judged by the rest of his life, not by one mistake when he was still a boy. The worst thing he did or the best thing he's done? Judged for a day or for a life?

A life of lies, I remind myself. A life where he had chance after chance to admit what he did, tell what happened, put Valerie's family out of their misery. Instead, he hid it and hurt them. *Fuck him*.

The talking stops, the singing's over and they're done with lionising Jackie Stevenson. The curtain slides back, a singular moment always guaranteed to make it all very real. The moment they all realise the person in the coffin is destined for the burny fire, no matter how good or bad they've been. There's crying and hugging and shaking of heads.

Soon, they're all on their feet, trooping out with due solemnity, doing the hypocrisy shuffle towards the front door. I'm scanning the mourners, looking for the two, but not seeing them. All I have to go on is the brief meeting at Meechan's funeral and some fifty-year-old photographs. I'll know them, but not by the back of their heads.

I'm five seats in from the aisle, close enough to see, hopefully far enough in to be overlooked even though there's no one beside me to hide behind. I'm barely earning a glance from those shambling by, and I'm happy with that. Then, abruptly, I'm aware of movement that's at odds with the rest. A man in black hesitates mid-stride. Is he turning towards me? No, he's stopped to let someone by him, another suit, someone who is striding into my row, coming directly towards me. His head rises but I know who he is before I see his face.

He's a big man gone to seed, ruddy-faced and bloated, breathing through his mouth. His eyes are hard and fixed on me. Norrie Caldow is coming straight at me, moving slowly but with purpose, his bulk filling the row and allowing no way past. I shuffle onto the seat to my right, backing away, and turn to head for the other exit and to flee. The other one is sitting there, right next to me.

Mick Brennan is smiling back at me. No humour in his expression, just a malicious satisfaction at my shock. He's pasty white with flinty cheeks and something scary in his eyes. I try to stand, but he grabs my wrists and holds them down to the pew. He's a skinny fucker but he's strong.

The big man is now right beside me and I'm wedged between them. I can smell Caldow's sweat and feel his chest pressed against my back. I'm going to shout, find my voice and scream. Maybe he senses it, maybe he's going to do what he does anyway, but he reaches out, twists me around and hugs me, enveloping me in a bear grip. He's clapping my back as if he's comforting me and I realise that's what it must look like to anyone watching.

My mouth is clamped to his upper chest, full of the heat and moisture of his shirt, silencing me, near smothering me, sending my memory racing to Jackie Stevenson under the weight of the hospital pillow. I'm agitated, panicking, no chance of shouting or even moving. There's a voice tight to me, whispering, rasping. Brennan is so close I can feel his lips brushing against my ear and it makes me squirm.

'I don't know what your game is you little fucking bitch, but it stops now. You do not fucking mess with us.' I try to speak, but Caldow just pulls me closer, muffling any sound.

'I don't know what you think you know, or how you fucking know it, but this is the end of it. My pal here could snap your scrawny little neck without even trying. Snap it like a fucking twig. So, you sit still, you do not move, you listen.'

I'm struggling to breathe, trying not to retch at the horror of my mouth and lungs being filled with the reek of the fat man's lather. I nod my head as best I can.

'I don't believe in coincidences,' the voice is Caldow's, thick and hoarse, my threatening anonymous caller for sure. 'So, when you start asking questions about something that happened a long time ago, sticking your fucking nose in where it shouldn't be, and then very bad things start happening to our friends, then we've got to wonder what the fuck you're up to.'

'I don't know what's been happening,' it's Brennan's rasp again. 'But our pals have been dying and you're in up to your neck. Whatever you did, whatever somebody did, it isn't going to happen to us. So, you tell me. Who are you? And what exactly is it that you think you know? And your answers better be the right ones or you're going to be joining our pal Jackie in the oven. You going to talk?'

Caldow takes some of the pressure off the back of my head, just enough that I can nod in agreement.

'Good,' Brennan rasps.

I breathe in through my nose, take in as much air as I can find, then open my mouth wide against the big man's chest. And I bite. I bite hard. Sink my teeth into his chest through his shirt and take as much of his flabby flesh as I can. He shrieks and his arm instinctively leaves me and heads for the pain. I stand, and Brennan, maybe taken by surprise, lets go of my wrists. I scramble past Caldow, squeezing between him and the seat in front, and reach the aisle.

There's only a handful of people left and they're open-mouthed at the noise from Caldow and the sight of me climbing past him. I don't give a fuck; I just want out. I can hear the men coming after me and know I can't outrun them with people in the way.

I'm almost at the door when I hear a voice cutting through the throng. It's calling my name and for a second, I'm confused that the voice isn't Caldow or Brennan's.

'Ms McGill. Ms McGill!'

I look up and see DC Phelan standing a couple of feet inside the chapel door. He's added a black tie to the suit I've seen him in before but still looks every inch the policeman. I'm hoping that's as obvious to Caldow and Brennan as it is to me.

'Are you okay?' he asks me.

I think, *No, I'm not. Arrest me. Arrest those men.*

I say, 'I'm fine.'

His eyes narrow, examining me and my thoughts. 'You look upset. And I heard that man cry out.'

I think, *This is my chance. To end it all right here. Tell him. Tell him everything.*

I say, 'Funerals. You know how it is. Grief hits people hard.'

Phelan chews at his lip as he thinks.

'Why are you here, DC Phelan? You're taking what I said seriously?'

He blows out some air. 'We're just making enquiries, Ms McGill. Being thorough.'

I think, *Not thorough enough.*

I say, 'I'm glad to hear it. I need to go.'

'We'll keep in touch,' I hear him say as I turn on my heels and stride out into the fresh air.

Caldow and Brennan are standing on the path leading to the car park and I have to walk by them to get away. Phelan's close by though, watching, and I know they can't touch me.

But it turns out they don't have to touch me to get to me.

Brennan hisses at me, quiet enough that only I can hear.

'Run if you want. We know where you live.'

Chapter 36

I run to Phil.

He's been messaging me, keen to meet, keen to go back to Bute. The prospect of that hadn't filled me with joy, but now ... now I'm keen to get out of Glasgow, so Rothesay seems as good a place to go as any.

We meet at Wemyss Bay, me from the train and him in his car waiting in the ferry queue. It's immediately strange as I see him standing next to his Skoda, smiling and waving. He's still a stranger to me, still the man who followed me, and yet we have this thing, this indefinable thing. He's much older than I am so wouldn't be interested in me, so that's fine, something I don't have to worry about. He's handsome, for an older guy, but that's not a consideration, so it's okay.

'Hi,' he says. 'Glad you made it.' He's finding it awkward too. Not sure what to say or whether to greet me with a handshake or a hug. We're not a normal couple. We're not a couple at all, just two people.

'Hi Phil. Good to see you.'

'Should we ... um. Do you want to go over in the car?'

'Yes. Thanks. I do.'

That passes for sparkling conversation for me. So far so good.

I slide into the passenger seat of the Octavia and we watch the ferry sail into port, cars and foot passengers streaming off, and then it's us. Phil steers the car into the body of the beast, all vehicles packed in tightly together, side by side and nose to tail, then we climb upstairs and watch the waves go by.

As we sail, I tell him about the Mansfield Park team photograph and the names on the back. He nods grimly as I add Caldow and Brennan's names to his list. I see his eyes darken at the new knowledge and decide not to tell him about my encounter with the two men at Stevenson's funeral. It would only lead to questions as to why I was there, and that's a road I'm not ready to wander down.

Phil has a plan. He readily admits it's a plan full of holes and optimism, but it's the only plan we've got. But it's *us* that have the plan and that's good enough for me. I'm happy to have someone by my side and on my side. It's been a very long time since that happened and I'm intending to enjoy it for as long as it lasts. Not that it's a thing.

We go up on deck for the last bit of the journey, getting up top in time to see Rothesay loom into view. The bay is bathed in sunshine, but clouds are hanging low over the town, closing in and threatening change. Time will tell if that's a good thing.

We book into the Glenburn, the big, imposing Victorian hotel a few minutes out of town. Phil's room is a few doors along from mine and we say brief goodbyes in the corridor with an agreement to meet downstairs before part one of the plan swings into operation. It means him going his way and me going mine.

The Golfers is busy as I enter, the snug full, and most of the tables and chairs taken. McTeer is standing at the far end of the bar, same spot as before. His spot. I position myself at the other end and watch him in the mirror. It takes all of five seconds before his eyes are locked on mine.

I can't read his reaction other than seeing his eyes widen. He brings his glass to his mouth and holds it there long enough that he's wearing a blank expression when it's revealed. He keeps looking at me though.

There's a large red mark on his forehead and his hand reaches for it as I watch, reminded of the pain and how it got there. I smile inside when I see it.

The barman approaches and I order a Diet Coke and stay where I am. I can see McTeer, and him me. No need to change that.

I'm nervous, both at being in a bar surrounded by people I don't know and being in a staring contest with a man who attacked me. He must be wondering what the hell I'm doing, trying to work out why I didn't go to the police, why I'm back here, yet not confronting him. He's holding the whisky glass in his right hand as though he might crush it.

He orders another, downs it, and turns to walk to the front door. I don't look at him except in the mirror, seeing him walk right by me and feeling the breeze of his passing. I stand still, mirror-gazing, for as long as I can, before allowing myself a solitary look out of the front window onto the street.

He's standing outside. Furiously drawing on a cigarette, moving nervously from foot to foot, and staring back into the pub. There's no way out without going right by him, and that's exactly what I need to do.

I send a text on my phone, take a final swig of my Diet Coke for some Diet Dutch courage, and head to the door. It takes all my strength not to look at him as I pass, but I manage it and cross the road onto the narrows of West Princes Street as I did once before.

There are no footsteps following me, not right away at least. I'm not going to turn around, no matter what, just focus on the path ahead. I do have to steel myself though as I pass the doorway that I was attacked in. Now I hear it. Someone walking behind me, a way back but there for sure. It could be him, but it could be anybody. I keep walking, lengthening my stride, past the Black Bull, quickening my pace till I'm safely out of this street. Whoever it is isn't getting any closer, not just yet, they're still ten or fifteen yards behind. But they're still there. I pass the Taverna Bar and try not to burst with relief as I reach Guildford Square.

Instead, I take a sharp left turn onto Watergate, past the jewellers on one side and the newsagent on the other, on past the Electric Bakery. It's narrow here too, and quieter. The footsteps are still behind me, but closer. The urge to look back is almost overwhelming but I resist. I resist even when they're no more than a few yards behind.

I'm almost at the old building that looks like a Victorian jail when the red Skoda Octavia turns down the street towards me. *Towards us*. It's no more than a couple of seconds after the car passes me that I hear its brakes squeal and the sound of a door being thrown open, instantly followed by a shout of fear.

I turn to see Malky McTeer trapped against the wall, unable to move between the nose of the car and the open door. The street is predictably, thankfully, quiet, and there's no one to see what's happening. Phil leans across from the driver's seat and roars at him.

'Get in the car.'

'What the fuck's going on?'

'In. *Now*. Or I'll drag you inside, then we can tell the police how you attacked this woman.'

McTeer looks from Phil to me and back again. He knows he's no choice. He gets in the front seat; I follow into the back, and Phil drives off.

We go east, following the winding coastline and a succession of old bus shelters, palm trees, and Victorian homes with a view, until Rothesay is behind us. We've driven for no more than five minutes but it's long enough for our silence to have put the fear of God into McTeer. Each and every one of his questions have been ignored.

I'm nervous but excited too. I'm worrying about what might happen, but I'm also hopeful we're getting closer to Valerie. She's nearer now, I'm sure of it.

Phil finally pulls off the road into a small parking area, the nose of the car facing the sea. He yanks on the handbrake and stares out at the view long enough to make McTeer's worries deepen.

'How good's your memory, Malky?' he asks at last.

'*What?*'

Phil turns to face him. 'How good is your memory? Do you remember a man named Tommy Agnew?'

McTeer looks genuinely confused. 'No. And there's nothing wrong with my memory. I've never heard the name before. What the fuck is this all about?'

I watch Phil hold the man's gaze for a while, calculating, thinking.

'Okay, I believe you. Let's try you on something else. Do you remember, long time ago now, five guys that wanted you to take them on a fishing trip?'

McTeer shrugs but glancing at him in the rear-view mirror from my seat in the back, I see something different in his eyes. Phil sees it too.

'Five guys that wanted to use your boat. But they weren't after fish. Five guys that came to you and Alec Thomson.'

McTeer loses the colour from his face. 'What?'

Phil's voice changes and I don't recognise the person that speaks. 'Stop fucking me about, Malky. The first thing you need to know is that I know more about the mess you got yourself into than anyone who's ever spoken to you.' As he's speaking, Phil reaches into the door pocket beside him and pulls out a long piece of metal that I think is a car lever. 'So, you talk to me or else going to the police will be the least of your worries. Do you fucking understand me?'

He understands. Shit scared. 'Yes.'

'Okay, let's start again. Do you remember the five guys that approached you and Alec Thomson in 1964?'

'Aye.'

'And do you remember when in 1964 that was?'

He starts on a different answer but looks at me, then at the lever in Phil's hand, and changes his mind. 'It was the night the lassie disappeared.'

'Say her name.'

'Valerie Moodie. It was the night Valerie Moodie disappeared.'

Phil doesn't take his eyes off McTeer's. 'Show him the photograph, Grace.'

I take the print from my bag and hold it in front of him. Five young men, sun-kissed torsos, brothers in arms. Any doubt that it was them, any doubt that it was McTeer, has just evaporated. We can see the years roll back in his eyes.

'Is this them?'

McTeer tries to fight it. 'I can't be sure. It was so long ago.'

Phil grabs the photograph from me and shoves it in McTeer's face. 'Look harder.'

The man sighs unhappily. 'Yes. I think it's them.'

'You think or you're sure?'

Another huff. 'I'm sure. It's them.'

'Tell us what happened. All of it.'

The floodgates open.

'It was a Thursday night during the Fair. Me and Alec Thomson were in the Taverna having a few beers when two guys came into the pub. We'd clocked them when they came in, watched them come right over to us, asked if we were Alec and Malky. They were obviously up to something and they were a bit wired, nervous that anyone was listening and being all sly about it.

'They said they wanted to hire someone with a boat for a late-night fishing trip. We'd already had a few pints so said no, but they said they'd make it worth our while, so long as we had a van as well because they had cargo they wanted to take with them.

'We might still have said no but they said they'd give us sixty quid. That was ridiculous money back then. We weren't stupid, we knew it had to be dodgy if they were willing to pay that much cash, but it would have taken us three weeks to earn that from the boat, so we said we'd do it.

'I was a bit drunk, we both were, but drink driving wasn't a thing back then and it probably wouldn't have stopped us even if it was. So, we went outside and there were three others hanging about. They said three of them would go with us.'

'Which three?' Phil asks him.

McTeer looks at the photo again and jabs a finger at Stevenson, Brennan and Caldow. 'Those three. They said their names were Billy, John and Jim, or something like that. Of course, we didn't believe them, but it didn't matter. They gave us thirty quid up front with another thirty to come, and that was all we needed to know.

'Me and Alec were in the front seats of the van when the three of them lifted the cargo into the back then squeezed in behind us. It was a large army duffel bag, one of those green canvas ones that hold tents. They said they'd been camping. The boat was at St Ninian's Bay as we'd been fishing off the west side of the island, near Inchmarnock. When we mentioned that to these guys, they got all interested and wanted to know more about it. They said it sounded like just what they needed.'

'What is Inchmarnock?' Phil asks him.

'It's an island in the Sound. About two and a half miles long, half a mile wide. Back then it was uninhabited, still is now apart from cows. When we told them that, they said it was perfect. Alec and I knew those waters well so it was no problem to us. Easy money we thought.'

'What did you think they were doing?'

McTeer shrugs and looks away. 'We didn't know. We knew it was probably crooked, that there was maybe something valuable in that bag and there might be a way for us to get our hands on it. So we drove to Straad, took the van down the dirt road to the bay, and parked as near to the boat as we could. The three guys told us to lead on to the boat and they'd follow with the cargo. They were taking care of it, whatever it was.

'We took them and the cargo on the boat and sailed to Inchmarnock. They'd taken a shovel from the back of the van and when we got there, two of them went off in-land, taking Alec with them and the biggest one staying with me in case I tried to leave them there.

'They came back about two hours later, saying nothing. Got back on the boat and we took them back. They paid up and warned us against saying anything. They knew our names, knew our boat, would find out where we lived. We'd to take the money and shut the fuck up.'

'And you did.' The raw anger in Phil's voice is unmissable. 'Even when you heard about Valerie Moodie. Even when you read about her mother being desperate to know what happened to her.'

McTeer looks away, his face crumpling. 'We didn't think it was her. We thought it was something they'd robbed, maybe from one of the big houses on the island, some loot. Alec asked me if I thought it was the lassie when we heard about her the next few days, but I told him not to be daft. He got drunk though and started babbling in the pub later that week, really lost it. People knew he was really freaked by *something*, and there was a lot of talk starting to go round the island, so we made up the story about seeing the body when we were fishing to cover that up. Then we denied that too. It was a mess, but it was too late by then.'

'How the fuck could you live with yourself?' I was surprised to hear it was me talking, the rage inside me taking over.

'Who's says I could?' McTeer shoots back. 'Why do you think I drink as much? I've had to live with this for over fifty years. It's near driven me crazy at times. And not made me easy to live with. Anyway, we didn't *know* it was her in that bag.'

'You should have gone to the police,' Phil told him flatly, no room for argument. 'And you know it.'

McTeer says nothing.

'Where did they bury that canvas bag on Inchmarnock?'

McTeer shuts his eyes and rubs at them with the heels of his hands. 'I don't know. It was dark and it was Alec that went with them.'

Phil sighs but there's barbed wire in his voice. 'Where did they bury it?'

'I told you. Alec went with them, not me.'

'But Alec told you where they dug?'

'A bit, yeah. But it was a long time ago.'

Phil stares at him. 'Do you still fish?'

The question comes out of the blue and McTeer looks wary. I'm confused too.

'Aye,' McTeer says. 'I can't afford to stop. Why you asking?'

'We're going to Inchmarnock. And you're taking us there.'

Chapter 37

It's a short drive, just ten minutes, across country from Rothesay on the east coast to Straad on the west. Phil is driving, me behind, and McTeer sitting reluctantly, silently, beside him. The road rolls and twists with my mind, past hedgerows, drystone dykes and grass verges, there are regular glimpses of sea and loch with distant mountains overseeing it all. On a bend, a dead-end sign leads ahead to a single-track road and we take it.

Straad is just a handful of houses and we steal past them until we're on a dirt path that's barely wide enough for the car, bouncing along on ruts and holes, overgrown grass waving us by. There's no chance of turning or of letting another car past, and I hope there's no one else crazy enough to be coming the other way.

'Here,' says McTeer from the back seat. 'We won't get any further.'

St Ninian's Bay is a flat horseshoe with white sand visible below the shallow water, rocks sticking above the surface. Clouds are low and thick over the mountain ridges of Arran and, in the near distance across the bay, there's a long snake of green which McTeer points to. 'That's Inchmarnock.'

The fisherman lifts his head, his nose to the wind, looking around for something I can't see and wouldn't recognise. Whatever he finds, it doesn't please him. He's screwing up his face and the leathery lines gather around his eyes. 'The wind's changing. This isn't a good idea.'

The island looks so near that I can't see the difficulty. Phil must be thinking the same. 'We're going. It can only be a short sail and I don't see any problems.'

McTeer shakes his head. 'It'll take longer than you think. We're going to be running against the tide and this is a nasty wee stretch of water in the wrong conditions. And these are the wrong conditions.' He sees Phil isn't for budging and sighs. 'Fucksake. Okay, if we're going to do this, we better get moving. And you're going to get your feet wet.'

We do. As we near McTeer's boat, I feel the icy chill of water rising above my ankles, my shoes soaked, and another few yards still to walk. I hear Phil say, 'Let me help,' and before I can reply or understand, I'm lifted clear of the sea and carried in his arms till he drops me gently and safely into the boat. I like it.

The other two get on board and the boat chugs slowly, quickly, across the black sheet that McTeer calls the Sound of Bute. We don't seem to be getting anywhere, yet the speed across the water is unnerving me. There's a strong breeze in our faces and it's chilling me to the bone. Phil is sitting next to me and twice I've thought he was going to put an arm around me to keep me warm. He hasn't. I'm crazy.

I've been thinking about telling him who I am, what I've done, *all of it*. I feel I should. We're in this together, whatever it is, and I think he'd understand. He knows loneliness, he's experienced loss and depression and pointlessness. I'm sure he'd understand.

We're heading straight towards Inchmarnock, and then, suddenly, we're not. There's a lurch to the side and in a second, we're side on to the island and going nowhere. Phil fires a look at McTeer who's working hard at the wheel. 'I'm trying,' he shouts. 'I told you this was a bad idea. Just let me fucking sort it.'

I'm gripping the side of the boat but still shifting in my seat, and I'm scared. My right hand is holding with all the strength I can find, and my left shoots out and grabs Phil's arm. He turns to look at me and he nods. I knew he'd understand.

The boat pitches and turns under the darkening sky, McTeer swearing, sweating, and manoeuvring furiously. We're ploughing straight into waves and it feels like we're hitting concrete. There's progress, but it's slow and painful and feels risky.

Eventually, one length forward and two to the side, battered and bruised, we make our way to the island. McTeer guides us into a small cove that's been made into a landing area. There's a craft already there, a blue-and-white flat-bottomed vessel that looks like a mini ferry. 'It's for the cattle,' McTeer explains, shouting above the wind. 'Takes them back and forth from the mainland. There's no people here.'

He and Phil jump off the boat, splashing into shin-deep water, before Phil helps me down and carries me to the rocky shore. We all take a breath, find our land legs and wrestle with our own thoughts. I feel troubled, nervous, my skin buzzing with anticipation. It's the same feeling I had when I toured Rothesay in Valerie's footsteps. Maybe she's with me again now.

Ahead of us, trees and bushes loom green and thick, with no obvious way to go. McTeer knows though, however unhappy he is about it. 'This way,' he huffs, starting to the right. 'It won't be far.'

We follow him up the slipway and onto a road. 'This wasn't here back then,' he tells us. 'But I've been on the island a few times since. We go across this, then into the trees. Then we look.'

The light soon fades under the canopy above, the birch trees closing in on us. McTeer leads us one way, then another. For twenty minutes, he seems to second-guess himself, looking up and around and changing his mind. He's giving a fair impression of someone who has no idea where he's going. With a shake of his head he leads us on another turn before stopping in his tracks.

'Maybe here,' he announces half-heartedly.

Phil stares him down. 'Are you sure? If I dig here and there's nothing, it's not going to make me very happy.'

McTeer considers this and concedes. 'Maybe it's further over there. Yes, I think that's it. This way.'

'*Stop*. If you're thinking you can get out of this by fucking around until we get fed up and go back to Rothesay, that's not going to happen. If you want off this island tonight, then you'd better find where they were digging. Let's go back to the slipway and start again.'

McTeer nods sullenly and turns back, trudging through the wet undergrowth, his shoulders slumped, Phil and me following behind. From the landing point, he takes his original route, barrelling straight as he can for maybe a hundred yards. I think he's trying this time, I can see it on his face, but it's still a struggle. Time and tide and twisted memories have muddied the route in his mind.

We reach a natural three-way fork in the trodden path and he stops, swearing under his breath, clearly unsure which way to go. 'We need to find two large, dark boulders sitting right next to each other. Alec said they dug next to two rocks like that. But it's near here, has to be. They wouldn't have gone far.'

He chooses left but doubles back in less than a minute, going straight on before giving up again. We go right, trees thick around us, whispering as we pass, until they suddenly thin out and we're in a small clearing, filters of fading light sneaking through the treetops.

There are two large, dark rocks. One about four feet high, the other slightly smaller, huddling against each other for warmth.

'This is it,' McTeer says. 'This is where they dug.'

Phil lays the spade on the ground, strips off his jacket and takes a deep breath. When he picks the spade up and drives it into the earth, the noise and the reverberation run through me as if he'd driven it into my spine.

He digs, McTeer and me watching, the sound of the metal into the earth all that can be heard. The world is centred on these few square feet of dirt in a wood on an island in the Sound. We're swimming in time and about to drown.

Phil digs for half an hour, maybe more, maybe less, but we all know the precise moment when he hits what he's looking for. The chink of spade on bone is muffled by earth but still rings so loudly I'm scared it will be heard back in Rothesay. I'm sure birds leave the trees above us and flee at the noise.

When the echo dies away, there's nothing. Not a sound. None of us moves for an age. I recognise the look of fear on McTeer's face and the blank, business-like expression on Phil's. My heart is in my mouth.

Phil starts digging again, slower though, working more carefully around the area where he struck, picking at the ground with the tip of the spade. After a few minutes, he gives up on that and gets on his knees, clawing dirt away, scratching at the soil, peeling back its layers until he sits up straight, his back blocking our view.

He turns, face sombre, drawing his body back to reveal what he's found. The dark earth is broken with different colours and it takes a moment for my brain to decipher what I'm looking at. I think I can only make sense of it because of what we're hoping to find and fearing to find.

Phil's work has exposed the tattered remains of dirty green canvas and a long dirty white bone that looks like an arm or a leg.

'Human.' He says it like a professional. Clinical. Matter-of-fact. 'I think it's a humerus. Upper arm.'

My stomach is turning, and I consider vomiting. I clean houses after people die. I clean up things that make policemen want to puke. But this is different. This is the wee lassie I've been looking for. This is the wee lassie that the whole island was looking for nearly sixty years ago. Lying in a lonely grave on an uninhabited island. Everyone looking for her but no one to stand over her and say nice things. Undiscovered. Alone.

I'd hoped it wouldn't be like this. Part of me thought I'd find she'd run off somewhere, that she was still alive with children and grandchildren, happily hiding under another name. I don't know whether to cry or not.

'Is it her?' I hear myself ask the question and it sounds stupid.

Phil twists his mouth and looks at me under a furrowed brow. 'From everything we know? I'd be amazed if it isn't. It'll need forensics to say for sure, but I'd give you a million to one on it being anyone else.'

'What do we …' I stop mid-sentence, no idea what happens next.

He sighs hard, shaking his head. 'We can't dig her up or take her back with us. That needs to be done properly. It needs the police and forensics. She deserves this to be done right, and the law says the same.'

There's a splutter behind us and we turn to see McTeer on his knees, eyes red. He's talking as much to himself as to us.

'I didn't know. Not for sure. They could have been digging anything. Hiding anything. I didn't *know*. How was I supposed to know? Nobody had heard about the missing lassie when we took those guys over here. And after that it was too late.'

The bastard has seen all his chickens come home to roost and he's feeling sorry for himself. He wants us to feel sorry for him too. I'm tempted to take the spade and batter his head with it.

It's raining. Water streaming through the trees above and soaking us. Valerie's shallow grave is already dampening, and it disturbs me. I crouch and start throwing earth back over the exposed bone, desperately trying to cover her before she's too wet. *I know*. But I have to do it.

I hear McTeer's verdict from behind me. 'She's fucking crazy.'

'Shut it,' Phil tells him.

'She is though. Covering up a skeleton in case it gets wet.'

I turn on him. 'So says the expert on covering things up. She's been lying in this hole all these years because of you.'

'Fuck you! You don't know what I went through. You've no idea what this has done to me. And I didn't put her in there. That wasn't me.'

'You *knew* she was here.'

The truth of that hit me hard and sudden. 'You actually knew *exactly* where she was. You found her far too easily for someone that supposedly hadn't been there.' It all makes sense now. 'You went back to the island thinking those guys had buried something valuable. And you found her instead.'

McTeer's lips are locked, his eyes burning.

'You found her and you left her to rot to protect yourself. You fucking bastard.'

'It wouldn't have changed anything.' He's whining and angry at the same time.

'It would have changed everything for Valerie's mother. And it would have been the right thing to do.'

'Okay, enough.' Phil steps between us. 'We can't do anything more here today. We need to get back while we can and contact the police. They need to take it from here.'

McTeer stands up. 'Police? You're going to the police?'

'Of course I am. What the hell did you think I'd do?'

'Leave me out of it. *Please*. I've done what you wanted. I brought you here. Found her for you. Please don't mention my name. My life will be hell.'

Phil deliberates this for longer than I'm comfortable with. 'I'm making no promises,' he says. 'Let's get back to Bute, then we'll see.'

It's getting dark as we trudge back through the woods then clamber onto the boat. The wind's higher, stronger, the rain is lashing down, and the current is swirling in front of us. Even I can see it's bad. McTeer looks like he's peering into his own grave.

We back out into the Sound, the boat rocking beneath us, the rain pinging the deck. We're going with the tide now, but it doesn't feel like that's a good thing. The boat surges, shifts and slides. There's another current working against us, turning us. I can tell how dangerous it is by the look on McTeer's face. He's having to work overtime to keep us pointing where we should be going. Even then the boat tips to one side then the other and I'm holding on for my life.

Things are moving across the boat, seating dislodged, metal banging into metal, ropes flying. I don't think we're going to capsize but I also don't know how the hell we're going to get back in one piece. My knuckles are white, and my hair soaked. Phil is yelling at me to hold on, but I can barely hear him over the crash of the waves and the roar of the wind.

We keep turning to the right, yanked around 90 degrees, and McTeer has to battle to get us on course again. The night has closed in, clouds on top of us, wind screaming. I can taste salt and fear.

For five long minutes, we toss and spiral. My hands are raw, and my mind is churning along with the sea beneath us. Then, it changes. Still rough, still wet, still heaving, but there's a weakening of the movement below that I can feel.

'We're past the worst of it,' McTeer shouts. 'We can roll in from here.'

The shallows of St Ninian's Bay are in sight, and seemingly in easy reach. I can see the water is calmer ahead and we'll make it back to land. McTeer is relaxed enough that he only needs one hand on the wheel as he uses the other to lean over and shove seating back into place. I look at him and see only what he did and what he didn't do.

I let go my grip on the side of the boat and I'm across to the other in two quick strides, shoving McTeer hard in the back with both hands. He's off balance and taken by surprise. He doesn't have any chance to do anything other than topple over the side. In a couple of seconds, he's yards from the boat. In a couple more, he's out of sight.

I feel hands on my arms, yanking me back into the middle of the boat and onto the floor where I sit, heart racing, blood pumping. Phil is past me, looking over the side and back where McTeer fell. He leans as far as he dares over the side until he gives up and turns to face me, eyes wide.

'Jesus Christ, Grace. What did you do?'

I think, *That's a silly question. You saw what I did.*

I answer the question he should have asked. 'He knew where Valerie was buried. All this time. And he did nothing. All those people who went through hell because they didn't know. He knew. And he could have ended all that right at the beginning.'

His mouth is open, and his eyes are trying to make sense of what he sees. I thought he'd understand. I'm not sure that he does.

He takes the wheel and turns us back towards the shore, throwing glances back at our wake. There's nothing to be seen other than white horses dancing on the rippling black. No man, no swimmer, no liar. Phil doesn't say a single word for the remainder of the sail back and it frightens me.

We glide into the shallows and he jumps off, beckoning me to him without a word. I swing my legs over the side, and he carries me clear of the water and dumps me on the rocks. He turns back and pushes the boat out again, wading until he's waist deep and the boat drifts off on the tide. We watch in silence till it becomes a shadow, then a memory. We watch till we're sure there's no sign and no chance of McTeer swimming back to shore.

'Get in the car,' he orders me. 'We need to get out of here and hope no one sees us.'

'They'll think it was an accident,' I tell him. 'He's got alcohol in his system; the sea was rough, and the winds were wrong. What did he say? A nasty wee stretch of water in the wrong conditions? They'll think it was an accident.'

For a moment, I think he's going to hit me. He doesn't, but I wish he had. 'Just get in the fucking car, Grace.'

The silent drive back into Rothesay feels a lot longer than ten minutes. Phil parks in front of the Glenburn Hotel and pulls on the handbrake with a ferocity that makes the car shake.

'Phil ...' I'm scared to ask the question. 'What are you going to ...'

'I don't know. I don't fucking know.'

'I'll clean the inside of the car,' I tell him. 'It's what I do, what I'm good at. No one will ever know he's been in here.'

The sadness in his voice nearly breaks me. 'Grace, *I'll* know he's been in here. I'll know. But it's not the fucking point. This isn't about how we get away with it from here, it's that it should never have happened.'

I know. I do know.

Phil closes his eyes and holds his head in his hands. He sits like that long enough that I'm convinced he's trying to wish all of this away. When he re-emerges, he looks and sounds tired.

'People fucked up that night in 1964 and it wrecked lives. Valerie Moodie. Her mother. My father, his friends, no doubt their wives and their kids. McTeer and his pal. And now you've fucked up, and more lives are wrecked. Have you any idea of the amount of shit you've dropped me in?'

'Phil …'

'I don't want to hear it. I'm going to call the police to tell them to go look for Valerie. But now I can't do it until we're both off this island. I can't do it until you're in Glasgow and I'm back in Lancashire.'

'You're going …'

Of course he is. My voice trails off as I realise the extent of my own stupidity.

'How could you do it, Grace?'

I remember sitting opposite him in the park in the West End, the first time we spoke to each other and how I thought he was looking at me like he was trying to see inside me. Now, he's looking deeper, struggling to believe what he sees. I need to convince him he's looking in the wrong place.

'You know McTeer should have told the police,' I say. 'What he did was illegal, right? It was obviously immoral, but it was illegal too, surely. Perverting the course of justice, is that it?'

His face darkens. 'That's not how it works, Grace. It's not your decision to make. That's why we have courts and judges and juries. They would have found him guilty of perverting justice. Or maybe he'd have got off, but that's how it is. He's an old man who'd had to live with his lies for all these years.'

'Exactly …' I see a straw of hope and grasp at it. 'And he'd have had to live with them for years more. You heard him. He's been haunted by it, driven to drink and hating himself. All of that would just have got worse if everyone knew what he'd covered up all that time.'

His mouth drops open. 'So, you were doing him a favour?'

Shit. 'I wouldn't … I mean … I didn't think before I did it, but this way there's justice for Valerie and justice for him. He was lonely and miserable and now he isn't.'

The words sounded okay in my head, but I can hear them hanging ridiculously between us now. I'm sitting with my hands under my thighs, trapped there for reassurance, and I'm staring out through the windscreen to avoid meeting his eyes.

He takes an age before he speaks, and when he does, it scares me that he talks quietly and slowly. It's like he's so angry he can't trust himself to be loud.

'Grace, you murdered him. You didn't save him from a life of torment, you *murdered* him. You're not God. You don't get to decide who lives and who dies. You don't get to be judge, jury and fucking executioner. There are laws to stop people like you doing things like that.'

People like you.

He might as well have slapped me. *People like you.* I'd allowed myself to dream about things that are disappearing before me.

'What McTeer did and didn't do was wrong, there's no debate about that. It was cowardly and selfish, and it was illegal. Did that give you the right to kill him? No, it fucking didn't. Yes, he was a miserable old bastard who had no happiness in his life. Did that give you the right to kill him for his sake? No, it fucking didn't. You never have the right to do that.

'And you talk about justice for Valerie? That would have been people going to jail for what they did. It would have meant the truth coming out, and those men – including my biological father – being held to account. That hasn't happened and now it can't. The only witness to what they did is dead, thanks to you. You don't get to play God, Grace. You just don't.'

I start to cry. I hate myself for doing it, but there's just no stopping the tears that trickle down my cheeks. It's because I know there's probably no coming back from this. Better or worse than that, I realise there's probably nothing more to lose.

'Phil, there are things I've got to tell you.'

Chapter 38

I tell him some things and I don't tell him others. I know what I should tell him but my courage leaves me. I should tell him everything.

How I knew nothing about Mr Agnew other than that he was desperately lonely. An old man needing someone to talk to, someone to listen. He didn't want to be a bother to anyone. He wasn't the kind to complain, born of a get-on-with-it generation. There were many people worse off than him, he'd no doubt of that.

We got talking on the Facebook group and he seemed such a nice old man. He didn't say too much at first, just happy to be having a conversation even if it was with someone he didn't know. I'm a good listener though, and he slowly opened up. His pain was obvious and heartbreaking.

He told me how he would watch television for hours and then realise he'd seen none of it, that it had flashed in front of him like a passing bus. That some days, he'd go to bed by 8.30 because there was nothing else to do. Or how he'd stand by the window of his flat and watch people coming and going, not recognising anyone, seeing his own street like a foreign land.

The things he used to do were lost to him, new things seemed out of reach, and above all, the people that filled his life were gone. Whether they were dead, had moved away or drifted apart, the common factor was that they weren't there.

His days were endless and joyless, and I encouraged him to think it was okay to complain about that. It wasn't something he had to endure or suffer in silence. I told him that being old didn't mean you had to be alone, it didn't come with the job.

But it was worse than just being on his own, his present was haunted by his past. He talked of regrets and consequences, how any problems he had, he'd brought upon himself. He hated the slog of loneliness, but he hated himself just as much for it being like that.

He told me the worst thing was that he couldn't stop thinking about what he'd done and what he'd lost. That he sat and thought and waited for the day to end.

I recognised guilt when I saw it but presumed that was all because of his wife having died. That he was suffering from survivor's guilt, going on when she hadn't, living when she'd gone. I still thought it to be that when I decided to ease his pain.

Mr Agnew told me many times that his life wasn't worth living, that he wanted a way out. He was done. He didn't come out and ask me to help, but I could read between the lines and knew that he needed a friend who cared enough to help him end his life.

So it was then that he finally invited me to his flat. I made him a meal, sat and listened. I had to know whether he was as unhappy in real life as he was on-line, that he wasn't laying it on thick because he was in that group. He wasn't. He was pitifully sad, a man doubting a lifetime's choices and drowning in his own misery.

His place was a mess because he'd lost any motivation to look after it. I could see that the relics of his chaotic living had been pushed aside to make room for a fleeting visit; clothes, boxes, bottles, all just shoved to the fringes of the room. His mind was the same, clearing just enough to let me in for the day.

I laced his tea with something guaranteed to put him to sleep. It was gentle, flavourless, painless. He got drowsy and apologetic. I told him it was okay, that everything would be okay. He lay on his bed and slept.

I said a prayer, closed the door behind me and left. That door wasn't opened again for five months. Sad as that was, I believe it justified my actions. No friends, family or neighbours were going to come to his door and make his life bearable. I spared him from that.

I kept in touch with Bob Meechan after the funeral. I think he liked that someone was paying him some attention and cared enough to worry about him. Bob was ill, seriously ill. He hadn't told anyone, not his son or his grandchildren. He didn't want to worry them.

They'd have had good reason to worry. He'd been diagnosed with terminal stomach cancer.

It took him almost a week to tell me. He mentioned the pain and said he wasn't well, but it took him five days and three conversations before he told me just how serious it was. *Terminal.*

He said the pain was constant, barely kept under control by drugs, and he couldn't take too many of them because they were so powerful. So, he lived with the cancer eating away at his stomach, bit by bit. Bob told me there were times he'd sit and feel it happening. He knew it might just have been his imagination, but he said he was aware of it gnawing at him, ripping him apart inch by inch, feeling its teeth on him. He said he was being eaten alive from the inside out.

He had two years left at the most. Two years of pain.

I asked him about Bute. Pressed him on why he and Jackie Stevenson had been so evasive, told him I knew they weren't telling me the truth. He claimed he didn't know what I was talking about, told me that he couldn't remember this or that. Every weak denial made me surer there was something.

The second time I visited him in Grantley Gardens, he threw up. It was probably the most violent vomiting I'd ever seen or heard. He tried to shield me from seeing it but there was blood, lots of it. The look on his face was horrifying; twisted, contorted in agony. When he finished retching, he curled up on the floor like a baby and cried. I think the embarrassment of doing that in front of me was almost as bad as the pain.

I cleaned him up, the vomit too and the blood. *Soak. Disinfect. Soak again. Decontaminate. Wash hands.*

I asked him again about Bute. Asked him what had happened with him and Tommy and Stevenson. He told me nothing.

The drugs to ease his pain really were powerful. They took it away completely.

I think I know why Tommy kept all the newspapers he did, even the many issues with nothing about Valerie Moodie in them. I think that was the whole point.

He was racked with guilt, eating himself up for his part in leaving the poor girl on that island for eternity. He couldn't have bought or kept those newspapers when his wife was alive, not without her asking why. Once she was dead, Tommy's guilt multiplied.

I'm guessing he bought and searched the papers for anniversary mentions of her, scared that his secret would come out, but then angry when there was nothing. He wanted to see her name, just didn't want to see his associated with it.

Tommy wasn't all bad. He maybe wasn't quite the nice guy I'd thought he was, but he at least had the decency to know it.

He kept those newspapers, the six copies and the wardrobe full of others, because they reminded him of two things. First, of what he'd done, and secondly of the fact that Valerie had been forgotten about. That no one cared enough to write about her.

I don't tell Phil much of that. I don't dare tell him what I did to Tommy. I do tell him about Jackie Stevenson. How my anger and frustration got the better of me. How I placed the pillow over his head and held it there. How I walked away. How I cried after it.

I cry as I tell it, too.

Chapter 39

I thought Phil would understand.
He doesn't understand.

He's driven home alone. The village called Warton, near Preston in Lancashire. A place I'd previously never heard of and now find myself dreaming about. He hasn't told me what he's going to do, if he's going to do anything at all. No promises but no threats either. I'm left to wait and wonder.

It's not him going to the police I'm worried about. I'm waiting for his judgement, to know what he thinks of me, whether he can forgive me, understand me or hate me a little bit less.

I'm also awaiting my own judgement on the same thing. If he's a more forgiving judge than me then I'll be happy.

In the meantime, I've turned off my phone, turned a deaf ear to work calls and my father, cuddled in with George and turned my face from the world.

Loneliness never felt so good.

Chapter 40

I don't know how long I've been asleep, but something has woken me from it. I'm vaguely aware of being disturbed by a noise, but I don't know what. I'm drowsy and uncertain, and George is making a commotion. He's agitated and noisy, but I get the sense that it wasn't him that woke me, rather that he's reacting to the same thing, whatever it is.

He's still lying beside me on the bed, but his ears are pointing straight up and he's staring towards the bedroom door. All I can hear is my heart and the sound of the house breathing in and out. It's midnight-quiet and I'm being silly, head messed with the confusion of a sudden awakening. Then I hear a noise, maybe wood against wood, coming from the other side of the door. It's just one sound though, then silence, and I'm not sure I heard it.

Then there's another and I know I heard this one. There's someone in the flat.

George is off the bed with a run and a leap and is meowing at the door to be let out. My phone's by the bed and I could call the police, or Phil, but I'm not going to. The police might mean more questions than I've got answers to, and as for Phil …

I'm going to look myself; it might be nothing. *I know it's not nothing.*

I wrap my robe around me, knot the cord twice and ease the door back. The hallway is in darkness but there's noise drifting the length of it, coming from the living room. I follow it, padding along the carpet, not sure why I'm trying to be quiet, but knowing that I'm desperate to be.

When I get to the other door, I push it away from me with my fingertips so that it drifts into the room. I stand, breathe, wait and wonder, then walk inside. There's nothing there that shouldn't be, no one or nothing on the settee or by the television. I step further forward, able to see around the corner to the kitchen side of the open-plan, and my heart stops.

Sitting at my kitchen table are Mick Brennan and Norrie Caldow.

One heavyset and ruddy-faced, the other spiky lean and flinty-cheeked. In my house. They don't turn around at first even though they must have heard me come in, they just continue chatting to each other face to face like they're sitting in the pub. I don't have much breath, and am not sure I remember how to speak.

'Morning,' Caldow says as he turns, his voice gruff and sarcastic. 'Sorry if we woke you. Tried to be quiet coming in.'

'Sorry, not sorry?' Brennan chips in, edgy and aggressive. 'Not fucking sorry at all.'

I find my voice. Almost. 'Why are you ...'

'Why'd you fucking think?' Brennan asks. He's a horribly aggressive little shit who wouldn't mellow with age if he lived to be a hundred.

'Sit down,' Caldow orders me. I don't move, and he repeats it. '*Sit down.*'

I walk over to the table, pull back a chair and sit. They're at either end of the table, me in the middle, and I'm forced to turn my head when either of them speaks. I don't like that. Over Brennan's head, I see the clock, and it's a bit after 2 a.m.

Caldow is looking down at the table morosely, jowls sagging. When he lifts his head, I'm drawn to it, looking straight into his eyes.

'I don't want to be here,' he says gravely. 'I'm seventy-four and too old for this shit. I should be in my bed with my wife. Instead, I'm out in the cold, and that's your fault.'

I say nothing. Think nothing.

There's a bottle of red wine on the table where I left it, one glassful out of it. Brennan pulls the cork and sniffs it before tilting it questioningly to Caldow. The fat man nods. 'Where's your glasses?' I point to the wall cupboard, and Brennan fetches two tumblers, pouring them both a drink.

'Too sweet,' Brennan complains. It doesn't stop him knocking it back.

Caldow takes a mouthful too then sits the glass down and looks at me. 'I'm going to ask you two simple questions and you are going to answer me or things will get bad for you very quickly. What do you think you know, and how do you know it?'

I think, *I'm not telling you anything.*

I say, 'I don't know what you're talking about.'

His left arm lashes out before I see it, the back of his open hand crashing into my face, battering into my nose and mouth. At first, I'm surprised more than hurt. Stunned that he did it, not sure how to react. Then the pain begins to throb in my nose, and I know it's bleeding, tasting it in my mouth. My lip is cut too, ripped by one of my teeth. I sit shock-still.

I sense movement to my right and turn just as George competes a leap onto the table beside me. His tail's up and he's unsettled. He's not up for a cuddle, he's checking I'm okay. I'm not.

Before I can move, Brennan shoots out a hand and grabs George by the scruff of the neck and lifts him clear of the table. 'What's this? A rat?'

'Put him down!' I spit out the words through blood and snot.

George is immediately freaked, swivelling in mid-air, claws out, stretching to turn and get at Brennan. The bastard is laughing, sneering at George. He's still laughing when George wheels and claws at the hand that holds him, causing Brennan to bleed, yelp, and let him go. George leaps from the table and the man scrapes back his chair to go after him.

'Don't you dare fucking touch him!'

Brennan hears something in my voice that makes him pause. Maybe he's got an inkling of what I'm capable of.

We stare at each other and I think I'm going to get hit again, when Caldow speaks.

'Leave it,' he tells Brennan. 'We're not here for the bloody cat.' He glares at me and reaches into his pocket, bringing out a knife, which he lays on the table by his right hand.

'You're the one who was phoning me,' I say it without thinking. 'The one who damaged my car.'

Caldow shrugs dismissively. 'It was a warning. You chose to ignore it and now we're here. I'm going to ask you again. What do you think you know?'

The knife has a long blade, curved at the end, its handle wrapped in tape. I'm struggling not to look at it. I'm scared of telling the truth and terrified of not telling it.

I opt to tell some of the truth. 'I know that you and this guy and Agnew, Meechan and Stevenson have been carrying a secret for a very long time.'

It's enough to save me from another backhander. They swap glances, Brennan shrugs, Caldow knocks back more wine and thinks.

'I want more than that,' he says. 'No guessing. What do you *know*?'

'I talked to Tommy Agnew before he died. I knew the five of you had gone to Bute and it had bothered him ever since.' It was both truth and lie.

'Tommy wouldn't have talked,' Brennan snaps. 'He wouldn't.'

Caldow ignores him. 'So, we went to Bute,' he says. 'So what? Have you really dropped yourself in all this shit for that?'

He's goading me, I know it. But I can't help myself. 'I know the five of you were responsible for the death of Valerie Moodie.'

There's a new silence in the room and for the first time since I was woken, I feel I have a small fraction of control. The big man is troubled, his mouth open, breathing heavy. Brennan looks anxious too, but a wave of Caldow's hand keeps him quiet.

'What makes you think you know that?'

I know I'm probably digging my own grave, but I talk and tell. Most of it.

'I know you bumped into her and her pals at Ettrick Bay Tea Room. And in the Taverna Bar.' I see that register on both their faces, so I push it. 'And I know you met her again on the street late at night, when she was on her own.'

'Did Tommy Agnew tell you that?' Brennan is furious, knocking back his wine and pouring another. 'Why the fuck would he do that, Norrie? After all these years.'

'Quiet,' Caldow orders. '*Did* Tommy tell you?'

'Yes.'

He backhands me again. I see it coming but can't move in time. There's a horrible crunch and I think my nose might be broken. There's no shock this time, just pain.

'Don't fucking lie to me again,' Caldow says. 'Tommy wouldn't do that.'

'How would you know? You hadn't seen him in years. The man lay dead for months without his so-called pals even noticing. You couldn't even be bothered to go to his funeral.'

Caldow bristles and reddens, and I look warily to his left hand. 'We agreed not to see each other again. It was the way he wanted it. But still, I *know* Tommy wouldn't tell you. But someone did. And I want to know who. Now.'

I go to the only name I can think he'll buy. 'Malky McTeer.'

'Who?' Brennan doesn't remember the name, but Caldow does.

'The fisherman. The guy with the boat. He didn't know anything.'

'No?' I continue to dig and dig with a little lie. 'He saw Valerie's body, so did his pal Alec Thomson. You really thought he didn't know what or who you were burying? He knew.'

'Who else knows this?' Caldow's voice is lower, trying to make it sound like it isn't a big deal.

'No one.'

I think I've answered too quickly. He doesn't believe me, but he can't be sure. He turns the knife in his right hand, and I watch the light catch it as it spins.

'No one? Just you? Make much more sense for you to tell if there's someone else.'

'No one else. Just me.'

'Hm. And why would McTeer tell you this after all these years?'

'He likes a drink. And he likes to talk when he's got one in him. And maybe he thought your threat – that you knew their names, knew their boat and would find out where they lived – had worn off.'

Caldow's mouth tightens and I watch his hand. He doesn't swing it, but I know he's thinking it.

'What happened to Tommy, Bob and Jackie? Don't tell me you don't know, and don't tell me it's a fucking coincidence. Because I know it's not.'

'You tell me which of you killed Valerie. Then I might talk.'

Caldow laughs. It's a bitter, hate-filled excuse for a laugh. 'You think you can make a deal? Fuck me, that's funny.'

He takes the knife and reaches across himself and stabs it into the table about an inch from my hand. It makes a noise that reverberates down my spine. He's just trying to scare me, I tell myself, but I'm worried about his accuracy.

'*Now*. What happened to Tommy and the others?'

'I killed them.'

Brennan and Caldow stare at each other and then burst out laughing. Caldow scoops back some more wine and wipes his face. 'Ask a stupid question, Mick. I guess I asked for that. Okay, seeing as you gave me an answer, let's play. Valerie Moodie's death was an accident. She was hysterical and we were just trying to contain her, calm her down. She got worse and fought and she fell. Hit her head off a rock. It was an accident.'

'Then why not tell the police that? And why was she hysterical?' I ask it looking straight at Brennan.

'Fuck you,' he says quietly.

I think, *Yes, it all fits. Brennan.*

I say, 'You wanted her in the Taverna and she wouldn't have it. Your mates were pulling her pals and you got knocked back. Hurt your wee man ego didn't it?'

'I said fuck you. Shut up.'

'So, when she came out of the show at the Winter Gardens, alone, and Agnew and Meechan were at your hotel with Marion and Dorothy, you two and Stevenson cornered her, didn't take no for an answer the second time. You took her somewhere and *you* raped her.'

'I didn't rape her,' Brennan snaps, jumping to his feet. 'She wanted it. She was just too scared to say she wanted it.'

I can't believe my ears. 'You *raped* her. She was seventeen years old and you raped her. And then one of you bastards killed her.'

There's a look on Caldow's face and I know in that instant that it was him. There's quiet in the room for a while and I know things have changed.

'I told you it was an accident,' Caldow speaks slowly. 'I pushed her because she was out of control and she hit her head. No one meant to hurt her.'

I'm not stupid. I know that the more they talk, the more they tell me, the more likely that they're going to kill me.

Brennan is back in his seat and trying to outstare me, his wild eyes fixed on mine, but they're not quite focused, and he's blinking weirdly. I can see his head wavering side to side like he's struggling to hold it up.

'You're pathetic,' I tell him. 'You're a rapist. Couldn't pull her, so you raped her.'

'Shut it.'

'No. You're a rapist and you know it.'

Brennan breaks and swings a punch at me, his right arm flailing at my head. And he misses by a long way. Enraged, he swings with his left and misses by even further, smashing his fist into the table instead. He looks confused. I reach across and slap him hard across the face. He's utterly helpless to dodge it.

I feel something smash into my shoulder. Norrie Caldow's meaty fist. I turn and see his fat red face twisted up with rage. He hadn't been aiming for my shoulder but for my face again. He'd missed his target, just like Brennan had. He swings again, this time in the right direction, but it's easy to duck my head back out of the way. I slip out of my seat and step away from the table.

They're breathing hard, me too. 'Sit the fuck down,' Caldow shouts and slurs.

'No. Ask me again what happened to Agnew, Meechan and Stevenson. *Ask me.*'

It's confusing them, it's *all* confusing them. Caldow bites though. 'What happened to them?'

'I killed them. You laughed, but I told you. *I killed them.* I helped Agnew die in his flat, before any of this started. I killed Bob Meechan because he was a sad, lonely old man, seriously ill, and wanted out of it. And I killed Stevenson because he didn't stop you bastards doing what you did to Valerie Moodie. And now I'm killing you two. You just don't know it.'

It sinks in slowly. The truth of it. They know I'm not joking. They know I'm crazy.

Brennan is the first to come after me, but he stumbles as he gets out of the chair and slips down on one knee. He lets out a roar of anger and pushes himself back up again. Caldow is up too, slow and swaying.

'What the fuck's going on Norrie? I feel weird.'

'Don't know but something. Get this bitch back in the chair.'

Brennan starts towards me but I'm easily quicker than he is, sidestepping him and slapping his face again, harder this time. That one was for George.

'Fucking get her,' Caldow bellows, one arm holding him up on the table.

'That shit wine,' Brennan whines. 'Can't move right. Too slow.'

Caldow takes a step in my direction but stops immediately, knowing his new limitations, sensing the problem. 'Something. Not right. The fuck?'

I'm still stuck between them, my eyes moving back and forth from Brennan to Caldow, but I'm relaxing, still wary, but knowing they're much less dangerous now. Now I've fixed them.

Brennan comes at me in a rush and I move aside, letting him crash to the floor. Caldow pushes off the table, arms outstretched, catching me with a glancing blow to the head, but it barely registers. I shove him in the back as he passes me and grab his knife from the table.

They're scared now. Partly by what's happening to them and partly at the sight of me brandishing the knife in front of me. They both edge away, Brennan on his arse and Caldow on unsteady feet. It's so tempting to use the knife, the idea of stabbing them so inviting. But so stupid.

'Fuck have you done?' Caldow demands. 'You did this. Know you did.'

'No, you did it,' I tell him. 'You drank my wine. Didn't bother to ask me if it was okay.'

'Wha?' He sounds stupid and confused, his mind slowing rapidly.

'I knew you were coming,' I explain. 'Didn't know it would be tonight, but I knew you'd come. So, I made some preparations. Taped a knife under the table here, hid a baseball bat in my bedroom. Just in case. The wine is topped up with ethylene glycol. The stuff you get in antifreeze. Makes it taste a bit sweet but doesn't have any smell to it. You've emptied the bottle and your reflexes are fucked. And that's just the start.'

'You couldn't … How did … Bitch.'

'Yeah. Now get the fuck out of my flat.'

Caldow helps Brennan to his feet, steadies him, maybe whispers something because they come at me together trying to swamp me in one stumbling, uncoordinated attack. I simply move aside, and they miss.

'If I was you, I'd go for help as quick as you can. Might be too late already. But you better be careful how you explain it to the police or ambulance staff. Get the fuck out.'

They back away from me, terror and confusion on their faces, stumbling to the front door and through it. I drop the knife inside and follow them, hoping no one in the other flats hears the noise as they bounce off the walls on the way to the lift. It takes Caldow three attempts to push the button for the ground floor, but he finally manages it, the door slides closed on them and they're gone.

I fall back against the hallway wall, my eyes closed, breath rushing from me, my hands suddenly shaking. George is at my feet, tail winding around my leg. I pick him up and hug him to me, both of us needing it. His head draws back from me and I remember my mouth and nose must still be bloodied. I apologise to him and draw the back of my hand across my face, removing what I can.

I need to be sure. I say it aloud, whispering it to George. 'I need to be sure.'

I take him back to the flat, pull on jeans, trainers and a sweatshirt, and go back out. The lift is there in moments but seems to take an age to sink to ground level again. They won't have gone far, can't have done, but I don't know which way they've gone.

There. Fifty yards along Wilson Street, moving slowly, holding each other up. I stride after them, wanting to get nearer but not too close. They're going two steps forward and one back, surely looking to the world like a pair of drunks. They weave left at the corner of Candleriggs, Merchant Square in front of them, getting slower all the time.

Brennan is struggling now, Caldow propping him up, half carrying him. The old church that's now

Ramshorn Theatre is up ahead and they're going straight at it. Maybe something in their heads tells them it's sanctuary. It isn't.

They stagger across Ingram Street, some fractured homing instinct leading them, and they lurch into the dear green space that is Ramshorn Graveyard. Mick Brennan takes a few disoriented steps before sinking to his knees and Caldow can't keep him up, the skinnier man collapsing face down into the grass. Caldow stumbles on for a few moments more before he crashes down onto a feathery bed of dark foliage that surrounds a weathered headstone.

I stand and watch. They're still. Sleeping the deepest sleep. Loss of consciousness becoming a coma. Not at peace though, they'll never be at peace.

They can't hear me but I'm talking. To myself, to them, to Valerie, to all the other ghosts, remembering the sequence of events that the ethylene glycol causes, the ones that come after unconsciousness and coma. 'Heart failure, fluid in the lungs, respiratory distress, loss of oxygen supply, multi-system organ failure. Death.'

The graveyard is where George and I found each other, a place that's always held happy memories for me. I can't help but think George would appreciate the irony.

Which reminds me; when I get back I need to get my kit and clear up any blood that George drew from Brennan's hand when he clawed him. *Equip. Remove. Soak. Disinfect. Soak again. Dispose. Decontaminate. Check. Wash hands. Report.*

It might not matter because CCTV will probably pick up images of me walking behind them. But, if it does, so be it. I'm past caring. It will take them a while to think there's a connection or to find me, and by then I'll have done what I need to do.

Chapter 41

Dorothy Denton recognises my voice. I can hear the intake of breath and then the impatient sigh.

'Yes?'

'It's Grace McGill.' I know she knows this.

'What do you want? I thought I'd been clear.'

I think, *Oh, you have.*

I say, 'I have information about Valerie. About what happened.'

She snaps. 'Do you know how many times I've heard that over the years? I'm going to hang up now.'

I think, *I've got one chance to keep her on the line.*

I say, 'I know about Tommy Agnew, Bob Meechan and the others. I know what happened.'

This time the silence is different. It's like she's stopped breathing.

'I can't talk here,' she says eventually and quietly. 'Give me your number and I'll call you. It might be half an hour or an hour, but I'll call.'

I give her my number and she hangs up without another word.

I do the only thing I can do; I wait. I make a cup of coffee and I wait. George jumps up onto my lap and demands attention, settling down to sleep on me after getting his chin rubbed. I'm sure she's going to call. I'm less sure after thirty-five minutes and beginning to worry after forty-five. Then the phone rings and I sit up like I've been electrocuted, causing George to jump off in fright.

'Hello?'

'It's Dorothy Denton.'

'Thanks for calling back. I appreciate it.'

We're dancing, being polite, but I'm sure we're both desperate to get down to it. I'm going to go for it because I can hear the nerves in her voice.

'I'm sorry for just saying those names. It must have been a shock.'

'It was. How do you ... what is it you think you know?'

She wants to see my credentials and that's fair enough. It's time to find out if I'm right.

'I know that you, Marion Millar and Valerie met five guys from Glasgow on Bute that day in 1964. Tommy Agnew, Bob Meechan, Jackie Stevenson, Mick Brennan and Norrie Caldow.'

Silence. I take that as meaning I'm not wrong yet.

'I know you met them at Ettrick Bay and then again in the Taverna Bar.'

'I haven't heard the name of those men in years. Not that I've ever forgotten them. Much as I'd like to, they'll be with me till I die. How do you know all this? Who are you?'

'I knew Tommy Agnew before he died. And then I discovered he had a secret and that it involved Bute. I did some digging ...' shit, I hadn't meant to use that

337

word and now all I can think of is Valerie's arm bone poking through the dirt … 'I found out a lot.'

I can hear her weighing this up. 'Have you though? All you've found, all you've told me are the names of men that we talked to.'

'No, I know a lot more than that.'

She snaps at me. 'Then you better prove it.'

'I know Marion Millar had sex with Tommy Agnew the night Valerie disappeared.'

'How do you … Are you a reporter? I won't talk to a reporter. Not about this.'

I think, *I'm not a real one. I just pretend.*

I say, 'I'm not. I swear to you I'm not. If I was, I'd just print this story. That's not why I called you.'

'Then why did you call? I don't understand what's going on.'

Here we go. 'I want to ask you things and I want to tell you things. Mainly, it's because I know what happened to Valerie.' I hesitate, part pausing for effect, part scared to say the words. 'And I know where she's buried.'

'Oh Jesus.'

I realise, or maybe remember, that she didn't know for sure that Valerie had been killed. A bit of her must have still been hoping all these years that Valerie had run away, that the sightings on the ferry and in Largs and Glasgow had been correct. Now I've blown up that hope by blurting out a few words.

When she answers, her voice is small, and she sounds like the seventeen-year-old that she was. 'She's definitely … you're sure?'

'Yes. I'm sure. I'm sorry.'

'Oh my God, that poor girl. Oh my God.'

She's crying now. Her breath is heaving and shaking. I've got tears running down my own cheeks.

'Who was it? Who killed her?'

'I've already told you the names. The names you hadn't heard in years.'

There's a gasp, then I hear a car door open, realising she's driven somewhere so as not to be overheard. Then I hear her throw up.

When the door closes again, there are tears and snuffling. When she speaks, she's breathing hard. 'Those bastards. Those fucking *bastards*. Which of them did it?'

'All of them. One way or the other, they all did it.'

'Christ I can't … Which of them did it? It matters to me.' There's another edge to her voice, something desperately anxious.

'What are you telling me, Dorothy?'

'It wasn't just Marion that … that went with one of those boys. She went with Tommy but she wasn't the only one. Oh God. They had three rooms, the boys. I went back with the one called Bob. I'm so ashamed. Even though no one knew, I've had to live with that shame.'

'But Valerie didn't go with any of them?'

'No. She didn't want anything to do with it. Marion and I were drinking, something neither of us had really done before, but Valerie wouldn't. She had an orange juice when we were on … Sweetheart Stout I think it was. The boys were all over us, very attentive, making us laugh, chatting us up. One of them, Mick, was very keen on Valerie. She was such a pretty girl.'

'But she wasn't keen on him?'

'She just wasn't keen on any of it. Drinking in pubs and flirting with drunk boys wasn't for her. The noisier and flirtier it got, the less she liked it. She said she was going to leave and go back to the guest house. The guy Mick got upset at that, and me and Marion weren't happy either as we thought the boys might go too. We tried to make her stay and it ended up in an argument. Those were the last words we had with her.'

I say, 'It's not your fault.'

I think, *It's partly your fault.*

'What …' she really doesn't want to ask this, '… what did they do to her? Which of them did it? Please tell me.'

'Norrie Caldow. I don't think he meant to kill her, but he did.'

'Oh.' She's relieved, I can hear it. Relieved it's not Bob Meechan. Bad enough that she'd had sex with him, worse for her if he'd then murdered Valerie. She's glad it was Caldow.

'He and Brennan came across Valerie in the street on her own. The woman in the box office at the Winter Gardens said she was sure she'd sold Valerie a returned ticket for that night's show. They were drunk. Brennan was mad because his pals were in the hotel with you and Marion and he'd missed out. He was already angry at Valerie for turning him down and showing him up in front of the others. He wanted revenge; the others were drunk enough to go along with it.'

'Did he … did he rape her? Did *they* rape her?'

I think, *You're going to be better off not knowing the answer to that.*

I say, 'I don't know. We'll never know. But I think she fought back, and Caldow hit her. Maybe harder than he meant to, maybe he knocked her against a wall or a rock. But he killed her. And they all covered it up.'

She's silent for a long time, save for some quiet sobbing.

'I think that maybe I always knew it was them or might have been them,' she says. 'We went looking for them on the Friday when we couldn't find Valerie, but they'd gone. They were meant to stay for another day, but they'd got on a steamer back to Glasgow.'

'But you never told the police about them.' It sounds like an accusation because it is one.

'No.' Her tone admits her guilt. 'We were young and stupid and away from home. It was the first time any of us had been away from our parents, and that's not how we normally behaved. We were scared of the truth coming out, so we lied. We dug ourselves deep enough into a lie that we couldn't get out of it again. Not till it was way too late and then there wasn't much point. It wouldn't bring Valerie back.

'We lied to save ourselves, I can't deny that. We couldn't face admitting it to the police because we knew our parents would find out. Worse, it would have been in the papers and we'd never have lived that down. It would have been unbearable. And I know ... *I know* ... that's no reason not to have told the police everything, but Marion and I told each other that nothing would change whatever had happened to Valerie. And if she had run off, then stories about us having sex with boys we'd just met would only have made her run further away. So, we didn't tell them about Tommy, Bob and the others.'

'But you wish you had?'

'Of course I do! Those bastards need to pay for this. The police need to ...'

I say, 'They're all dead.'

I think, *And I killed them. You're welcome.*

There's shock in her voice. 'All of them?'

'Yes. They all died in the last few months.'

'No, I ... I don't understand. You still haven't told me who you are.'

I think, *Maybe I'd tell you if I knew. I used to know who I was. But that seems a long time ago now.*

'I don't matter. Dorothy, what you need to under-stand is that this is all going to come out very soon. You need to prepare for that, and you need to decide what story you're going to tell the press.'

'*The press?* You said you weren't a reporter.'

'I'm not. But Dorothy, the police know where her body is, and they won't be able to keep it quiet for long. The newspapers will be all over this, television too. I found you, so you can be sure that they will.'

'Oh my God. My husband ... my kids. I need time to tell them. If this is going to ... oh my God. They deserve to hear it from me. They need to. If this has to come out.'

'I think it does. But I do know a reporter, someone who can be trusted to be fair.'

'I don't know …'

'Dorothy, this will come out one way or another. Valerie has been buried long enough and so has the truth.'

Chapter 42

I knock and wait.

Morning is never a good time to visit him but today I've little choice, it has to be done, and it has to be done early. I knock again, louder and longer.

I eventually hear movement and shouting from deep inside the flat. They aren't happy sounds; they're the sounds of a man dragged rudely from slumber to hangover without having time for a pee in between.

'Who is it?'

Normally, when he asks that, he knows it's me. But normally, he knows I'm coming, and he knows my knock. Today, my knock is different.

'It's me. Grace.' My voice is different too.

The door opens on the chain and he stares out, eyes red and wide, hair dishevelled, face creased, all wrapped up in a navy towelling dressing gown. Half asleep and half scared. When he sees it's me, there's a moment of relief before his features twist into a glower. Then curiosity as he notices the bruising to my cheek and nose.

'What are you here for? What kind of time's this?'

There's whisky and beer on his breath, stale as a corpse and twice as fetid. He yanks the chain back, snapping it from the catch and throwing it against the back of the door as he turns and stomps inside. He's gone to the bathroom and I head to the kitchen, knowing that's where he'll be going next.

A couple of minutes later he's there too, pulling back the fridge door and drawing deep on a carton of orange juice. When he stops to have a breather, he glares at me before knocking back another lungful of cure then falling into a chair by the table, checking his watch to make sure it's as early as his body tells him it is. It's only eight in the morning and he's not seen that in a long time.

'Why the fuck are you here at this time?'

'To say goodbye.'

He wasn't expecting that. I know it won't shut him up for long, but I'm enjoying seeing the confusion on his face. And knowing it will get worse.

'What are you talking about? I'm not feeling well, and I don't have time for this shit. What do you mean you're here to say goodbye?'

'Just that. I'm here for the last time. We're done.'

He laughs in my face. 'Is it that time of the month again? It's too early for your whining. Listen if you're going, then go. Piss off. What are you waiting for?'

'I've things to tell you first. I need you to understand why this is happening. Why there's no way back.'

'*No way back*,' he parrots. 'You've been watching too many movies. You'll be back and we both know it. You'll always come back because we both know it's your fault that I'm on my own. You *owe* me. Your mother would have come back if you hadn't done what you done. She'd have been here looking after me. She loved me.'

I laugh. I can't help myself. I know it sounds hysterical, but I don't care.

'She might have come back, that's true. But she didn't love you. You killed that as sure as I killed her. She *hated* you.'

I realise it's the first time I've said the words out loud. The first time I've admitted it to him. It should be emotional and meaningful, but for him it's just an excuse for another fight. My admission flies right over his head and he only thinks of himself.

'How fucking dare you? Saying a thing like that. She loved me. Which was more than you ever did.'

I think, *Is that true? I know it's not, but it's so long since he crushed my love that I can't remember a time I didn't hate him.*

I say, 'If she did love you then she hated you too. You didn't give her much choice.'

'You don't know what you're talking about. You were a kid and part of the problem. She always came back because she loved me. You'll come back because you have to.'

It's time that he knows.

'I won't be back because after I leave here, I'm going to prison. Possibly for the rest of my life. Definitely for the rest of yours.'

His jaw falls slack, and he stares at me, mouth open, eyes shock wide. '*Prison?*'

I nod, shameful and defiant all at once.

'*Prison*. Why the fuck would you be going to prison?'

'I killed people.'

The room becomes smaller and quieter. When he sees I'm not smiling, his eyes narrow and he looks for the joke. 'You mean your mother?'

'I mean other people. Lonely people. Sick people. Those in pain or with nothing to live for. People who were better off dead than alive. People like you.'

He's staring at me. Wondering. Then he settles on what makes most sense. 'Bullshit. *Killed people*. Sure you did. What's *wrong* with you?'

I think, *He still doesn't get it. He can't get his head around that I did what I'm telling him.*

I say, 'I killed them. I murdered them.'

'Bullshit.'

'Do you remember the old man you read about in the paper? The one that had been dead in his flat for five months?' He nods, warily. 'His name was Thomas Agnew. Tommy. He'd been living on his own for years, lonely after his wife died, unhappy, miserable. I tripled the dose of his medication and watched him pass away.'

'I don't believe you.' *He doesn't want to believe me.*

'There was a lady named Helen. Every day was like a life sentence for her. She hated being alive. So, when she was in the bath, I held her head under the water. I held it there until she stopped fighting, until she was at peace.'

His mouth is open, but he still doubts. 'You couldn't. You don't have it in you.'

'No? They were easy. Comparatively. Once you've drugged and then smothered someone that you've loved with all of your heart, then anything else is simple.'

Now he understands. I can see it in his eyes. 'You're mad. You're a crazy fucking bitch.'

He's right. For once in his miserable fucking life, he's right.

I move closer to him and he doesn't like that. He's much more used to me trying to keep my distance.

'Are you scared? You should be. I've done terrible things; I know that now. But I could do them again. I could do them right now.'

He shrinks from me, retreating as deep into his chair as he can. It's not that he's got weaker, not that I've got physically stronger. He senses something else in me and he's afraid of it. I can see the fear in his eyes, and I like it.

'I've suffocated old men like you. Stolen their breath.' I move my hand close to his mouth as I say it and he recoils.

'I've poisoned old men like you. Slipped them some-thing that stopped their hearts or put them to sleep for ever.' I follow that with a glance at the carton of orange juice that sits on the table in front of him.

'What the fuck have you done?' His hand flies in-stinctively to his throat, feeling it for signs of damage. 'What the fuck have you done to me?'

I shrug and stare, as if I'm expecting him to die before my eyes. He tries to get up, but I push him back into the chair. He's panicking. He's terrified. And he should be.

He's spitting out the liquid in his mouth, desperately gobbing out what he can, but it's just saliva. The orange juice is down his throat and heading for his stomach. He believes me now, no question about that.

'Tell me who killed my mother.'

'What?'

'Who killed her? Who *really* killed her? I gave her the drugs and put the pillow over her face, but who took her life away?'

'Fuck you.'

'Who took her life away?'

His voice is small. 'Me.'

'I can't hear you.'

'I did. Have you poisoned me?'

'Okay, who abused her, mistreated her, gaslighted her, put her in hospital and treated her like a piece of shit?'

'I did.'

'Who wasn't worthy of her and knew it? Who treated her that bad because he knew he was a piece of fucking dirt compared to her?'

'Me.'

'And who regretted losing her for the rest of his life? Who knows he's nothing without her?'

'*Me!*'

I'm crying and I'm not even sure why. I wipe the tears away with the heel of my hand, bruising my cheek, angry at myself.

'Look at me,' I tell him. His head is hanging, like a beaten dog. I want him to face me. 'You're not dying, you pathetic shit.'

His head snaps up. 'What?'

'You're not poisoned. There was nothing in that orange juice. And I'm not going to kill you.'

'I don't …'

'If I wanted you dead, you'd be dead already. But there's worse things than death, I've learned that much.'

He doesn't know whether to be angry or relieved. 'You fucking bitch.'

'You're not listening,' I tell him. 'You're going to be living alone, living with memories, living with pain. Living without hope. And you've earned every bit of it. You moan that your life's bad now. Just wait. Twenty-four hours a day on your own. Seven days a week on your own with no visitor. You'll be wishing I'd killed you.'

He's got the message now and I can see it wash over him, the reality of it squeezing his throat.

'You'll have all the time in the world to remember every time you hit her, every time you criticised her, every time you put her down or put her in hospital. You'll have all day every day to think how you should have treated her right. And I hope she haunts the fuck out of you. I know I will.'

'I'm sorry. Okay, I'm sorry. Listen, don't do this. I'll …'

'Too late. It's done. I couldn't stay even if I wanted to. Yes, I could spare you, end it for you now, but I won't. You'll reap what you sow. You deserve this.'

'I'm already without your mother. I won't cope without you too.'

'I know.'

He tries to push himself up from the chair, but his body betrays him, and I don't even have to push him back. 'Then do it. Please. Kill me. You did it for them, you can do it for me.'

'No.'

'Do you want me to beg? I'll beg.'

I lean in close, my mouth near his, my flesh by his. My own flesh and blood. The man who gave me life and the man who ruined it. I can smell him. The way he smelled when he came to kiss me goodnight when I was young and he came home late, booze on his breath and spikes on his chin. My father.

'Don't beg,' I whisper. 'Save your breath for living.'

His face contorts into a snarl, a twisted picture of useless, pathetic rage. He's barely recognisable and yet I've never seen him more clearly. 'I'll do it myself if I want,' he says. 'If I want to die, I'll do it. I'll decide. I'll fucking decide.'

'You won't. You're a coward, we both know that. You haven't got the guts to do it. Maybe because we both know you'll be going straight to hell if you do. You'll have to wait. And you'll have to wait alone.'

I turn and walk away. He's still shouting, still threatening, still begging as the door closes behind me for the last time. I hesitate, argue with myself briefly, and say a silent prayer before leaving for the last time.

Chapter 43

The knock on the door sends my heart racing. I know it's him and there's a sense of no going back. I blow out a long, nervy blast of breath and open up. He looks awkward, unsure of how to frame his face, whether a smile is appropriate or not.

I think, *I wish this had worked out differently. I wish you didn't think I was crazy.*

I say, 'Hi Phil. Thanks for coming over.'

Coming over. Like he was here for dinner or to pick me up. Phil Canning taking me on a drive or to a restaurant. Wishful thinking so far removed from reality.

'Are you okay, Grace?' he looks genuinely concerned and I see his eyes narrow as he sees the marks that Caldow left on my face. I'm fine, surprisingly. But I like that he's worried about me. 'Are you sure you want to do this?'

I think, *Yes. No.*

I say, 'Yes.'

He brings a newspaper, the *Standard*, from his jacket pocket and lays it out in front of me. I've already seen the online version, but there's something more real about it being in physical form.

Body find may end 55-year-old mystery

Police believe buried island corpse is missing teenager Valerie Moodie

There's a photograph of a police line with forensic officers at work behind it. A taped-off crime scene, the trees and bushes of Inchmarnock in view. There's another shot of a police boat and huddled figures lifting something from it.

The article is shrouded in speculative phrases but there's no doubting the message. It's Valerie, we've been tipped off, they know, and we know. There are guarded quotes from Dorothy Denton and a cousin of Valerie's, expressing hope that there might be closure. Whatever that is. The local MP says he hopes it will bring an end to a dark chapter in Bute's history, one that it's doubtful he knew anything about until he was called by the reporter. Unnamed locals express shock and sadness, like locals and neighbours always do, although one is quoted as saying how, coincidentally, someone had been asking about Valerie just weeks ago.

There's no mention of me or Phil, just the suggestion that the police received an anonymous call. That's as it should be. We're not part of her story, we're just bit-part players who wandered onto the side of the stage and off again, touching nothing, saying nothing. Valerie is as Valerie was before either of us stuck our noses in. Some justice has been done along the way, but none of that is much use to her either.

It's done, and Phil's going home. We have a deal.

I'm going to the police to tell them about my mother. I'm going to tell them about Helen McCrorie, Eddie Connarty and Graeme Holmes. That's it.

'You sure you don't want to tell them about Stevenson?' he asks me. 'Get it all off your chest and not have it on your conscience.'

I shake my head. 'My conscience won't be changed by the telling. And I'm not going to tell them anything that will drag you into it. I did this. I made choices, and there's a price to be paid.'

'You don't have to carry all this on yourself, Grace. They killed that girl. They murdered her and covered it up.'

'And they've paid their own price. It's not going to help, hurting anyone else. You know the only thing I want you to do for me.'

He nods. 'I'll do it. I'll make sure he's looked after. Don't worry.'

The relief rushes out of me in a big sigh and I'm glad I'm sitting as I feel my knees buckle. 'Oh God, thank you. I don't know what I'd have done if I'd had to leave him alone. I'd never have forgiven myself. Are you sure you're okay with it?'

He smiles. 'Sure. Maybe a cat is just what I need. George can live with me and he'll be okay. I'll make sure of it.'

I want to hug him.

'I need a bit of time to say goodbye to him then I'll put him in the cat carrier for you. Be careful when you get him out though. He can be fierce. Chances are you'll get scratched.'

Phil smiles at me. 'What's life without a few scratches? Grace, are you going to be okay?'

'I'll be fine.'

'Good. Grace … give me something. Something I can understand and live with. I hope you can find peace, but I need some too.'

I sit quietly for a minute, gathering my thoughts, considering posterity. Then I speak.

'I know what I did was wrong. Maybe I always knew it, but I tried to take some pain away from people. I was trying to help, I really believed that. But it wasn't my place to do it. Not my job.'

'Do you feel guilty about it?'

'I am guilty. And I'm going to tell the police that.'

He nods. He understands. 'Do you feel guilty about killing your mother?'

I stare at him and wonder. It's a huge question.

'I don't feel guilty that I did it. Just guilty that I didn't do it sooner. But I'll have to live with that.'

Chapter 44

I'm not going to prison.
I'm not going to the police.

That would be both too easy, and too difficult. It's not that I want to avoid being punished for what I've done; I'm ready to accept that. It's the questions I'm not ready for. I don't want someone poking around in my head, looking for answers that I don't have. The thought of being interrogated, psychoanalysed and second-guessed scares and horrifies me. I don't want to be anyone's guinea pig or be put on public display.

Even if I pleaded guilty, there would still be a trial, still be evidence and cross-examination, along with public humiliation. I don't want any of the probing and prodding. I don't want any of it.

I've got one final diorama to finish. I've been working on it from the moment I helped my mother on her way to a better place. It's a simple room, just a lonely single bed, one chest of drawers, one wardrobe, a lone photograph of my mother on the wall.

I've painted the walls the same colour as my bedroom, a pale yellow on three of them, and wallpapered the fourth with the same pattern that lines the wall behind my bed. I've used a small rectangle of the same carpet that's under my feet right now, and even found a doll's house bed that's close to my own. All that's missing is the space where I've been.

My only regret is that I won't be around to see how long it takes before I'm discovered. It's a test of sorts, I guess. If I'm found right away, if Phil or my dad or Harry or one of the handful of other people who might possibly have an interest in my existence care enough to contact the police or break down the door then maybe I'll have done the wrong thing. If I lie here for months, then I'll have been proved right.

Either way, I'm bringing an end to the pain I've been swimming in for far too long. It will be like turning off a light, flicking a switch, closing a book.

It will be a quiet end to a quiet life.

A single daisy is in my left hand. The pills are in my right.

All I need to do is find the courage to swallow them.

Acknowledgements

I want to thank the brilliant Eve Hall, my editor at Hodder & Stoughton, for her support and insight during the completion of this novel. My agent, Mark Stanton at The North Literary Agency, got Grace from the beginning and his encouragement was invaluable.

Thanks to everyone on the beautiful Isle of Bute, particularly to Anne Speirs for her unrivalled knowledge, and to my partner in crime at Bute Noir, Karen Latto.

For technical expertise, I'm grateful to Ev Campbell for advice on miniature crafting, Alastair McMurray on how to poison people, former Inspector Aileen Sloan for police procedure, and Miyo Kojima for lonely death cleaning. For everything else I owe my wife, Alexandra Sokoloff.

Last, but never least, thanks to my best buddy Clooney for being the inspiration for George.

Order the new book from C.S. Robertson . . .

The Trials of Marjorie Crowe

Those who live alongside Marjorie Crowe in Strathdorcha put her age at somewhere between 55 and 70. They think she's divorced or a lifelong spinster, that she used to be a librarian, a pharmacist or a witch. They think she's possibly lonely or ill or maybe just plain rude.

She lives in a cottage on the edge of the village. The local kids call it the Hansel and Gretel house and make fun of her. With her few friends long gone, she's regressed into a quiet, almost mute, world of her own.

Marjorie manages to look tall despite being only around five feet six. With her slim frame and long, unkempt grey hair tied behind her, she always walks with her head up. And she walks and she walks.

Her daily strolls are the stuff of local legend. Twice a day, at the same time and the same pace each day, she walks. The locals can set their watches by her. She even goes in one door of the local pub and out the other, as if it isn't there.

When Marjorie is seven minutes late walking through the back door of The Foresters Arms, it's noticed.

That's the same day that 11-year-old Charlie McKee disappears.

That's the day everyone wants to know what Marjorie knows . . .

HODDER &
STOUGHTON